LOST MOON

/ / / /

J.R. RAIN
MATTHEW S. COX

THE VAMPIRE FOR HIRE SERIES

Moon Dance
Vampire Moon
American Vampire
Moon Child
Christmas Moon
Vampire Dawn
Vampire Games
Moon Island
Moon River
Vampire Sun
Moon Dragon
Moon Shadow
Vampire Fire
Midnight Moon
Moon Angel
Vampire Sire
Moon Master
Dead Moon
Lost Moon
Banshee Moon

Published by
Crop Circle Books
212 Third Crater, Moon

Copyright © 2019 by J.R. Rain

All rights reserved.

Printed in the United States of America.

ISBN: 9781696261708

Chapter One
Another Lifetime Ago

Dread has been stalking me as of late, but the details of why are woefully unclear.

Ever have one of those days where it feels like you've left the coffee machine on at home and at any minute, the fire department is going to call about your house burning down? That's exactly how it's been for me constantly for about the past month. Only, add in wondering if I've also left the windows open during a rainstorm, sent off the mortgage payment, and worried about having a daughter old enough to start driving.

Mix all that together into a giant hairball of anxiety and that's precisely what's stuck in my metaphorical craw.

Presently, three serious issues—some might even call them catastrophes—in varying stages of progress occupy my mind. I'd say the most alarming is my seventeen-year-old daughter having a boyfriend—I'd rather kill the Devil again than have to admit this truth to myself. Tammy, seated behind me in the middle row of the Momvan, rolls her eyes in response to that thought. Okay, okay… that's a bit melodramatic. She smirks as if to say '*just a bit, yeah*'. Second, and not quite as life-changing as realizing my kid is almost an adult, I don't seem to be an undead anymore.

It's really damn difficult to be ungrateful, though I can't help but have a little bitty moment of wishing this had happened *before* my kids grew up, Danny turned into the king of douchebags, and I lost my day job. Being a legit vampire had, after all, taken so much from me. But hey, I shouldn't be too ungrateful. Gift horses and mouths, right? A good change is still a good change, whenever it might occur.

Speaking of change, it shouldn't surprise me that a journey high into the 'upper dimensions' or whatever they are resulted in some serious crap going down. It's mind-blowing to think about, but I'm pretty sure I got kinda close to the Creator. Probably the way a person standing outdoors is 'kinda close' to the Sun. Near enough to feel warmth and light, but not enough to be annihilated. And I mean annihilated in the most loving way possible. Now, going *to* the Creator is a little different. 'The Big Sleep' as Raymond Chandler might call it.

While I'm not undead anymore, my body is

quite far from normal. After all, I didn't stop being a supernatural creature, or even a vampire—though my vampirism has gone through a sort of metamorphosis, you could say. Perhaps spending the past thirteen years loathing the idea of drinking blood finally registered with the creative forces of the universe at large. I'm still not sure how believable it is for me to have 'creative' powers like that. Samantha Moon is no Van Gogh, or even a Charlie Reed, author of *The World of Dur* novels, and a powerful creator in his own right. However, it's hard to argue that the new me hasn't fixed everything I've loathed about myself ever since the attack that took away my mortality.

Instead of blood, I now consume psychic energy. No, that doesn't mean I run around to call centers for psychic hotlines and raid their stash of Red Bull. My sustenance is mental energy. Everything alive is a food source, including animals. Allison thinks it's even possible for me to drain energy from plants, but we haven't tested that yet. My sun allergy is a thing of the past, too. Some suit in a boardroom of a sunblock manufacturer is probably trying to figure out what caused a noticeable sales slump. If Costco had that stuff in five-gallon drums, yours truly would've killed one a week.

But the new me is back on speaking terms with the sun.

This, of course, is why I allowed myself to be talked into a trip to the beach on a Friday afternoon.

Spur of the moment idea from Tammy within minutes of her coming home from school. It's also why my sister Mary Lou is in the passenger seat and the Momvan is packed full of teenagers—our teenagers, that is. Meaning, only my sister's kids and mine. It's blowing my mind to see Mary Lou's children looking so much like adults. And, it really does make me happy beyond words that the five of them have stayed close even into the often surly teenage years.

Ellie Mae is a few weeks shy of turning nineteen. Other than being blonde, she's so much like my sister at that age it's scary. Highly 'motherly' toward her siblings and even my kids. Billy Joe is the same age as Tammy, seventeen. He tries to act like his father, Rick, but the kid's not exactly the most muscular critter in the world. His grades aren't exactly superb either, but he's not in danger of flunking out. My sister and her husband aren't too worried about it since Billy wants to skip college and apprentice as an electrician.

Meanwhile, the Alchemist is hinting that Anthony should attend Light Warrior school, whatever and wherever the hell that is. I think I would prefer my son being an electrician, thank you very much.

Mary Lou's third child, Ruby Grace, is still the anomaly. I still see her as the precocious two-year-old saying stuff way too advanced for a girl her age. She's fifteen now and smart as a whip. Kinda dainty though, so she routinely gets mistaken for twelve. If she keeps going as she has been, the kid will end up in any college she wants on a free ride. I'm not asking how my sister and Rick produced a genius, but stranger things happen all the time.

Anyway, back to the subject of catastrophes. I mentioned three of them and only went over two.

Tammy sighs again since I'm thinking of her having a boyfriend as a 'catastrophe.' And okay, maybe my recent change is more of a good thing. Those two aside, the actual catastrophic event is fortunately also the one that appears to be the least progressed: the Elizabeth situation. Ever since she escaped from me, we've all been on high alert.

Hmm. Now that I think about it, 'escaped' is not the right word. That business about me being chosen by fate to guard the universe from the revival of the dark masters? Yeah… lies. Elizabeth played me and I fell for every bit of it. Guess there's that pride biting me in the rear end again. I used to be rather darn proud of being a federal agent and that pride nearly got innocent people hurt. Elizabeth, crafty bitch that she is, sensed my prideful streak and exploited it. Of course, I believed suffering undeath to contain her dark master self an unwanted but vitally important burden to the survival of the entire world.

Hubris sucks.

As it turns out, my head was more of a hotel room than a prison cell. She needed me to fix the balance of magic in this world, since an entity known as the Red Rider broke it, vastly diminishing the potency of magical things here. With him destroyed and magic sliding none too slowly back toward equilibrium, Elizabeth no longer had any reason to lay low. I'd unwittingly given her the power to abolish the Void and set her brethren free. Never mind that destroying the Red Rider was also a moral requirement. The Universe often has a cruel sense of irony. Doing something ostensibly noble also set in motion what could very well end up being a new Dark Age.

Getting melodramatic again, Mom, says Tammy in my head.

Yeah, well, it's possible. I mean just what the world needed, a sect of evil mystics from the 1400s coming back from the dead… sort of. If they've rematerialized into this world—the Third Dimension—it's gone unnoticed. More likely, they're still hiding out in one of the upper realms, building power, getting used to having physical bodies again, and so on. Elizabeth pretended to be a prisoner trapped inside my head for thirteen years. I'm not expecting her to rush hastily into anything.

Anyway, Tammy didn't think it was healthy for me to sit around the house all day worrying—again. Which is why everyone's in the Momvan. And going to the beach.

Yes, the beach. As in wide open sand under the glare of the unblinking eye of fiery doom. Two out of three of my sister's kids are big fans of the beach. Ruby Grace not so much. Anthony is kind of 'meh' to the beach trip. He'd rather be on the computer playing a video game or horsing around with his friends. The boy has a few close friends from school, but most of the other kids seem intimidated by him. He's kind of a jock, kind of a nerd, but doesn't really belong to either group. I suppose it would be more accurate to say he's really a nerd but due to supernatural reasons, he's got the body of a jock. He doesn't bother with organized sports at school or in leagues anymore since he feels it would be unfair.

Today is also the first time in a long while for me to bust out a bikini. Red one, too. You know what's a seriously strange fact? Since becoming a vampire, I've spent more time stranded outside completely naked than in a bathing suit. Mostly, that's Talos's fault. If I don't undress before shape-shifting, the clothes shred. Then again, I couldn't tell you the last time I'd been in a bikini.

Actually, maybe I could. Way back when, just before my attack, when I'd lost track of Tammy at the beach.

So, yeah. This is the first time in over a decade that I've worn one.

I used to be the queen of beach bums as a mortal. But it's a little difficult to go sunbathing when the sun wants to kill me. Even though my new 'psychic vampire' self is back to being on friendly terms with the sun, thirteen years of warfare has left me with a flinch response that's still taking a while to go away. After all, there was only so much that industrial strength sunblock could do back in the day. Even though I managed to survive, being exposed to daylight had hurt like a bitch.

Another thing that's been bothering me: my sister turned fifty last month. She looks so damn much like Mom. No, that's not the part that bothers me. It's that *I* still look like I'm in my late twenties. Someone seeing us together would probably assume my sister is my mother, and that's seriously depressing me. Worse that Mary Lou isn't the least bit jealous about her looking older and I'm not.

And yeah, I know she's being truthful. I can't read my sister's mind, but Tammy can, and she let me know that her aunt M Lou wasn't jealous of our situation in the least. However, that she's really not jealous still makes me feel guilty somehow. It shouldn't, but it does. Probably because it makes me think about our parents getting old and how I haven't seen them in a long time… and how they still don't know what happened to me. Every time I think about going to visit them, my head fills with a vision of them seeing me still looking twenty-seven or so and dropping dead out of shock. There's no way to visit them without letting them in on the supernatural stuff. Well, at least no way without somehow making them not care how young I look. My mental powers don't work on family, and Tammy can't insert thoughts, only read them. There's always asking Fang to play with their perception of me, but part of me wants to keep all the supernatural weirdness as far away from them as possible.

Not sure if it's a good thing my parents and I

parted on somewhat unpleasant terms. Nothing super awful, just a bad argument over the federal agent thing. It's possible that they *still* don't know I had to step down from that job thirteen years ago. Nah, Mary Lou would've told them by now. Considering they haven't called me, reconciliation can't be too foremost on their minds, so whatever.

It's beach day. Enough bad thoughts.

My brain does a weird thing during the ride, like momentarily forget a decade or two had passed and daydreams that Danny is in the passenger seat and my kids are still super small. Wow, it really has been *that* long since I've been to the beach.

Speaking of which, while my body might not be aging, this van definitely is. Still, my Toyota Sienna has been through the war and back. I can't really bring myself to replace it just yet. Maybe once my kids are all grown up and out of the house—no rush—it'll be time to get something else. At least with the sale of that huge house nearly done, there's no need for me to feel bad about spending tons of cash at the garage to keep the Momvan on life support.

The passing scenery fills my head with memories of the past, happy times before things became so darn strange.

We're sneaking in during the waning part of the beach-going season, mid-September. It's still warm enough, so I didn't put up too much resistance when Tammy got the idea. The whole time I park, we unpack, and march across the lot out onto the sand, my head spins in an effort to understand why I hadn't gone straight to the beach as soon as it hit me the sun no longer hurt.

My body even has warmth again.

It could be that I'd acclimated myself to the mindset of the beach being an off-limits place for the rest of eternity. Or perhaps it makes me think of Danny. As soon as I unfold the beach chair that's been sitting untouched in my detached garage ever since Tammy was four, the answer comes to me: that dream. Not long after my attack, one hell of a nightmare hit me of being on the beach, in this very chair, burning to ashes with the most unimaginable pain.

Suffice to say, that left a mark. Even if only in my psyche.

I've come to learn that vampires—at least traditional ones—don't dream unless it's prophetic. The same probably holds true for the kind of vampire I am now. One of these days, I need to ask Kingsley if he dreams.

Tammy bursts into laughter. When I glance at her, she smirks and shares her thought with me: she's wondering if he dreams about chasing cars or squirrels in his sleep.

Oh, that's bad. So bad, I laugh, too.

I stop laughing when she takes her T-shirt off to expose a black bikini with blue trim that's so revealing it might just resurrect Danny from the grave so he can yell at her to cover up. If the shocked look on Anthony's face is any indication, that's exactly what's going on in his head. My ex-husband ended up as a quasi-dark-master and took up residence inside Anthony. That's seriously got to be hell on the poor boy. What kid wants their father snooping over their shoulder every second of every day? That's going to be super awkward when he finds a girlfriend. Considering what teen boys are inclined to do when they're alone sometimes, it's probably already awkward.

Tammy mutters, 'La-la-la-la' with her fingers in her ears.

Anyway, I'm sure Anthony is hearing an earful from his dad now.

Chuckling, I sit on my lounge chair and hit myself with the spray-on sunscreen while my sister does the same. The kids kinda mill around us. Ellie Mae, Billy Joe, and Tammy all seem happy to be out at the beach and are debating between braving the water or just hanging out, possibly throwing a Frisbee. Ruby Grace isn't terribly thrilled at being out here. She does have a swimsuit on, but plops down on a towel before breaking out a Kindle.

Ellie Mae starts teasing her for being a geek. "Come on, Roo, have a little fun for once!"

"Reading *is* fun," says Ruby.

"Such a nerd," mutters Ellie Mae with a hint of a Valley Girl sigh and a smile.

While the kids debate nerdiness, Mary Lou leans closer to me. "Ruby's already got a tentative scholarship offer from several colleges."

"She's fifteen." I blink. "Isn't it a little early to think about college?"

Mary Lou chuckles. "Not early for her. She's already planning on something like molecular biochemistry or some such thing I can barely pronounce."

"Like I said," says Ellie Mae, overhearing us. "Nerd."

"Good for her." I grin.

Tammy sets her hands on her hips, looks around, and sighs. "Wow. I can't remember the last time we came to the beach."

"Seriously," mutters Anthony. "This feels like the first time."

"Probably because you were a baby. An ugly baby, mind you." Tammy playfully punches him on the shoulder.

A sad smile forms on my lips as I once again remember the last day we'd been to the beach, before my attack. Tammy had been four, Anthony two. He'd burrowed a nice little hole in the sand between Danny and my chairs, and Tammy kept trying to fill it back in. Of course, she also pulled a disappearing act that day and damn near gave me a heart attack at thinking she'd been abducted. I had no idea back then that my daughter had probably seen the vaporous, black apparition of Elizabeth scoping me out. Or maybe she'd been scoping Tammy out. At that point in time, the woman didn't exactly know which member of the bloodline would be the perfect fit. Then again, a four-year-old vampire would hardly be of use to her. From what I understood, the real contenders had been me or my sister, Mary Lou.

"Wow," says Tammy. "I was a serious brat. The last time we were here, I kept dumping sand on your head."

"Huh?" Anthony pauses in applying sunscreen to look up at her. "Sand on my head?"

"Yeah, like this—"

And *splat*, she smacks him upside the head with a handful of sand.

I chuckle, watching Anthony chase her over the hot sand. They both end up splashing each other in the water.

Meanwhile, Ellie Mae and Billy Joe peer pressure Ruby Grace into swimming at least for a little while. Shortly, Mary Lou's three kids join my own within the lapping waves. Good grief, my two are almost as pale as vampires. Apparently, living a primarily nocturnal existence for the past decade has had an effect on not just me, but them, too.

I recline in my lounge chair and try my best to enjoy sunbathing. Used to be, me and the sun had been besties. Some people like watching sports on television, cooking, building models, video games, whatever... me? I liked soaking up rays. Guess I am a California girl through and through. Despite how much I used to *love* this, getting comfortable proves difficult. Somewhere between having that dream of spontaneous combustion and playing chicken with burning daylight for so many years, I'm as nervous as a soldier navigating a bombed-out city in a warzone full of snipers.

Maybe the day will come when this is once again as fun as it used to be.

Let's hope.

Thinking of snipers makes my thoughts drift to my old job at HUD. I wonder how my former boss Nico is doing these days. He's gotta be sixty by now or months away from it. Knowing him, he hasn't retired yet. I'm half tempted to check in on him, but he would notice my appearance hasn't changed since the day I resigned, and that would cause some problems.

Now that I can exist in daylight, I suppose it would be possible for me to reprise my old job without a problem. But… why? The money we're getting from the sale of the mansion aside, it's hard for me to give up the freedom of being my own boss. Besides, working HUD cases feels so 'small time' now. Like, I've got bigger problems: hunting demons, stopping Elizabeth's army of dark masters, working for an angel, and wandering multiple dimensions. Compared to that, being a HUD agent is about as impressive as mall security. And yet, at one point in my life, losing that job had been as emotionally painful as a death in the family. My whole sense of self-worth had been wrapped up in the achievement of making it into the agency.

I sigh, smiling to myself that I'm thoroughly over whatever sense of loss bugged me over it. Then again, having a steady check had been nice. Luckily, there's no end to cheating spouse cases. Yay, me.

LOST MOON

Mary Lou and I lay there sunning ourselves, watching the kids tentatively venture into the water. Predictably, Anthony is the most fearless, going out way farther than the others without hesitation. Ruby Grace doesn't appear afraid as much as disinterested. Hmm. Maybe there *is* something wrong with her? What kid doesn't like to go swimming?

Even more than being out in the day without worrying or even being uncomfortable, sitting on the left chair—with Mary Lou on my right—is bizarre. Danny always sat on the left, me on the right, with the little ones between us. It doesn't feel like it's been thirteen years. The last time I sat in this chair, Danny hadn't been a world class asshole. He'd been a good husband and a good father… neither one of us with the slightest idea how drastically and strangely our lives would change so soon after that day.

I hadn't known it at the time, but the dream that came to me a few days into my new existence as a vampire *had* been prophetic. Danny with another woman, breathing black vapor into Anthony. Sure enough, he did cheat on me… and now he's a dark spirit inside our son.

"What's bothering you, Sam?" asks my sister.

"Not really *bothering* me as much as feeling weird and nostalgic." I stretch. "Odd being here without Danny."

She sneers at the name. "You don't miss him, do you?"

"I don't, not really. After everything he pulled,

there isn't much fondness left for even the man he used to be before my life got freaky."

"Freaky to the nth degree." Mary Lou grins, then turns serious. "What that man did to you, using the kids as weapons. That's unforgivable."

"Chill out," I say. "Not missing him exactly. Just… it doesn't really feel like that much time has passed. Certainly not a whole childhood worth of time."

My sister laughs at my attempt at slang. Tammy doesn't so much as laugh as roll her eyes. She let it be known that she was fine with the occasional 'chill out.' but put her foot down on chillax. I told her I respected her opinion and suggested that she both chill out and chillax. Her eyes had nearly rolled up into her skull.

"Tell me about it." Mary Lou smiles. "I'm not even immortal and it feels like it's only been a few months since the kids were all tiny."

Thump.

My sister howls in surprise.

The volleyball that bounced off her head sails back over me and lands a few feet away in the sand.

"Sorry," calls a tall, blond, muscular guy in his mid-twenties. His blue swim trunks are a bit on the revealing side. Maybe he's European? He picks up the volleyball and looks me in the eye. "Didn't mean to hit your Mom in the head like that. Blame Carlos over there. He doesn't know his own strength." He gives us a big cheesy grin that, I suspect, is meant to get us hot and bothered.

I'm neither hot nor bothered, though plenty irritated, and take in a breath to correct him, but Mary Lou grasps my arm. "It's all right. Accidents happen. Sunglasses didn't break. I'm good."

As soon as the guy's out of earshot, back with the other twenty-somethings playing volleyball, I look over at my sister. "Sorry."

"We've been through this already. You don't need to apologize. Any rational person looking at us would make the same assumption. Besides, did you see his buns?"

"Oh, brother."

For an hour or so, we relax in the sun talking about normal things mothers of teens talk about. Mary Lou ends up verbally tap-dancing around something she's worried about Billy Joe doing, and she's being so vague I can't tell if she's hinting that he's smoking weed, planning to join the circus, or sneaking girls into his room without permission. Whatever it is, her husband is laughing it off as 'something boys do,' and this upsets her, but not enough to get into an argument with him over it. She's about to ask me how I think she should deal with it when a girl's squeal comes from the water along with a clap.

Ellie Mae yells, "Piss off, creep!"

That gets my attention, and Mary Lou's as well.

The kids are hanging out in a cluster, almost waist-deep in the ocean. Anthony and Billy Joe, who'd been completely underwater, surface at the same time, no doubt in response to Ellie Mae yelling. She's standing a bit closer to shore, only knee deep—evidently playing lifeguard for the younger ones—and a boy about nineteen give or take a year appears to have given her butt a pat. Now, he's hitting on her. She's having none of it, dodging every attempt he makes to put an arm around her or take her hand. The girl's already got a boyfriend—Josh I think? Probably would've brought him along today if the trip didn't come about on such short notice.

Speaking of boyfriends, my daughter has one of those, too. Ugh, forget the dark masters, the world's already ending. Did I mention he's an elf? Yeah, long story there. What can I say? My daughter has offbeat interests.

Ellie Mae leans back, rubbing her rear end. Yeah, definitely an unwanted pat occurred. Maybe even a slap. Tammy looks about ready to jump on the guy and start punching. Ruby Grace sinks down into the water until only her head is visible. The poor girl might be ridiculously smart, but she's totally non-confrontational and a little shy in the presence of strangers. Billy Joe swoops in, putting himself between the dude and his sister. He's seventeen like Tammy, but has an older look to him. Anthony walks up to stand beside Billy Joe with his arms folded. Even though he's not the biggest fifteen-year-old, my son has the 'go ahead and try something' posture of the old wise master from every Kung Fu movie ever made. He'd probably look more intimidating if he could produce facial hair. I'm sure he *can*, but it hasn't started appearing yet. The poor kid looks like he's twelve if you only see his face. He's got Danny's youthful good looks. Pretty sure if my husband had lived—we'd be in our later forties by now—he'd still look thirty. Mary Lou once called him an evil Ralph Macchio for looking way younger than he is.

Anthony dislikes fighting, at least against ordinary people, since he doesn't want to hurt anyone.

After muttering something that turns Ellie Mae's face red with anger, the jackass saunters away over to a group of three other guys, his obvious friends. The situation appears resolved, so I don't fly out of my chair and run over there. Another weird thing going around my head these days is the thought my kids don't need me to solve every problem for them anymore. They're not toddlers or even small children. Sure they're not adults either, but the list of issues that require Mom to step in is shrinking every day.

Despite knowing that they will eventually grow old and their souls will someday slip free to go around for another ride, I don't want them to leave me. (Though the jury might still be out on Anthony, who may or may not be a partial immortal.) Anyway, being the mother of teens is so damn bizarre. One moment, it's like I can't wait for them to be out on their own because the stress is reaching epic proportions, the next, I want to keep them little forever. Not *too* little, just small enough to need their mother.

A long, slow sigh slips out of me.

No, I don't *seriously* want that. It's merely the mom in me struggling to relax my protective grip. Totally normal. However, given the weird stuff that's happened to us over the years, my grip has been quite a bit tighter than most. Maybe too tight at times. Allowing the kids to stretch their proverbial wings is the hardest thing I've ever done.

And considering all the bizarre things that have happened in my life post-vampire change, that's a statement.

The idiot who 'hello-slapped' Ellie Mae on the backside—yes, I peeked into his head—remains close, making constant remarks to his buddies about Ellie Mae and Tammy being 'hot.' Though, he refers to my daughter as 'that goth chick.'

Mom, says Tammy in my head. *This guy is seriously pissing me off.* She proceeds to share with me various embarrassing things the guy has said about her and Ellie Mae to his friends. *The guy in green shorts isn't too bad. He's been telling the moron to stop harassing us. The other two are laughing. Anthony wants to know if he'll get in trouble for punching him.*

That's a yes, and not just from me. If he starts a fight, the cops will probably come after him.

Mary Lou, who'd been watching the creep like a hawk, looks at me. "What's going on? Tammy's looking at you in that 'talking to your head' way."

"Yeah." I explain to my sister what's going on. "No problem. Easy-peasy."

"What are you going to do?" asks Mary Lou.

Smiling, I get up and meander across the beach in their general direction, acting like I'm not actually walking toward them on purpose. The guy is *still* hovering near them trying to get Ellie Mae to pay attention to him. When I get close enough—about fifty feet away—I latch onto him with the mental focus that has become my version of drinking blood. While 'eating' psychic energy is so, so much better in my book than drinking blood, it comes with a slight downside: I have to feed more often. With blood, a pint or so every couple days was often enough to keep me fed, barring sustaining damage or overexerting myself.

As a psychic vampire, my nutritional needs require two feedings per day. However, it's hardly an inconvenience given how easy it is. Usually, I'll siphon little bits of energy from whole crowds at a time so no one even notices anything. One trip to Starbucks equals Sam happily full. And hey, I can enjoy the coffee again, too! In this guy's case, though, I concentrate on draining only him… and don't stop until he faints, asleep.

This form of feeding, unlike consuming blood, can't kill someone. That said, overfeeding on mental energy from a human has a much worse effect: destruction of their psyche. Basically, it leaves a person in a permanent vegetative state. Just a live body with no mental faculties left. Yeah, super cruel. Collapsing unconscious isn't dangerous —unless he happens to be attempting to set a world record by walking on a cable across Niagara Falls at the time—but here, he's merely going to sleep for about twelve hours.

Tammy, Anthony, and Ellie Mae all clap when he careens over backward. Billy Joe keeps 'standing guard,' watching the dude's friends. Predictably, they freak out at his sudden fainting. Another upside to psychic vampirism: no teeth marks. Granted, any wounds caused by a vampire tend to heal within minutes, if not seconds. The point being, of course, no one has a clue what just happened.

I walk onto the wet sand, up to my ankles in the water only when waves come in. "You guys okay?"

They all say yes, nod, or give me thumbs-up signs.

"What happened to him?" asks Ruby Grace, still neck-deep.

"Oh, I dunno. Must've spent too much time in the sun." I shrug, smiling. "Could be heatstroke."

Tammy snickers. Mary Lou's kids look at us both with that slightly confused 'missed an inside joke' sort of expression. They have no clue just how weird their auntie and cousins are.

"All right, as long as you're okay." I wave and head back to the lounge chair.

"That was bad," mutters Mary Lou, grinning.

"So was the stuff that guy said to the girls. A long nap is getting off easy. If anyone said that stuff to me when I was nineteen, he'd have had a giant red handprint on his face."

"And a broken nose once I caught up to him." She winks at me. "Hey, I realize you just ate, but do you want something from the grill? I'm getting kinda hungry."

I recline, fingers laced behind my head, smiling. Normal food tastes good again. Does absolutely nothing for me nutritionally, but that just means indulgence comes without guilt. I fish some cash out of my purse. "Sure. Grab me a chili dog. Been ages."

Chapter Two
Bare Essentials

Used to be, sunrise would knock me out even faster than watching baseball on television.

For all the upsides to my recent change, it does have one drawback: my consciousness is no longer wired to a cosmic off switch. That's more an inconvenience than a problem, since it leaves me vulnerable to sleepless nights brought on by worry. Yes, I'm trying to sleep at night again for that added feeling of sanity. Hey, I'll take normal anywhere possible. But, if my thoughts are lost to worry, it makes for hours of ceiling staring.

One way to explain what it's like is, say you went thirteen years with a television that automatically removed all commercials… and now they're back. Though, to be fair, the ad-zapping TV only worked during specific hours.

Anyway, the main reason this is a problem is

due to Elizabeth. Whatever she's planning, it might happen in weeks, or even decades. Not like the woman's trying to beat a deadline after all. From what I've pieced together over the years, the last time she grew overconfident and rushed into something, Archibald Maximus and the other Light Warriors ended up tossing her into the Void. That's a vast oversimplification of what happened—giant war, lots of suffering and fighting and so on.

It's kinda sad in a way to think that her own son fought against her, but the woman had been seriously messed up in the head. Most likely, she's plotting everything out three times and waiting for a time that offers her group of returned mystics—or whatever they've become—the best chance of accomplishing their goal, whatever it is. For no particular reason, my opinion of that has changed. 'Taking over the world' feels like too much of a generalization. Besides, no empire *that* big would be sustainable. Sure the Roman Empire lasted a long time, but it hadn't encompassed the entire world. No, I'm sure they're up to something horrible, but what her endgame is, no idea. No sense driving myself crazy by letting runaway thoughts terrify me.

Actually, I did have some inkling of her endgame, and it's so grandiose as to boggle the mind. The last time we spoke in any meaningful way, she had indicated that she had designs of creating her own universe somewhere within the vast, unused space created by the Origin. No, not the unused space in this universe. Creating her own universe, with its own rules, utilizing some of the unused space within the vastness of the Origin itself. Strange concept to be sure. But I likened the Origin as a skyscraper, with many floors already occupied and utilized. Our universe was, say, the tenth floor, with its millions of galaxies, stars and planets. A helluva of a big floor, to be sure. But there were other universes out there, occupying other floors, universes set up in ways that boggle our mind, universes with, say, no free will. Or universes with no concept of the individual. Group consciousnesses. Group thinking. Universes with just a few dozen life forms that never, ever die. In one of my meditations, I'd received such images, impressions.

I knew Elizabeth and company sought to find their own unused floor, and to make of it what they desired. Would be a strange and twisted universe should they succeed.

Well, for now, they were here on Earth, and what they sought next was a mystery to me.

The alarm clock going off scares the ever-loving crap out of me.

Can't remember the last time I screamed in fright.

It's not quite six in the morning on Saturday. And yeah, I know… it's a violation of the Geneva Convention or something to be awake this early on a weekend. Though, to be honest, sleep had been elusive. This new me has a different reaction to insufficient sleep than a normal person: it makes me hungrier. Basically, whatever energy I didn't regain by sleep needs to come from other people. Allison thinks this might allow me to stay awake for extended periods provided there's sufficient people around me to draw from, but I haven't tested it out.

Speaking of Allison, she's the reason I'm dragging myself out of bed at this hour on a Saturday. Among the many things that have happened to me in the aftermath of Elizabeth escaping and yours truly being at ground zero of the Red Rider exploding, my magic has returned. Yes, magic. Perhaps 'returned' isn't exactly the best word for it since I never really *had* magic in this lifetime to begin with. Though, that's more a case of me not realizing it than lacking potential. A couple times when I'd been little, faeries had shown themselves to me. Naturally, Mary Lou and my parents thought it was a product of my imagination.

Surprisingly, Mom came closer to believing me than my sister.

Alas, they convinced me that I imagined it, and, with doubt, the magical critters never appeared again. Allison is pretty sure they had been real faeries, like the ones who swarmed around that little girl, Annie and her giant tree.

Being a witch, having what some people call 'nature magic,' followed bloodlines as well as souls hopping among various reincarnations. In numerous former lives, rumor has it that I'd been a fairly powerful witch. My magic hadn't yet manifested in my current life before undeath got me. Alas, becoming an immortal has taken me out of the cycle of reincarnation, and initially, ended any chance of me using magic.

That changed, however, when the Red Rider literally blew up in my face. That wretched creature had been hunting young witches for centuries, stealing their power and devouring it—including myself in a former incarnation. This resulted in a net weakening of magic in the world. Ever wonder why there are all sorts of stories about Camelot and dragons and whatnot, but the real world is boringly mundane? Yeah, blame that guy. Because of him, the world had become largely devoid of magic except in a few small pockets. Witches and creatures like faerie continued to exist, but greatly diminished.

Not anymore.

When it—I refuse to call such a monster a 'he'—died, all that magic rushed back to wherever it belonged, reuniting with the various reincarnations of witches past, even me. Still not sure how it is that any magic at all works for me since I am still an immortal even if no longer undead. And that's part of why I'm getting up early.

My plans with Allison involve us going off somewhere remote to do some experimentation. She's been wanting to test me for a while ever since we got back from the upper dimensions, and today is the first opportunity we've had. Due to her crazy hours at the radio station where she works, she's coming straight here from the studio without sleeping. That's pushing her a bit too far, so I'll be driving—in her car.

My Momvan isn't quite up for a long trip. Something's squeaking under the hood and I don't feel safe getting too far away from civilization with it.

Thinking about today is what kept me up last night. Truth be told, I couldn't wait to see how magical I was... or wasn't. Of course, I would be leaving Anthony alone all day, but there weren't any direct threats against my family, and the last I checked, the kid took down a whole werewolf pack himself... granted, as the Fire Warrior. Still, kind of badass. Plus, I can teleport home if he has a serious problem. Tammy's got a date with Kai later today. It's taking a tremendous amount of self-control to let my daughter stretch her metaphorical wings. One good thing about her being a potent telepath: she knows I trust her. My negative reactions and thoughts about her going off on dates are entirely based on my fears of outside threats attacking her with more than a little denial on my part that she's growing up.

Allison sends me an 'I'm outside, should I come in?' text.

I send back 'Come in. Gonna grab a shower real quick.'

It's a really good thing my friend doesn't have any interest in being a thief. With the resurgence of magic in the world, she can pretty much snap her fingers and open any ordinary lock. Still, not wanting to be rude, I jog to the door and let her in. We do the 'hey how are you, haven't seen you in a whole two days' routine, after which she flops on the couch while I run to the shower and change.

By 6:18 a.m., I'm dressed for the woods with jeans, a flannel shirt, and hiking boots. We head out the door and hop in her Honda Accord, her taking the passenger seat. While I'm backing out of my driveway, she sets her phone in the dashboard mount and opens a GPS app pointing the way to a spot in the mountains to the east past Irvine Lake, close to Black Star Canyon. She has a place set up out there that the trifecta of witches she's part of sometimes visits for a deeper connection to the natural world. Between the energy of the place and its remoteness making interruption unlikely, it offers an ideal spot for me to play around with forces that ought to be kept secret.

We swing by Starbucks, mostly so I can absorb energy from people waiting in line. Yeah, it's kinda cruel to make tired caffeine-seekers even more tired, but there are a good fifteen or sixteen people here, which dilutes the effect on each person to pretty much negligible. We grab lattes, return to the car, and embark on the roughly hour-long ride up into the hills.

Allison spends most of the trip talking about a creepy caller who keeps dialing into her radio show, claiming to need help, and saying that only she can help him. Problem is, he never says much more than asking for help before the line drops… and the caller ID is blank. Even more unusual, the phone company has no record of an incoming call at the times the dude's on the line. Stranger still, she can't get a handle on his location via her remote viewing, so it's either a ghost or another psychic messing with her.

One hour and twenty-six minutes after leaving the Starbucks, Allison points at a small spot where the dirt road widens enough to park and be safe from traffic. You know, in case a deer comes jogging by. Something tells me this stretch of road sees a car or two a month, if that.

Allison leads the way up a hilly trail, the hillside dotted with surprisingly thick trees for California. We hike for a while, eventually stopping at a small clearing encircled by greenery that's grown almost too perfectly round to be natural, with a carpet of unusual green moss covering the ground. Not sure what it is since this sort of thing doesn't grow around here normally—I think. In fact, this small patch of woodlands doesn't resemble anything that belongs in Southern California. More like we've gone to Ireland.

"Wow. Is this a faerie's circle?" I ask.

"No. Those are much smaller and made of flowers and/or mushrooms." Allison smiles and kicks her shoes off, emitting the kind of adoring, relaxed sigh that usually comes out of me when my head makes pillow contact.

Oh, that's right. When I acted as a conduit for

Allison to break down the barrier the Red Rider used to trap Annie, touching the ground with my bare skin let me channel more power. I remove my boots and socks, making faces at how weird the soft green stuff under me feels.

"So, the barefoot thing is real, huh? Next thing you tell me, we get even stronger naked."

She laughs. "There are some witches who do that, but I'm not one of them. The touching-the-ground deal depends on the particular type of witchcraft you're attuned to. My assumption is you're the same as me, more of an arcane type."

"What the devil does that mean?"

"It means we're harder to understand. Not easily classified. Definitely not a nature witch, though we do get a little boost if we touch the earth directly, but that girl, Annie, is a true natural witch. Animals, faeries, and such flock to her. The energy increase for her when in contact with nature is way stronger than for us. Well, me."

"That explains why she hates shoes."

Allison nods, distracted. "Yeah. Putting shoes on her is like muzzling a dog. From what your sire described, you were very much a natural witch, back in the day in your previous incarnation."

"Until my magic was sucked dry." Indeed, I'd spent many an incarnation building that magic back up again. In fact, this was supposed to be the lifetime where the magic finally expressed itself, even if weakly. Until vampirism robbed me of that break out moment. "So what kind of witch am I in *this* life, Ally? And please tell me I'm not one of the ones with a thing for death and crows." I scratch my head. "Necromancers?"

Some color drains from her cheeks. "Hell no. Necromancers are *not* witches. They're something else entirely. Closer to the sort of mystics that hung out with 'the bitch who shall not be named.'" She taps a finger to her lips. "You like the sun and you live in dry California, maybe you're a particular kind of magic user that's fond of the desert."

I tilt my head. "What, like a genie?"

"No." She wags her eyebrows. "A sand witch. Get it?"

I groan. "Wow. Are you sure you're not a necromancer? That was pure evil."

She laughs. "Sorry. Yeah. Sit and give me your hands."

We both plop down cross-legged, knees nearly touching. She grasps my hands, closes her eyes, and enters some manner of meditative trance. With 'she-who-shall-not-be-named' out of my head, the barrier keeping me out of Allison's thoughts has finally been taken down. However, what's going on in there is mostly mental pushing and pulling, something akin to a person who can't see in the dark feeling their way around an unfamiliar room.

For about two minutes, I sit there listening to birds chirp.

With a *crack* like a .22 rifle firing, a thin electrical spark leaps between the tips of our noses. My eyes water from the hit a little, but it doesn't hurt any more than a playful flick from an irritating older brother. Allison, however, flies over backward as if someone strong slugged her in the forehead.

"Allie? Are you okay?" I leap from sitting to all fours and crawl over to where she stopped sliding. Her nose has a small char mark on it and her hair's all fluffed, but it doesn't appear that she's seriously injured, more dazed. "Allie?"

She blinks. "Ouch. Yeah. Okay, that's both what I was expecting and not."

I help her sit up. Again we end up cross-legged and facing each other. "Can you make that a little more confusing? I almost understood you."

"Hah. I'm pretty sure you're an arcane witch like me. That's what I expected due to your bloodline with Hermes and all, and some of your prior incarnations being in the same trifecta. It would be pretty weird for you to be a nature witch, a white witch, a seer, a cosmic witch, a kitchen witch, or a black witch."

"So you know which witch is which?"

This time, she groans. "What I *didn't* expect was the differential feedback. That, most likely, has something to do with you not being quite human."

"Gee, thanks."

"You know what I mean. Your soul is fully contained inside you. You don't need regular food —or any food. You have wings, for crissake!"

"Fine. I get it. Not human. What next?"

Allison coaches me for a while in regard to tapping my magical abilities. Despite knowing this stuff is real, there's just something about the moment that keeps me from taking things too seriously. I feel like that kid in the movie doing the 'wax on, wax off' thing. However, being able to get the gist of things directly from her thoughts makes learning somewhat easier. After another almost-hour, I've managed to summon a candle-flame-sized fire on my fingertip... except it's amber, not red-orange.

"You did it!" cheers Allison.

"This'll come in handy if I take up smoking again." I hold my fingertip up, staring at the little energy plume. "Is it normal to be this color and why isn't it making heat?"

"It's energy, not fire." She points her arm skyward and launches one of her magical 'darts' into the air. "Like that. Pure arcane energy. Only, you're not exactly at the point of being able to call enough of it at once to make a weapon out of it."

"Right..."

"Still, that's good for light."

"I can see in the dark, Allie."

"Umm. It's fun at parties?"

I chuckle. "Can't exactly go public with this."

"Oh. True." She rubs her chin. "Well, you can't bake a cake without taking the first step."

"Or, for that matter, bake a cake with it."

"True."

I shake my hand until the 'flame' stops. Then try to recall it. Only takes me about five minutes. Third try takes less than a minute.

"Progress." Allison grins.

Another forty minutes later, and I'm able to make an illusion about the size of a cat, by drawing more of that same energy and colorizing/shaping it instead of simply projecting it in a raw form. Allison keeps coaching me until I've made a fairly passable image of a calico cat. An hour later, I've managed to make the illusion appear solid. Unless someone tries to touch the cat, it looks like it's real —except for not casting a shadow. Meanwhile, Allison has been stifling a yawn or two. The poor thing had worked a radio show all night, and taught magic all morning.

"Okay, so you've definitely got magic again." She smiles, but it flattens. "However, I have a feeling that it's weaker than it should be because your soul is fully contained."

"Wouldn't that make it *more* powerful?"

Allison shakes her head, making her hair dance about. "No, not really. Witchcraft involves drawing energy from the world, channeling it through your body and soul, then projecting it outward in a different form. The problem is, you're already sort of clogged up with internal power. There's nowhere for the earth magic to move. It sort of gets lost within you."

"And you know this how?"

"I can see it in my mind's eye."

"Of course you can," I say, grumpily.

"Don't be that way, Sam. We all have our talents."

It's weird to feel disappointed at this since magic has never been anything I expected to have or relied on. Considering everything else about me, there's no reason for me to be glum over feeling that the supposedly powerful magic of my bloodline can't reach anything close to its full potential and will ultimately be lost because I can't reincarnate. Or not. My bloodline isn't dying out. I have two kids.

"It'll diffuse among any remaining souls connected to that bloodline, making them all stronger. Or maybe the nearest one to you will get it all and become world breaking." She shrugs, reading my thoughts. "It's really hard to guess what's going to happen after the resurgence."

We experiment for a while more. Eventually, I feel fairly proficient at making illusions of small animals. The 'spells,' for lack of a better term, work in one of two ways. Either they're 'self-contained,' and last about ten minutes before dissipating, or I can make only one at a time and keep it going by concentrating on it. Interestingly, the concentration needed sort of happens off camera; as in, behind the scenes at the back of my thoughts.

Once I've got some of that down, Allison yawns in earnest. She doesn't even have to ask. I know she wants to head back and get some shuteye. We put our shoes on and hike back through the woods to the car. I'm not a hundred percent sure, but I think a faerie might've checked us out on the way. That is, if I could trust the subtle movement from the corner of my eye.

Allison emits a groan of relief when she sits in the passenger seat of her Honda. "Think I'm gonna sleep on the way back to your place if you don't mind. Hey, would you just carry me inside and plop me on your couch?"

"Sure."

I stick the key in and turn it. The engine whirs for not even a full second before a loud *pank* comes from under the hood, followed by a noise like a bunch of rocks rattling around in a metal can. My second try to turn the key goes straight to the clattering noise. No one has ever accused me of being a mechanic, or even close to one, but my gut says the starter is dead.

"Crap!" yells Allison, sitting up. "Ugh. I knew I should've gotten that new car."

"What new car?"

"I was looking at one last week. Another Honda."

"Well, why didn't you get it? You make good money now."

She shrugs. "Just been afraid to."

"Afraid to get a new car?"

She takes in some air, exhales. "This might sound weird, but I have the worst luck with new cars. Like the worst. And I'm not talking like lemons or anything. My whole life, every time I've gotten a new car, I've been fired within a month or two. Maybe three. And it's not necessarily a *new* car. Usually, they're used. But the instant I'm dealing with car payments again, bam! Bad stuff happens." She leans forward and starts bonking her head on the dash. "Dammit. I wanted to sleep. Why can't I just go to sleep?"

While she bonks away, I pull out my phone... no signal. "Good news! We're in a dead pocket."

"Could've told you that. Side effect of our shrine."

"Seriously?"

"Yeah. Messes with phones, radios, you name it." She flashes a sheepish grin. "Anything technological kinda gets a bit weird close by. And, crap! We're going to end up having to walk like six miles."

I hold my head high. "Walking is for lesser mortals. I can fly us out of here."

I hop out of the car, look around to make sure no one is watching, and proceed to strip. We have the sort of best-friend-sister-roommate relationship where random spontaneous nudity is utterly bereft of embarrassment, though it doesn't happen too often. Usually only as an aftereffect of shape-shifting, sharp claws, or something going seriously wrong with a kitchen appliance, covering us with mess.

Talos is big enough to carry a rider, though I'm not sure he'd appreciate being treated as a giant sky horse. His slate-scraping laughter slides across my thoughts.

"Oh, wow. That's not a bad idea. Scary as hell, but beats walking. Hurry up and change before someone sees you with nothing on."

"Did you forget I grew up a hippie?"

She laughs.

"Besides…" I bundle my stuff up into a wad and hand it to her to carry. "If I had a dollar for every time I've ended up stranded somewhere naked, I'd have another mansion to sell."

"Hey, idea." She grabs my hand and pulls me into the woods far enough that we're out of sight from the road.

Gah. I'd forgotten how weird it feels to streak the forest, having plants brushing over bare skin. "Okay, this is starting to get strange now… walking off into the woods with you. Naked, I might add. If you turn me into a forest nymph, so help me..."

She laughs. "No, I got an idea. Didn't want someone to see you while we practice this."

"Allie, this isn't exactly a major highway."

"Yeah, but my luck…"

"You're not the one letting it all hang out." I fold my arms.

She shifts my bundle of clothes to her left arm. "Illusion magic. We've been working on it all morning. Instead of making a cat, make clothes."

Huh… that's an idea. I peer down at myself, concentrate on the mental image of an ordinary skirt, and invoke the magic the same way as when making false felines. Amber energy streams from my hands, gathering around my lower half like a cloud. A second later, it 'solidifies' into a grey skirt like I used to wear at HUD. It doesn't have any weight or substance. Still *feels* like I'm streaking, but at least no one can tell.

"You should make a single garment that covers everything," says Allison.

I'm about to ask why, but I catch her drift. "Otherwise, the separate pieces will disappear in like ten minutes."

"Boy, you must have had a great teacher."

I ignore her. "But how long can I make one article of clothing last?"

She shrugs. "Indefinitely. Remember, the concentration sort of happens behind the scenes."

"I'm still not sure I'm doing it right."

"You just learned it, what, two hours ago? You'll get better at it."

My second try summons a red evening gown. Damn subconscious.

"You should do that next time you're with Kingsley. Blow his furry little mind."

That gets me cackling with laughter. He would be absolutely perplexed by a dress he could see but not touch. Still, for emergencies, this will come in really handy. The only real problem I can see is needing to have a real solid mental picture of the garment. From there, I just let my subconscious go to work on it. However, such behind-the-scenes magic kinda drains me, which means tired, ergo, hungry.

So, red dress it is. For now.

That done, I back up a few paces from her, close my eyes, and picture the distant dancing flame, beckoning it closer. A momentary feeling of disorientation comes and goes, and I become aware of having enormous wings instead of arms, a tail, and a much keener sense of smell. Allison's muted gasp of awe confirms Talos is here. Or at least, he's loaned me his physical body.

A copy, Sam. He mentally 'smiles.' *I'm still here where I belong, keeping an eye on your human body.*

Eyes open, I look down at Allison. As far as dragons go—at least to anyone who reads fantasy—Talos is pretty small. My son said he looks like something called a wyvern, basically a dragon that only has two legs since the wings replace arms. But he's not exactly the same as that, either. I'm sure this dimension's perception of reality has an effect on how he appears here. Additionally, without me being an undead vampire, he's less of a giant bat-creature.

I stare at Allison until she understands I'm asking if she's ready to go. Can't talk in this body. At her nod, I flatten out as much as possible and let her climb on my back. This is no knight riding a dragon into war, more like a big sister giving her six-year-old sibling a piggyback ride—in terms of size comparison—but it works.

The tricky part is going to be finding a place to land back in civilization that won't cause problems. Hmm. Hillcrest Park will be perfect. I can teleport home, grab the Momvan and pick Allison up. Hope she's listening in right now so she knows to get a good grip.

"Oh, you don't gotta tell me twice," says Allison. "Or think that twice. I'm holding on as tight as I can."

Chuckling to myself, I stretch Talos's great, leathery wings out and leap into the air.

Chapter Three
Auto Zoned

Every now and then, the way a day ends up going is pretty far from how I expected when it began. Like me spending hours with Allison trying to get her car situation sorted. Flying back home worked out reasonably well. Only one guy—who doesn't remember anything—saw me swoop down and land as Talos at Hillcrest Park.

After getting dressed, I teleported home to my special empty nook in my closest, checked on Anthony who had his friends Bryce and Camden over to play video games, then went to pick Allison up. We spent the next two hours on the road with a mechanic driving a flatbed to recover and return the Accord.

Suppose it's good we started so stupidly early. It's only a little after three now, but it feels like it should be closer to ten. Poor Allison spent most of the time on the road asleep. Can't blame her. Of course, now that we're sitting in the waiting area of a car repair place in southeast Fullerton, she's wide awake from nerves. If they come back and say the car's going to cost a couple thousand bucks to fix, she's probably going to trade it in and get a new one. Paying for the tow will hurt. At least the place is willing to discount the recovery fee if they do the work.

Two women in their twenties and a guy about the same age sit behind desks at one end of the room. Apparently, they're 'maintenance coordinators' or something like that, scheduling service appointments and acting as a buffer between customers and the actual mechanics. The guy's pretty easy on the eyes. He's no ridiculous bodybuilder, but it's obvious he works out.

For about twenty minutes, we sit there watching the three clerks come over and call people by name, then discuss their car situation. Every time one of them walks out from behind their desk, Allison perks up—and slouches in disappointment after realizing they're looking for someone else.

She glances at me as if she's about to ask me for the fiftieth time if I think the car's totaled, but rather than speak, she bites her lower lip and gets a far-off look in her eyes. Uh oh. Allie always bites her lip like that when she's getting a psychic hit. That expression… someone's either dying, about to die, going to be lit on fire, or I'm going to end up stranded somewhere naked again. Hopefully, this time, it isn't in 1862. Or maybe the face she's making isn't supernatural in nature and she shouldn't have eaten that gas station burrito so fast.

It occurs to me that she's staring at the somewhat hunky 'maintenance coordinator.'

Her expression returns to normal; she shifts her gaze to me. "Sam, I just saw something potentially disastrous."

I look back and forth between her and the guy a few times. "The car's going to be super expensive to fix?"

"No, not that." She takes my hand and gives me the most epic of 'the poop is about to hit the fan' expressions. "I just a had a legit vision. And not a good one."

"Talk in privacy?"

She nods. We get up and head for the door, stepping outside to the right a little for some privacy.

"Okay. What did you see?" I ask, inheriting her worry.

"A young woman with light brown hair. Someone you spent time with, an immortal. Uhh… Mandy? Minnie? Mindy?"

"Mindy Hogan?" I ask, picturing the poor girl in my head. So damn young, barely twenty before she became an undead. "The, uhh, zombie?"

Allison fades out again. Any normal person looking at us would think I'm helping my friend who overdid it on some particularly strong weed. The space cadet quality to her posture fades a moment later, leaving her pale. "I just saw an entire college burning. Lots of people dead, some running around while on fire. We need to get to her right now. Something seriously bad is going to happen."

"Umm. She's kinda far away. In Arizona."

"Guess I ride you again."

"Or we can teleport," I say.

"Do you know somewhere safe to jump to?"

"Hmm. Not anywhere near the college."

"Well, I'd rather not teleport into a parked food truck. Maybe we should take Talos?"

"Talos it is."

"Miss Lopez?" asks one of the women clerks, sticking her head out the door. "Got a minute?"

Allison jumps, but doesn't yelp. "Uhh, yeah. Sorry. How bad is it?"

"Not bad at all. The starter died. Should be good to go with a new one. Also, it's about time to replace the air filter."

"What's it going to cost?" asks Allison.

"Starter and labor's going to be $550. Since you're getting the work done here, the tow charges drop to $85. Air filter's $50. All together, it's $685, plus tax."

Allison gives me a 'just a sec' look, then deals with the woman. It's going to take the mechanics a few hours to do the work, so she decides to pick the car up tomorrow. After she signs the work order, the clerk smiles at us and returns to her desk. We head straight to the Momvan. As I climb in behind the wheel, I wince as I'm reminded of the first time

I ran into Mindy… literally.

"So, this one feels bad?" I start the van and pull out of the parking space. "The vision, I mean."

"Yeah." She kneads her hands in her lap. "Real bad."

"You-know-who bad or something else?"

"Umm. I don't think dark master bad, but pretty bad. Just hurry." She puts her seatbelt on.

"You know, Talos doesn't have seatbelts."

She emits a nervous laugh. "Yeah, I know."

Chapter Four
Incoming

Allison worked her magic, and not in a metaphorical way.

She did two witchy things. First, she enchanted my backyard with a brief glamour spell that blurred the memory of anyone looking there while also giving them the inclination to go do something else aside from peer into my yard. This allowed me to go outside in my birthday suit without being noticed, change into Talos form—also without being noticed—and leap into the air, carrying her.

The second bit of magic she did was to conjure a motorcycle helmet for protection from the wind. Apparently, it *is* possible for a witch to create temporary physical objects instead of mere illusions, but that's going to take years of practice before I can do anything like that. Although a relatively new witch herself, Allison has been at this a lot longer than me.

She's also using the magic of technology for navigation purposes. Unfortunately, considering how fast I'm flying, she's pretty much hunkered down against my back as tight as possible. She's an old pro at riding horses, but they don't usually exceed 200 miles an hour, or do so at 2,500 feet—I'm guessing—off the ground.

After getting me generally pointed in the vicinity of Tucson, Arizona, she puts her phone in the leather jacket she borrowed from me and clamps on. I suppose there isn't *too* much to worry about. Some people have ridden motorcycles at this speed and it's not like we'll be flying at 36,000 feet so she'll run out of air. A little pre-flight Google search gave an estimate of about 470 miles to Tucson, so it's probably going to take approxi-mately two hours to fly it. I'd have teleported with her, but my familiarity with the area is lacking considering I've only been there once and it had been slightly crazy. That, and Allison doesn't like it when I teleport her. She gets insanely seasick for a while after.

I'm not sure where Mindy is at the moment—home or at school—and Allison said calling her would be bad for everyone, for some damn reason.

So, we fly.

Allison is oddly blasé about flying in such a dangerous manner. It mystifies me until her thoughts give away that she's got another spell hovering at the tip of her brain that acts as a parachute type effect. It isn't quite levitation, but it would let her fall to the ground at a slow enough speed that she'd land even softer than a real parachute jump. For the most part, I sense Allison is gazing around at the landscape below in awe. There really is something about flying that captures the human psyche.

While she's captivated by the scenery, I spend the two some hours flapping my wings while alternating my worry mode, mostly about Tammy and Anthony. Honestly, they're old enough to handle things without me for a few hours. Heck, at this point in their lives, they should be used to me having to urgently disappear to deal with weird stuff. I hope they both decide to stay at home while going to college—if they choose college—rather than dorm somewhere. Yeah, it's a little selfish of me to want them to remain close, but it's not really *that* big a deal. Visiting them is as easy as a quick teleport, but the bigger problem would be intruding on the eventual sense of independence they'll need. Honestly, I'm more afraid of an empty house than almost anything else I've had to confront in this crazy life. When my kids move out, it'll just be me and the ghosts of the past in that place.

And lord help me if Anthony does decide to go to Hogwarts, er, alchemy school.

Allison thinks: *Aww, they'll be fine. You're an awesome mom.*

Thanks. So what are we getting into here other than a giant fire?

The entire point of us zooming down there so

fast is to prevent that giant fire.

That's not answering my question.

Still working out the details. I'll get a better feel when we get close to her.

The more I think about it, the more leaving Mindy to her own devices a few months ago feels like an error in judgment on my part. I'd allowed sentimentality and pity to get in the way. That girl may only be a little older than my daughter, but she is a walking zombie apocalypse. Allowing her to continue existing is probably about as smart as giving pre-school kids a live hand grenade to play with.

Oh, stop. You're not a murderer, Sam. And no, I'm not seeing anything about zombies.

If Talos had arms, I'd have wiped the sweat from my brow.

Okay, to be entirely technical, he does have arms, but they're his wings.

This is so much nicer than driving, only it's a little tricky to stop for Starbucks like this.

Allison cackles at my thought. "Just pull up to the drive-through. They probably see weird stuff all the time. You know we could probably tell them it's an elaborate costume and they'll believe us."

Know what sounds *strange?*

A dragon laughing. It's kind of like a blast furnace having indigestion.

***

Tucson is damn near impossible to discern from the beige expanse below, at least from this high.

Up ahead past a stretch of smallish hills sits a patch of ground that kinda looks like the hull of a spaceship from one of Anthony's movies. Though, it's not panels or random metal junk attached to the ship, it's thousands of buildings that look tiny due to the altitude. Taller mountains stand beyond the swath of civilization, their upper reaches darkened brown.

I slow from an approximately 250 mile-per-hour sprint to a lazier maybe ninety or so, and start losing altitude in hopes of spotting the University of Arizona. Since I didn't exactly spend a lot of time looking down on this area from the air, nor did much of it fix in my memory, it's probably going to take a little more help from the cell phone for us to find the place.

"Look out!" shouts Allison.

I swing Talos's head around, searching for whatever startled her. Motion low to the right catches my eye, two enormous birds flying up toward us. Something doesn't seem right about them. At first, it's because birds don't generally fly up to intercept dragons like a couple of fighter jets, but when they draw closer, it becomes clear that they're not birds at all but crimson-skinned creatures with a passing resemblance to pteroda-ctyls, having long, pointy beaks, wide leathery wings, small legs, and a trailing tail.

Freakin' gargoyles?

"Not exactly," says Allison. "Demons."

Crap, I think. This is going to get rough, isn't it?

"Don't worry. If I fall off, I'll catch myself with magic."

Except there's no possible way for me not to worry about dropping my best friend.

The incoming demons break formation, one pulling up high, the other staying under us. Looks like they're maneuvering to attack from two directions at the same time. I lean back into a climb to stay above the one going high. Unfortunately, it's quite a bit smaller and lighter than Talos, also it's not carrying someone on its back.

A streak of bright yellow light flies over my head, striking the demon in the wing and tearing a fist-sized hole in the membrane. Smoke peels from the burned edges of the wound. The creature emits an agonized screech, stops flapping as if paralyzed in pain, and glide-falls.

Nice one, Allie.

"Well, I was aiming for its head, but thanks!" shouts Allison.

The other demon rockets straight up at me from below. Allison screams as I roll into a dive to avoid the thing's undoubtedly sharp-as-hell beak. It whooshes past me close enough that a wingtip brushes Talos's belly. At that distance, it looks bigger than expected, with a body about equal to an average human man's torso. From the tip of its beak to the end of its laughably small legs, it probably would be about the same height as a person due to its elongated neck.

And it stinks. *Damn* does it reek.

The aroma of sulfurous rotten eggs, feces, and cat pee punches me straight in the nostrils, making even Talos's eyes water. Wow. If it's that horrible from a split second almost-collision in midair, I would *not* want to be anywhere near it on the ground.

Allison hurls a few more attack spells. Unfortunately, her projectiles aren't terribly fast—roughly like a fastball pitch. Sure they're kinda difficult to dodge on the ground, but when everything is moving in three dimensions at about a hundred miles an hour, it gets tricky.

Demon one—with the holed wing—has regained control and swoops in high left. I'm pretty sure it's going for Allison out of revenge, except she's too focused on trying to hit the other one on the right that she doesn't see it coming. Seconds from it scissoring her head off with its four-foot-long beak, I roll upside down and rake at it with my feet. I'm expecting to at best, shred it like a housecat using its back legs, and at worst, kick it away.

The thing is... Talos has some serious toenails.

Two of the talons on my left foot spear the little bastard through the chest, piercing out its back... and he sticks to me. Shrieking and squirming, the pterodactyl-shaped monster tries to bite my... I guess that joint's about equal to an ankle? Anyway, its teeth kinda bounce off my scales. Oh... that's cool. Not sure what made me expect those things to slice me up with ease, but it looks like my armor's going to hold up here. Big time.

Allison's screaming gets distant. It occurs to me that I'm still upside-down and no longer burdened by extra weight.

Shit!

I roll back upright and swing my head around searching for her.

Allison's about forty feet down, gliding. Despite a bright orange magical motorcycle helmet hiding her face, the way her arms are folded tells me she's not too happy and is giving me the 'look of doom' from behind the visor. The remaining demon goes after her. I dive, flapping hard to intercept.

Fortunately, the demon's not the smartest thing in the world—it's course straight at her makes hitting it easy for her. Allison's next energy bolt nails it in the face, blowing its head into a shower of black slime. The sword-sized beak goes flying in one direction while the remainder of the body pretty much falls straight down, the headless noodle of a neck fluttering.

Both beak and body disintegrate into black dust after a moment.

I swoop under Allison so she lands on my back again. Once confident she's got a good grip, I shake my left foot, again feeling like a cat. Ever see a cat step on something sticky? Yeah, that's what I'm doing, but no matter how hard I shake my foot, the demon remains stuck on my talons. And no, biting it to pull it off is out of the question. Did I mention how bad this thing smells?

"Thanks," yells Allison.

Oh, as if any choice existed, I think.

"I would've been fine. Might have been hard to explain to anyone who saw me glide to the ground, but the fall wouldn't have hurt me." Despite her confidence, she squeezes me pretty tight. Yeah, slow-fall magic or not, being this high up without an aircraft is kinda scary if you don't have wings.

Allie? Why isn't this stupid thing on my foot disintegrating like the other one?

She leans over to the left and hurls another spell, blasting it in the chest. "Because it wasn't dead yet, just faking."

Seconds after her magic leaves a crater in the demon's chest, it melts away into black dust.

I wiggle my—Talos's—toes, and emit a sigh of relief. Gah! Having that thing stuck to my foot had been annoying as hell.

Heh. Hell. Demons. Right.

Umm, Allie? What the heck were those things and why are they here? I mean, I know they were demons, but why are they here, and why did they attack us?

"Because it knows we're coming," yells Allison.

It? It what? What it?

"I'll explain when we get there. My throat hurts from all this yelling. It's loud up here."

Right. Aha! Stadium! That, I remember. And there's the University of Arizona.

Now I just need to figure out where Mindy is…

Chapter Five
Monster

I hastily swoop in for a landing atop the tallest building on campus, right as the sun's going down. Seems like it's the highest building in the area at about ten stories. Brick red, rectangular, white roof. Doesn't look like there's all that much activity going on below at like five or whatever time it is. Six? Wait, we crossed a time zone. It could be seven. Doesn't matter.

The high roof is a good out-of-sight place for me to change back to me and get dressed. Wow, I haven't been naked on the roof of a building at a college in a long time. Hey, don't look at me like that. I hadn't even met Danny then.

Allison holds my hand and we jump off the side, floating straight down like we don't weigh much at all.

"Wow, that's amazing," I say once we land.

"Like a leaf on the wind."

She chokes up, almost crying.

"Umm. What about that is sad?"

"You never watched *Firefly*, did you?" Allison wipes her eyes.

"Nope. Didn't have any of those in my backyard as a kid. Though we did have fairies. I think."

Her sniffles turn to laughter. "Dork. No, it's a TV show."

I give her a blank look.

She gasps like I've committed some great sin. "Oh, forget it. We have real problems now. Where is she?"

"I think I remember… come on."

It's tempting to teleport again, but the only two places in her house I remember well enough to land are her bedroom and the bathroom. Pretty sure she's not in class at the moment, so yeah, I can't take that chance.

That decided, we head out for the place she's renting.

Walking. Like normal people.

***

The good news is, her roommates remembered me as her cousin.

Bad news is, Mindy wasn't there. Her roomies told me she went home for the weekend, then tried to grill me about what they did that pissed her off. They think she's avoiding them because of something they did. I can't tell them she's avoiding people in general because she's become like the queen of zombies or some such thing, so I say she's having a rough time lately because someone in her family is really sick. She's wanting to spend time with them while she can.

That seems to smooth things over with the girls.

"Okay, so now what?" asks Allison once we're outside.

"Her parents live in Canelo. Kinda remember it being like forty miles south."

Allison pulls out her phone. "Ugh. Back up we go, I guess."

I fold my arms, smiling. "You sound thrilled."

"Oh, the flying's fine." She smiles. "It's the not finding her that's annoying. This feels bad."

"You still haven't told me what *this* is."

"Got it." She holds up her phone with a map on it. "I'll explain when we get there so I only have to do it once."

"Right…"

With the help of Allison using magic to create a 'zone of disinterest' as she calls it, I undress and call Talos again. Even though a few people walk past the alley we're hiding in, none of them notice a giant black dragon-like creature sitting there. Whatever she did just kinda makes people not pay attention to this spot for a while. Either that or they simply didn't see me in the dark.

The girl's a veritable Swiss Army knife of useful stuff.

And she's only getting stronger...

Flying to Canelo doesn't take long at all. Again, with her phone GPS, Allison navigates. Her app is having a conniption fit at us going in a straight line while ignoring roads, constantly trying to redirect us to the nearest bit of pavement. However, the endpoint is still clear on the screen.

My memory of this place is better than I thought. As soon as we get close enough to see the town, I veer toward Mindy's parents' house. God knows we spent plenty of time running around here collecting and burning the dead. Ugh, what a mess that had been.

I hate zombies. After that experience, I don't even watch that show my kids like anymore. Just don't wanna see that stuff, period. Even looking at it on a TV screen makes me smell it all over again. Not sure if it should concern me that my kids still watch the show. If protecting the world from a zombie apocalypse comes down to deleting zombies from the collective consciousness so the universe doesn't make them real, we are doomed.

A moment later, a bright beacon on the ground catches my eye. No, it isn't a light—it's Mindy Hogan in a two-piece bathing suit reclining in her back yard. It's not weird because she's a zombie… it's weird because it's dark out. Is she moonbathing? That must be some new hipster thing.

No point being subtle. She already knows I'm special.

I circle around to approach the house from the

rear and glide in low.

Mindy's eyesight isn't the greatest. She doesn't react to me until I'm like fifty feet away and flaring my wings out to slow down. The smoothie she's drinking nearly falls out of her hand as she looks up at me in complete shock. Pretty sure the only reason she hasn't either run off screaming or grabbed something to wallop me over the head with is Allison on my back waving at her.

I land and walk the last few yards over, Allison still riding me like a bizarre two-legged horse.

Mindy's shocked expression shifts to 'that's so cool!' "Umm. Who are you?"

"Allison Lopez." My friend hops down, pushes my wing up out of her way, and ducks under it, offering a handshake. Allison points to me. "You know Sam Moon, right?"

"I know a *vampire* named Sam Moon. Not a hideous flying dragon thing."

Who's she calling hideous? asks Talos in my head. *And you humans are nothing to write home about.*

I snicker and reassure Talos he's a very handsome giant dragon-thing. I next summon the single flame and change back to myself.

Mindy gawks at me. "Whoa. Okay, I used to turn into a monster once a month, but nothing like that."

I roll my eyes.

"That's totally badass!" Mindy squats to check out a Talos footprint. "How can I do that?"

"Sorry… I don't think it's really possible. Kind of a one-in-a-million chance for me, too."

"Wow. It doesn't bother you being outside with nothing on?" asks Mindy.

"You're in a bikini. Not that much different." I chuckle. "And what are you doing out here at night?"

She shrugs. "Not like I get a suntan anymore—or feel cold. Just relaxing outside. So, how do I turn into whatever that was?"

"Dragon shapeshifting is pretty rare, even for vampires." Allison hands me the clothing bundle. "Ugh, what's that weird smell?"

"Cow brain smoothie." Mindy tilts the cup at us, then slurps out of the straw. "I added some kale and quinoa for variety."

Allison and I both cringe. Kale? Seriously?

I hurriedly dress.

"Anyway…" I grasp Mindy's shoulders. "We have to talk."

Chapter Six
A Question of Survival

Allison steps closer and stares into Mindy's eyes.

I back off and give her some room. Damn, this poor kid. Sure, she's twenty, but still sets off my maternal protectiveness. It's pretty obvious from looking at her that she hasn't come to terms with what's happened. Worse, she's likely still beating herself up for being dumb and going to that medical testing place. At least in my case, the attack happened out of the blue. No stupidity on my part beyond going for a jog at night. But if I hadn't gone out, the vampire who attacked me would've gotten me at home and most assuredly killed my whole family.

Unless, of course, my sire had gotten there first, which very likely wasn't going to be the case.

So, no. As foolish as some may think a woman

going for a midnight jog alone is, I no longer consider it stupid. Indeed, maybe some instinct told me to get away from my family at that moment to protect them.

"Yeah." Allison breaks her piercing stare with Mindy. "That's what I thought." She faces me and flares her eyebrows.

I tilt my head.

She flares her eyebrows again like she wants me to do something. Oh, duh. I peek into her head.

Sam, thinks Allison. *That girl doesn't have a dark master inside her at all. It's a demon. A nasty one. She's like legit possessed by a demon.*

My initial 'yeah, so?' reaction gets a frustrated scowl from Allison. She taps her foot impatiently while Mindy looks back and forth between us like we told a joke she didn't get. A second later, it hits me. Holy shit! Demonic possession, not a dark master? Does that mean it isn't permanent?

Bingo, Sam.

That's why Mindy isn't rotting… she's not dead.

Two for two, Sam.

She's curable… I stare at the young lady, all my mom-ness coming to the surface.

Maybe, maybe not.

I shift my gaze to Allie. What do you mean? It's either curable or it's not.

Allison winces. *The actual curing part is not too difficult as this sort of thing goes. The hard part is going to be surviving it… and I don't mean just*

Mindy surviving it. This one's big, Sam. Kicking it loose from her could wipe out a small town and take us with it.

Say what?

I wouldn't even suggest we try this but… it's going to unleash chaos anyway within the next forty-eight hours. Thousands of zombies, riots, fires, mass panic. Might even be the end of civilization as we know it. Could be two hours from now, too. My precognition isn't exact. Just know it's soon. If we don't do this, it's gonna blow up anyway.

Shit. Okay.

I take Mindy's hand. "We need to talk. Are your parents here? They should be involved, too."

"Umm, you guys are kinda freaking me out." Mindy eyes Allison. "Why does she look so scared? Did you tell her what I am?"

"Mindy, she rode in on the back of a dragon. You can assume she's aware of the supernatural stuff already." I smile. "C'mon. Let's go inside. What we have to tell you is scary, but you might like it."

"Sure." She sucks down the last of the brain smoothie, and leads the way in via the back door. "Mom? Dad?"

Art's grunt comes from the living room. A moment later, he and Louise Hogan walk into the kitchen.

"Umm?" asks Mindy, looking around at everyone. "Feeling a little out of place in a swimsuit. Do

I have time to change?"

Allison nods at her.

"Be right back." Mindy dashes off down the hall.

"Sam," says Art, offering a handshake. "What a pleasant surprise… I hope."

"There's something wrong." Louise nods in greeting, though she eyes me suspiciously. It's not a look of distrust, more that she seems to be aware we bring bad news.

"Yeah." I nod. "Something is wrong, but we have a chance to stop it from getting worse."

"Sam, what's all this about?" asks Art.

"We'll explain everything when Mindy's back. Actually, *she* will." I gesture at Allison.

My witchy friend hooks her thumbs in her jean pockets.

"Who's this?" asks Art.

I introduce Allison as a 'genuine psychic' and my best friend. Allison beams at the 'best friend' part. I sigh, regretting it instantly.

Too late, you said it.

"We're here because of her vision," I add.

Louise is about to scoff, but evidently changes her mind when Mindy walks in—a reminder that supernatural stuff *is* real. The girl's changed into a flannel shirt and jeans, still barefoot. At seeing her dressed, the parents both relax a bit. I'm sure watching her tolerate the chilly Arizona desert night in almost nothing unnerved them.

"Okay," says Allison. "Here's the deal. When I

explain this, Mindy, you're going to immediately fall under attack. You need to steel yourself mentally and ignore every urge you might get. Can you do that?"

Mindy looks worried, but clenches her fists and nods. "Okay. You guys aren't here to kill me, are you? Finally decide I'm too dangerous or something and need to incinerate me?"

"No," I say. "Not at all."

Her parents both sigh in relief.

Allison opens her hip bag and takes out a black eyeliner. She steps up to Mindy and starts drawing little marks on her forehead. "Okay, so Sam tells me she explained all that dark master stuff to you a few months ago?"

Mindy nods. "Yeah, this creepy voice in my head."

"Well, you don't have a dark master. The entity possessing you is actually a demon."

"Oh…" Mindy's eyes turn solid black. She grabs Allison around the neck and starts lifting her off her feet.

I pounce on her arm, but the girl is *strong.* Too strong for me to stop.

Mindy's eyes fade back to normal; she lets go, then stands there shaking. "Sorry. Wow. I wasn't expecting"—she growls—"*that*. It's pissed."

Art moves to embrace Mindy from behind, but I hold up a hand to ward him off.

"Best if you stay out of arms' reach. Your daughter is fighting off the thing inside her trying to take over now," I say before facing Mindy again. "Here's the important part. Because it's a demon and not a dark master, there's a few key things to be aware of. One: you're possessed by a demon. That means you're not dead. Two: we can probably kick it out of you, but it's dangerous."

Mindy's eyes start to milk over, but she snarls and fights her way back to the surface. Sweat beads on her forehead. "It's seriously angry. It's a pain in the ass to hold it back. Are you saying you can make me normal again?"

Allison and I both nod.

"Theoretically, but it's dangerous," adds Allison.

The fight raging inside her seems to settle. Mindy stands tall, no longer shaking, though her glare could melt steel. "Don't care. Do it. I knew a day like this was coming. Might as well be now."

The hope in her eyes pulls at my heart. It's like the slight chance of getting her life back is the only reason she's able to contain that thing.

"Wait. How dangerous are we talking here?" asks Art.

"Don't care, Dad. If I can get my life back, anything's worth it. It would be better to be dead than be this way forever. I see the way you guys look at me sometimes… like I'm some nuclear bomb that could go off and kill everyone."

Art and Louise look down.

"I don't blame you. I *am* a ticking bomb." Mindy nods at us. "Whatever you have to do, do it."

The skin of her cheek and neck stretches forward as if a hand inside her tries to tear its way out. For a few seconds, the eyeliner writing Allison put on her glows bright orange. "Umm. That felt weird. What happened?"

Allison shivers. "Don't ask."

"What's involved?" Art peels his gaze off the floor to look at me. "Is our daughter gonna make it?"

"That's less of a question than are we *all* going to make it," says Allison. "Breaking the demon's hold on her isn't going to be the risky part. Pretty sure I can do that. Problem is, once it's kicked out of her, it's going to be here and we have to deal with it. Depending on how that goes, it could kill all of us. Even wipe out this entire town… but I have an idea to help with that part."

"I'll get the shotgun," says Art, starting to walk off.

"Artie." Louise grabs his arm. "A gun ain't gonna hurt a demon."

"I'm not going to be able to hold this thing in much longer, guys. Whatever you're going to do, do it fast." Mindy looks me in the eye, not a hint of hesitation in her. "What I am now is worse than dead. If you guys screw it up and turn me into a ghost, I won't be mad at you, I swear."

"Are you sure?" asks Louise, Art, and me all at the same time.

"Do. It." Mindy shivers with the effort it's taking her to contain the thing.

I glance at the parents.

They don't seem terribly happy with the idea, but both of them nod.

"Let's do it," I say.

Chapter Seven
Fun for the Whole Family

We relocate a fair distance away from town in the scrub desert, far enough that we can't even see any other houses.

Mindy stands on a spot Allison indicates and tries to hold it together while my witchy friend walks around tracing circles in the dirt with a knife. Art and Louise stand on either side of me a few paces away. Despite his wife's pleas, Art still brought the shotgun. It seems like a modern weapon wouldn't really bother a demon… but that makes no sense. The destructive power of buckshot vastly exceeds that of a sword, so why do I think guns don't work? Maybe because the entire idea of demons feels 'medieval.'

Or maybe because I'm carrying the Devil Killer. That kinda makes swords feel way more powerful than they would normally be.

While Allison continues setting up a circle, I gaze skyward and whisper to Azrael, the angel who gave me that blade, asking him to get my back if whatever comes out of Mindy is over my head. Then again, it's not going to be The Devil. That thought comforts me only until I realize that the prior Devil *wanted* to be destroyed. Good chance it would've been a lot more difficult to kill him otherwise. Also, good chance this demon doesn't want to die. He seems quite upset at the notion we mean to pluck him out of Mindy like a stubborn tick before he can unleash the end of the world.

Speaking of Mindy, her eyes keep flickering back and forth between normal, milky white, and solid black. Whenever they go onyx, her facial expression is so different that I know it's not Mindy looking at me. Yeah, that's hate. That's the kind of hate you throw at someone who steals the parking space you've been waiting five minutes for.

A shimmer appears off to the left. The bluish coalescence of energy I've come to recognize as a ghost attempting to remain invisible to humans glides over to Allison, who speaks to it. Aha. That must be Millicent come to help us out. They confer for a moment before Allison looks at me like she's about to ask me to do something horrible and cruel. Millicent flickers brighter, fleshing out, so to speak.

"Okay, okay, fine... I'll ask." Allison tromps over to me.

"This can't be good," I say.

Art sucks in a breath. Louise squeezes my arm. I

don't think they can see Millicent yet. But at the rate she's coming into focus, they would soon enough.

"I really, really hate to say this… but we need Tammy and maybe Anthony here, too."

"What?" I narrow my eyes, mama bear protectiveness rising. "What for? They're kids."

Allison holds her hands up in a placating gesture. "According to Millicent, Tammy needs to shield Mindy's mind from the demon while I cut it out like a tumor. Without her, Mindy might not come out of this and have anything close to sanity left. That demon is going to try to do as much damage as it can on the way out. It could leave her in a vegetative state."

Louise squeezes me harder. "I… I can't ask you to risk little children."

I bow my head. "My daughter's seventeen. Not exactly little. Dammit. Why Anthony?"

"Because this is going to get kinda nasty. Millicent says there's gonna be a bunch of demons. Think Fire Warrior here. Besides, you and I are going to have our hands full, and he can help protect Tammy. She's a potent psychic, but physically, she's no tougher than any normal person."

Ugh. I rub my forehead, picturing Judge Judy reaming me out for being stupid. "Does it legally count as child endangerment for me to bring two minors into contact with a greater demon?"

Allison bites her lip. "Umm. Probably, but what judge would ever believe it?"

LOST MOON

For the past seventeen years, my life has been primarily dedicated to protecting my children from danger, not bringing them into it. Deliberately exposing them both to the presence of a powerful demon goes against every fiber of my being. One look at Mindy desperately trying to hold back the tide of evil inside her, slams me with guilt. My kids aren't innocent little children anymore. As much as I don't want to admit it to myself, they're both kinda potent supernatural beings. Well, Tammy isn't so much a 'supernatural being' as she possesses potent powers. Dammit. Allison (and Millicent) are right. If my kids don't help out here, Mindy, her parents, and probably quite a few other people are going to die.

"Okay. I'm not going to force them to do anything, but I'll ask."

Allison nods.

I pull out my phone, and catch myself feeling strange that there isn't already an answer from Tammy. The amulet the faerie, Maple, gave her that quiets the relentless assault of telepathic voices also limits her range. Remembering how overcome she'd been with happiness and gratitude when she understood what that amulet did—spared her sanity —makes me smile and go a bit misty-eyed.

When she's wearing it, it's possible for me to go far enough away that she loses her almost-constant eavesdropping into my head. Most people would probably consider that invasive as hell, but not me. I understand where it's coming from. Yeah, she's seventeen, but she still wants to cling to me like a frightened child. Ms. 'Too cool for school' wouldn't dare show that vulnerability out in the open, but her constant link is basically like she's holding my hand all the time in a way no one else can see.

Of course, she'd never actually admit that to me. And maybe I'm misreading it. Could be, she's trying to be as close as possible since she knows she isn't immortal and I'll have to keep going someday after she's gone. Or, maybe she's being protective of me in case Elizabeth attacks. Yeah, my little Tam Tam is starting to grow up. In some situations, she probably *could* protect her mother now.

Feeling old, I let out a long sigh.

After setting up a group text with my kids, I send: *'You guys up for a quick exorcism?'*

Tammy: *'Mom! I'm with Kai.'*

Anthony: *'Lol. That's probably why she wants to do an exorcism. Or who!'*

I send. *No lol. This is serious. A girl is going to die, maybe a lot of other people, too.'*

Anthony: *'O sht. Ya sure. Can I take the car?'*

The boy thinks he's exploiting a technicality to get around swearing by omitting the i.

A tingle creeps over my head. Tammy must've removed her amulet. Letting her powers off the leash is fine when she's ready for it. Having such a wide range wasn't the problem as much as the constant barrage from thousands of voices she couldn't get away from. Turns out her range with me is almost limitless, especially now that Elizabeth is gone from my head.

Tammy texts: *'You know, Mom, most families consider movie night or going on vacation together to be family activities, not getting into fights with demons.'*

'Sorry. I guess we never did the vacation thing,' I type.

Tammy: *'It's okay. If it wasn't money, it was the sun. Hey, now that you can go outside again… how about Hawaii? Miami?'*

Hah. I send, *'Sure, after school's out for the summer.'*

Tammy: *'Cool. Okay. Let's kick some demon butt!'*

I shake my head at the absurdity of it all. *'Okay. I'll be right there.'*

Tammy: *'But you're in Arizona.'*

'I'll be home in like ten seconds. Stay out of the living room.'

They both assure me they will. I look up from the screen and examine my surroundings to get a good feel for them. "Okay. Kids are game. Be right back."

Allison nods.

I stare into space, picturing the dancing flame in the dark. Once it solidifies, I feel myself move toward it. The tiny candle grows into a roaring wall of inferno with a doorway in the middle leading to my living room.

When I step through, I'm home.

Anthony's voice drifts down the hall. He's telling his online gaming buddies something came up and he has to go. A minute or two later, he emerges from his room in a white tank top, cargo shorts, and white socks, giving me a casual 'Hey, Mom' sort of wave while grabbing his sneakers from the floor. He looks at them, shrugs, then drops them and removes his socks.

"Ant?"

"If the Fire Warrior has to come out, they're just gonna get destroyed, anyway. Oh, crap. Let me grab a spare set of clothes." He runs back to his room.

"Tammy?" I yell.

Chill out, Mom. I'm on the way back now. Kai doesn't want to break the speed limit, says my daughter in my head.

Mindy's hanging on by a thread, I think. How long will it take you to get here?

Umm. Couple minutes? Faster if you promise to make a cop forget if we get stopped.

No. Drive safe.

Tammy can read minds, but not influence them, which is probably a good thing. Meanwhile, Anthony returns with a small backpack over one shoulder. He stuffs his socks and sneakers in it. "Okay. Ready."

I sigh. "Waiting on your sister."

He nods, then heads to the kitchen to stick his head in the fridge. As we stand around waiting, Anthony munches on a slice of cold pizza—I swear that boy never stops eating. Finally, the near-silent whirr of an emerald green Tesla pulls up outside. Tammy runs in the door, wide-eyed with urgency and worry. Her lipstick, I note, is smeared.

As soon as I notice it, she blushes.

"Forget it." I take her hand. "We have a demon to kill. Come on, you two. Hop on already."

They're about the same height, but Anthony's heavier. My teleportation is fickle. It will take everything I'm wearing or carrying along for the ride—thankfully. But it doesn't like taking other people or big objects I'm merely touching. Like, if I lean on my van and teleport, it won't go with me. If I simply hold my kids' hands, I'd disappear out from between them. So… Anthony hugs me from behind, Tammy from the front. As soon as they lift their feet off the ground to hang on me, I call the flame. In that moment, my power considers them 'stuff I'm carrying,' so the teleportation brings them along.

When we reappear in the field, Art and Louise both yell in surprise.

Tammy looks around. The instant she makes eye contact with Mindy, my daughter recoils as if she'd been punched in the nose. Faint scratches appear on her cheek. Rather than cry out in pain, she recovers her balance and glares back with a look of 'Oh, hell no.' She's already read the basics of what we need her to do out of my head, so she gets right to work. Within a moment of her focusing on Mindy, the young woman stops shuddering and snarling, once again seeming relatively normal.

Millicent walks over, now a fully manifested apparition. Other than faint transparency, she appears fairly lifelike. And oh my God. This girl looks about the same age as my daughter.

I just can't handle the idea that my kid's this close to being an adult.

"It's time," says Millicent. "Prepare yourselves."

Chapter Eight
The Exorcism of Mindy Hogan

At Allison's urging, Mindy sits on the ground, cross-legged at the center of a series of concentric ritual circles etched into the dirt. To me, some of the lines and funny symbols contain a faint ghostly light.

Allison starts trying to explain to me how to stand there and provide witchy power to the ritual while she and Millicent work the spell, but Tammy decides to cut corners and shoves the information into my head. In mere seconds, it feels as though I've participated as an assistant in hundreds of rituals.

"Whoa." Allison looks at her. "Never even thought about that. She could make a fortune copying knowledge between brains."

"If only," mutters Tammy. "It doesn't stick. *Actually* learning stuff is permanent. What I just did only lasts a couple days. Maybe I *could* burn it in permanently, but it would overwrite something."

"Come on!" says Mindy in a tone part way between urgent and angry. She gasps and grabs her chest, but the pain appears to fade in time with Tammy emitting an annoyed grunt.

I move to a spot on Mindy's left. Allison stands a few paces in front of her with Millicent opposite me on the right. Wonder if this is what it would feel like to rejoin the trifecta? I know it's not going to happen. Even after my magical awakening, the whole 'immortal thing' gets in the way. Besides, my magic is nowhere near strong enough for the trifecta. But, I don't have to be a part of it to help out here. Essentially, my role at the moment is paranormal battery, providing energy that Allison and Millicent can direct.

Tammy heads around to stand behind Mindy, staring at the back of her head with the concentration of someone building a ship in a bottle. Anthony remains standing by Mr. and Mrs. Hogan, arms folded like the bouncer at a bar. Those poor people barely handled seeing Millicent manifest and me teleporting. If my son has to go Fire Warrior here, that's probably going to send both of them to the funny farm.

"All shall die," says a male voice from Mindy. "The Moon children will be first. Dear Samantha, you'll be last so you can savor all of their suffering."

"Blow it out your ass." Tammy glowers at

Mindy, her face reddening from effort.

Okay, that is *not* a good sign. I can't remember ever seeing my daughter having to work so hard to do something telepathically.

Mindy's eyes melt from solid black to normal. "Please, hurry up!"

Allison holds her arms out to either side and begins chanting in a language I don't recognize. Millicent responds, the two of them going back and forth as if singing a duet. Sensing the time is right, I raise my hands and pour magic energy into the circle on the ground. The runic sigils she drew earlier flare with light.

The Hogans don't react, unable to see paranormal energy.

A scuff breaks the silence behind me, fairly far off. A low moan that sounds all too much like a zombie cuts off after less than a second to the *blam* of Art's shotgun.

"Holy crap," mutters Anthony. "That's a straight up zombie… or was."

"Mindy, we talked about this," says Louise in a tone like she's scolding her for not putting dishes away. "No more summoning undead. I mean it."

"Not her," grunts Tammy.

A handful of staggering dead show up over the next several minutes, though Art and his shotgun handle them well enough. Louise, grumbling the whole time, jogs back to the house to get more shells and a 9mm handgun for herself plus an aluminum baseball bat she gives Anthony. The zombies continue coming after us, but the elder Hogans and Anthony hold them off.

Allison and Millicent increase the speed and volume of their chanting. I catch a few words that sound familiar like 'Gaia,' and other names... spirits and ancient gods they're asking to help out. Where and how I know these names, I can only guess. Surely, a past life memory coming to the surface.

In response to this, Mindy begins writhing and snarling. Her body shakes from her effort to hold herself still. Soon, the familiar stink of rotting eggs saturates every breath. Pretty much everyone except for Mindy and Anthony gags on it.

My son holds his hands up. "Wasn't me."

Mindy rakes at her own throat while speaking in a male voice. "I shall take this vessel down to the inferno with me!"

I dive on her, grabbing her wrist and pulling her hand away before she can do serious damage to herself. Good thing she's as tough as an Abrams tank—well, at least for now. Mindy swings her arm hard to the side, launching me like a human javelin. The throw is so forceful and abrupt there's no time for me to stretch my angel wings before I'm eating dirt.

"Help!" screams Mindy. "I'm slipping!"

A blast of orange light erupts behind me. I scramble to my feet and whirl around to run back... and pause. The Fire Warrior hovers above Mindy, pinning her to the ground the way a cat might a mouse. I start to scream in dismay while rushing toward them, but she's not burning. The idea that the Fire Warrior can control what his flames burn and don't burn shouldn't strike me as strange when I'm staring at a giant, hulking male figure wreathed in fire. More shocking, though, is watching Mindy nearly overpowering him to escape his grasp.

Allison and Millicent walk around the perimeter of the largest ritual circle, still chanting. Mindy gets an arm loose and reaches for her face, so I dart in and grab her wrist before she can blind herself.

"This girl belongs to me," shouts Mindy in a male voice.

She struggles to stand, but between the Fire Warrior and me holding her down, doesn't get too far. Still, it takes both of us to contain her and she's *still* slowly overpowering us. Growling, Mindy stops trying to gouge out her eyes and grabs my left forearm, spearing her thumb into the muscle.

It hurts more than it should, making me yowl involuntarily.

"That's for stabbing me in the arm, bitch!" snaps the demon.

Son of a... well, yeah, when Mindy and I experimented to see how tough she was to hurt, poking her with the Devil Killer probably pissed it off.

Energy filaments glide past me from Allison and Millicent, connecting to Mindy's forehead—specifically the markings drawn there.

I growl. "Oh, I bet that hurt. If I'd have known what you were back then, I would've stabbed you a few more times."

"And kill this vessel?" Mindy laughs in the man's voice.

"No, but, a few pokes in non-vital spots might have encouraged you to get out of her."

"Oh, it would have taken a lot more than that... as you will see."

Tammy gasps for air, sounding as tired as if she'd carried furniture up three flights of stairs all day.

The demon inside Mindy starts rambling at her, commanding my daughter to get out of her head, to stop making walls. It threatens to disembowel her, make her eat her own flesh, and all sorts of other horrible things I'm not going to repeat. Anthony tries to shut it up by crushing her down into the ground, but the demon backs off to allow Mindy to feel her bones at the verge of cracking. When she screams in pain using her normal voice, my son stops pressing.

Though the Fire Warrior has the face of a hardened man in his late thirties, he gives me this 'what should I do, Mom?' stare. He's still my fifteen-year-old son mentally. Much like me and Talos, Anthony's merely borrowing a body.

Allison and Millicent repeat the same short phrase over and over. While I don't understand whatever language it is—Gaelic?—they're speaking, it's pretty obvious this line roughly translates to 'get the F out of her.' Perhaps not literally, but by intent.

Screaming, Mindy lurches to her feet, throwing the Fire Warrior off to the side. Unlike me, he only goes a little ways before crashing to the ground. Ghostly threads shoot up from the concentric rune circles and bind Mindy's arms to her sides. The male voice laughs, mocking the restraint.

Mindy arches her back and a blast of black vapor explodes out from her chest, mouth, and nostrils, rapidly growing and solidifying into a bald humanoid figure that slaps me with a hand as big as my chest, launching me airborne as much as off to the side, spinning me head over ass. I sprout my wings to catch myself in midair and reorient to face the demon in the circle.

A monstrously large humanoid figure now stands over Mindy, who's slumped backward to the ground and isn't moving. The poor girl is covered in gooey black slime that's still bubbling up out of her mouth and nostrils. That gives me a flashback to Elizabeth vomiting out of me and nearly makes me hurl again. The demon's easily fifteen feet tall, generally man-shaped, with gloss-black skin, two horns three times the length of its face sticking straight up from its temples, wings, and random bits of ebon fur on its body. Eyes of glowing crimson flicker at me. It briefly appears appalled and confused—that tells me we succeeded in evicting it from Mindy—but its expression soon goes wrathful.

It spins toward Tammy.

The Fire Warrior, however, has other plans. He's right there behind it and levels the somewhat-taller demon with a thunderous right hook that throws the tall-but-lanky Hellspawn into a tumbling mess of limbs and flapping leather wings.

I thought those little pterodactyl demons stank. They are but mere amateurs.

This one smells like a whole house full of dead bodies in the middle of August. Another drawback to the 'new me.' I need to breathe. Well, maybe. The jury is still out. I haven't bothered to do an official test yet. That said, I often catch myself breathing again. In and out, like a normal person. Even if many minutes pass between breaths.

Laughing, the demon picks itself up and holds its arms out to either side. Red glowing rips appear here and there all over us on the ground.

I swoop down to land beside my kids.

Mindy's well and truly unconscious—but she appears to be breathing.

Arms in varying colors, dark red, black, white, and grey, reach out from the dozens of crevasses opening everywhere in sight. A small army of lesser demons drag themselves up from the inferno. Some look like men with heads of goats or serpents. Others lack a separate head, instead having giant eyes where shoulders should be and a mouth spanning their entire chests. A handful resemble huge spiders. The big one laughs while pointing at us—and the small demonic army starts closing in on us.

"Can I scream now?" asks Tammy, rhetorically.

"We've gone way past the point of screaming."

Allison moves to the center of the circle. "Get in here, Tam."

My daughter dashes inside the circle. "Is this gonna stop them?"

"No, but it'll slow them down."

Blam.

The shotgun blast peppers the big demon with a few spots of lead, though nothing pierced its skin.

"Uhh…" Art runs over to me. "What do you reckon I should do?"

I gesture at Mindy. "Get her out of here. You and Louise take her and go inside. This is about to get bad. Very, very bad."

Chapter Nine
Queen's Exchange

The Fire Warrior charges straight into the thick of it.

Damn teenage boys and their utter lack of self-control. Fortunately, the tallest demons only come up to his chest. Brandishing the Devil Killer, I charge in before they can entirely surround him, opening with a wild upswing that nearly slices a spider-shaped demon in half.

Anthony punches one of the goat-headed humanoids in the face, smashing its skull in with one hit... and snatches its weapon, a long-bladed spear that looks more like a small sword mounted on a pole. All of the goat-like ones have either those or crude swords. Speaking of which, two goats rush at me. I catch their spears with the Devil Killer, shoving their attack to the left while spinning around into a stab that impales one in the heart.

Something hot and slimy hits me in the face with a wet *splat*, blinding me. It takes me a second to realize I have a tentacle wrapped around my head. Since it's pulling me to the right, I slash at the air and hit something that offers little resistance. Demonic screeching comes from that direction and the tentacle around my head goes limp, falling over my shoulder to the ground. The source, one of the chest-mouth demons, grabs at its enormous maw, a length of black tentacle-tongue dangling out, gushing ichor from where I lopped it in half. And yeah, it looks as gross as it sounds.

Meanwhile, meaty thuds, demonic screeches, and thumps behind me suggest the Fire Warrior is quite capable of holding his own against these things.

A spider demon leaps at Allison and Tammy, but slides to the ground as if hitting an invisible glass bubble as big around as the ritual circle. Seeing a spider that big is enough to finally make my daughter shriek. Instant embarrassment comes over our mental link along with a defense that Ruby Grace screams like that when she finds *tiny* spiders.

No, Tam, I don't think you're girly or a chicken. That thing is the size of a Prius.

She doesn't respond with much more than a brief emotion of gratitude. Her focus is spent on not only keeping the main demon out of our heads, but also the others. Evidently, the chest-mouth ones have strong mental powers and are attempting to mind control us. Okay, those become target *numero uno.*

I leap around some goat-heads and chop at a chest-mouth demon. It's like slicing into a human-sized Jell-O mold. The blade passes easily straight down to the crotch. Before I can even pull my weapon out of the corpse, the remains have disintegrated to black dust. A goat-man breathes a stream of flames at me from the left and a little behind. My superhuman reaction time lets me dive away in response to the sudden light before ending up scorched. I hit the ground, already feeling hungry and tired. Ugh. This is not good.

Wait a second…

Psychic demons…

Psychic vampire.

I leap upright and focus on the four remaining chest-mouths, trying to drain them of as much energy as my powers can steal. Energy surges into me. It's like being a little kid at one of those places with a chocolate fountain and I just stuck my head into it. Instant sugar-jitters make my hands shake. The small thumb-hole wounds in my left arm seal in seconds, perhaps a reaction to me overfeeding. An idea hits me to siphon power from the demons and use it to fuel my magic side, reinforcing the protection circle—but that's kind of difficult to concentrate on while dodging a bunch of goat-men trying to impale me on pole-mounted swords.

The Fire Warrior plows into the horde like an insane fourth-degree black belt abusing day-one students. Even the goat-men, which appear to be far better at fighting than the chest-mouths, flail under his assault like untrained conscripts thrown straight from a turnip farm into the King's Army. It's not that my son is all that skilled, but he's just hitting them so damn hard, their attempts at parrying aren't working too well.

Most of the time I swing the Devil Killer at a goat-man, they block. The chest-mouths kind of obligingly stand there and die. They're big, too slow to dodge, and unarmed. They do *try* to scramble out of the way. If not for the constant attempts by the goats to defend them, I'd have motored through all of the mind-controllers in seconds. Allison throws energy bolts into the crowd of demons, mostly picking off new ones before they can climb completely out of the holes. Since the big spider demons apparently feed on fear, many of them orientate on Tammy—and promptly explode in showers of yellow goop whenever they get too close, thanks to Allison and her magical bolts.

"How do we close those damn rips in the earth?" I shout.

"Millicent is on it," yells Allison.

Pain jabs into my shoulders and my feet leave the ground.

Oh, that's not good.

I look up, but see nothing. Down to the right, I see spider legs.

"Ant!" yells Tammy. "A bug has Mom!"

Okay, a spider demon bit me on the back and lifted me up. I should be freaking the hell out, but

I'm not too worried about poison. Still, I swipe back and forth behind my head with the sword, unfortunately not hitting anything. The big spider rotates to the side and begins trotting off with me in its grip like a dog retrieving a ball. I keep flailing the sword around behind me, but the angle is too weak and the blade only bounces off a hard shell. Getting away from this thing is going to require ripping its fangs out of my upper back.

The *whoosh-splat* of an energy bolt happens nearby, but the demon holding me doesn't let go, only screeches in pain.

The Fire Warrior lets out a bellowing grunt. He leaps like thirty feet across the 'battlefield' and lands on top of the spider demon carrying me away. An explosion of hot slime covers me from behind in time with the mandibles holding me losing their strength. I land on my feet, but refuse to look back. I'm covered in oozing demonic bug guts.

Yes, I realize spiders don't have mandibles. And they're not technically bugs.

Ask me if I care right now.

Three goat-men rush toward us, spears lowered.

An energy bolt from the direction of the circle nails the middle one in the face, blowing off most of its snoot. It spins, tripping up the other two and fouling their aim. I move to attack the one on the right while Anthony grabs the other two, smashing their skulls together so hard they burst. The goat-man blocks my overhead chop. I pull the sword back and thrust. He tries to knock that aside, but I score a slash on his thigh. It hurts enough to make him falter to one knee, leaving himself exposed for a beheading shot, which I gladly deliver.

Anthony glances over at me with a 'what took you so long' expression. Brat.

"Mom!" screams Tammy.

I turn toward the circle.

The big demon has breached the protective barrier, reaching in toward her and Allison. Allie makes a shoving gesture at Tammy as a faint burst of energy, more of a distortion than light, explodes from her palm and hurls my daughter backward off her feet. The demon's giant hand closes around Allison, and I watch helplessly as it leaps into the air. Another crevasse opens right under Tammy—and she drops over the edge (along with my heart), clinging to a tuft of weeds to keep from going all the way. Red hands come up from below and grab her shoulders.

I bolt up to a sprint as Allison's screams go by overhead. A tremendous *thud* shakes the ground with such force it nearly makes me lose my balance and fall. That the noise ended with a wet squish is horrifying, but I can't spare the second to look at what happened. A demon is trying to pull Tammy down into a fucking hole.

She screams, but it sounds more angry than frightened. Her fingers drag gouges in the dirt from her struggle to resist being dragged literally to Hell.

Wings out, I leap into the air, flying in an arc as if to dive straight into the portal trying to steal my kid. From directly overhead, it looks like a fifty-foot deep pit with fire at the bottom. A mix of goat-men and chest-mouths climb the walls, two goats at the top attempting to pull Tammy down.

There isn't enough room for me to squeeze into the pit with them, so I land beside it, plunging the Devil Killer into the first goat's head while grabbing Tammy's wrist in my free left hand. My second swing severs both of the other goat-man's arms halfway between hand and elbow. He emits this pathetic bleating wail of pain and falls, his hands still attached to my daughter's coat. The tuft of scrub brush she'd been clinging to breaks. I catch her just as she drops, and haul her up out of the crevasse with one hand.

Did I just save my daughter from plunging into hell? Or wherever it is that these things live? Yeah, I knew the previous devil had created many versions of hell, each geared toward the expectation and belief of the individual soul. Either way, *this* hell looks terrible. Surely, my daughter would have been consumed in the fires below... or eaten alive.

My God...

Millicent appears out of thin air next to me and gestures at the ground.

The crevasse slams closed, crushing the hundred or so fiends climbing the walls and throwing a geyser of black demon blood into the air. Again, the ground shakes. Being so close to the hole, the force is enough to knock me and Tammy over. My daughter doesn't bother standing up; instead, she grabs my head and turns it so I'm looking up at the big demon flying off with Allison.

"Mom. Go get Allie before it rips her head off."

Oh, hell no. Allison is hanging limp in its grasp, either fainted or been knocked out. I can't carry other people using these angel wings… which leaves me only one option. I leap into the air, flapping hard, and stuff the Devil Killer back in its sheath. As I power upward, following the greater demon, I summon Talos. Alas, my wardrobe doesn't survive the transformation, but there's no way I'm going to hesitate for the sake of clothing when my friend's life is seconds from ending. Jeans can be replaced; Allison, not so much.

Seeing a look of WTF on the face of a mostly skinless demon at the emergence of Talos is, admittedly, amusing. I'll laugh about that once I'm sure Allison is safe. There is a good reason dragons are shaped like dragons. Talos is a much better aerialist than a man-shaped demon with wings sprouting from its back. It takes mere seconds for me to overtake and crash into him, sinking my teeth into his wing membrane while digging my talons deep into his back. Yeah, that had to hurt.

Screeching, the demon reflexively drops Allison and dives away from me, cradling its tattered left wing. Talos cringes a little at the back of my thoughts, having sympathetic pain to membrane damage.

Free fall wakes Allison up, but I don't wait to see if she's got the presence of mind to enchant herself to slow her drop. I snatch her in my talons like an eagle seizing a mouse—only I don't impale her. My grip pins her arms at her sides, but she doesn't seem to mind so much. Better than falling to a splat.

This isn't exactly going according to plan, I think to her.

Allison laughs. "No exorcism ever does," she shouts above the wind. "Besides… we didn't really have a plan beyond hurry up."

Below on the ground, the many glowing red crevasses that dot the desert like so many evil eyes begin winking shut, one by one. From this high up, the sound of the earthen walls crashing together is like a muted bass drum and the Fire Warrior appears to be about an inch tall. Watching him rip through the lesser demons reminds me of one of his video games. Tammy's gotten back inside the circle of protection, which appears to still be powerful enough to keep the entities away. Looks like her ability to block the chest-mouth demons' mind control has caused them to order the goat-men to kill her. This has resulted in them all focusing on the circle and crowding together into easy pickings for Anthony.

Allison wriggles her arms loose.

I fly in low over the fiendish horde as Allison rains a few magic bolts down on them, which kinda makes me feel like some kind of bomber in a war movie. After overflying the circle, I bleed off some speed and swing around, dropping Allie on the ground beside Tammy inside the protective ward before flap-sprinting at the big demon. After all, he seemed to heal enough to regain his balance. Talos's eagle eyes spots him flapping hard toward us.

He wants to play in the air? We can play in the air.

A plan forms in my head. Rip him up until he can't fly anymore, then after he crashes, weakened, I'll change back to myself and finish him off with the sword.

Good plan, comes both Allison and Tammy's thoughts.

I give them a mental wink. Thought so.

Like a pair of jousters, the demon and I rush at each other. We're both over-cautious about our wing membranes, so the first pass draws no blood on either side. The next time we cross paths, we both score hits. His claws cut Talos's scales much easier than I expected, resulting in a long and painful slash down my left side. It's shallow, but it burns. Meanwhile, my talons tear a gash in his side as well, but if it hurt, the demon isn't showing it.

We gain altitude, flying in figure-eight patterns making strafing passes at each other four more times, trading superficial cuts. Ugh, but it's starting to look like biting might be necessary. I really, *really* don't want to know what demon blood tastes like, but Talos's maw is deadlier than his talons, and the demon has been focusing entirely on avoiding my feet. The first time I go for a bite should catch him off guard.

Gotta make it count.

At least if I can keep the demon occupied up here, that will allow Millicent to close off the portals bringing more small demons over. Sure, as soon as we get lower, this thing can open more, but his attention is on me right now.

Again, we circle around... then race toward each other. As we pass, claws and talons clashing, pain screams down my back, almost following the spiny ridge. Damn, that hurts. Good thing its claws are on the smallish side, only about six inches long. I didn't land a hit that time, instead trying to get a feel for a bite attack at its throat. Comparing the size of Talos's mouth to the demon's neck, it should be possible to decapitate it in one snap. And if I do chomp its head off, there should be at least a ten-second window before it disintegrates. That should be enough time for me to impale it through the heart with the Devil Killer... and thus permanently destroy it.

I fly around the outer curve of the figure-eight and come about to face the demon. It maneuvers to face me in preparation for another jousting charge. Once again, we accelerate, flying toward each other. It's grinning over my failure to draw blood last time. Probably thinks its winning. Heck, I'm in so much pain from all the claw slashes, it's possible the demon *is* winning. Feels like I'm slowing down, too, struggling to maneuver or even stay in the air at this point.

But Talos is tough, and his body is thicker than this demon's, whose claws can't penetrate deep enough to cause serious damage—unless it maybe gets me in the eye. Talos's consciousness drifts forward in my head, almost like the more experienced pilot suggesting he take the stick when a storm approaches.

I mentally back off, letting him have control. Not to do so would be stupid. He *is* a dragon. I only play one on TV sometimes.

The demon rushes closer, its right arm poised to strike, a leering grin on its face. That smile enrages me. He thinks he's won already. Thinks he's going to piss me off into making a mistake. Hah. Joke's on him. Talos has the 'controls.'

And he's not at all angry. He's something else... but what?

Except I don't have time to ponder what it is.

We crash mightily together.

With the speed of a springing cobra, Talos's jaws close around the demon's relatively narrow neck. Instant revulsion comes over me at a flavor akin to a carrion-sulphur smoothie going down my throat. The demon's head tumbles loose, rolling over my back. Its body, limp, wraps half around me.

I try to shift back to my human form to get the sword out, but it doesn't work. Something is wrong. Desperately, terribly wrong. Burning pain deep inside my chest reaches my awareness once the initial horror of the flavor in my mouth lessens.

We're no longer flying... but falling.

And now I can see why...

A long, onyx spear at the tip of the demon's tail is impaled in my dragon body at the base of my neck. Every heartbeat hurts with the scrape of cardiac muscle sliding against the foreign object inside me.

No! Talos!

That emotion... he hadn't been angry; he'd been resigned.

He knew. Must've seen the tail I didn't see. And yet he still committed to the attack.

I struggle to shapeshift before grief can overwhelm me. Gotta kill this son of a bitch for good or what that foolish, reckless dragon did will be a complete waste.

Except... I can't focus. Electrical tingles wrap around my body, my thoughts, my everything. My vision washes out to blinding white light. Pain like an acid bath hits me so hard I can't even scream.

Unsure if I'm dragon or human at the moment, I curl up fetal in midair, clutching at the object stabbed into my heart.

The intense white glare fades to darkness...

Chapter Ten
Plead the Fourth

Gentle wind washes over my body.

Recent memories of pain are so beyond measure they don't seem real. Heavy, rumbling breathing comes from nearby on my left. With each exhalation, a wave of hot air rolls past. The chill presence of hard stone touches my skin, making me aware I'm naked, flat on my back. No sooner does the thought 'this is strange' form in my head than a burst of spider-tingles covers me in a fit of pins and needles.

Helpless to do anything in response to such a bizarre sensation, I convulse, my body entirely out of conscious control for a few agonizing seconds. When it passes, I sit up into a ball, arms wrapped around my legs, and gasp for breath.

I'm sprawled at the innermost part of a shallow bowl-shaped area recessed into the slope of a black stone mountain. Maybe thirty feet of worn rock stands between me and the edge. The range stretches off as far as I can see on either side. In front of me and a long way down is a landscape of charcoal grey desert, dotted here and there with black patches. Near the horizon, the sky has a pale purplish hue, darkening to violet and eventually black higher up.

Whoa…

Three moons hang overhead. A giant green one almost directly above me and two smaller blue ones off to the far left.

Another heavy exhale from the left reminds me that I'm not alone here. This, also, reminds me that Talos just sacrificed himself to kill a greater demon—but before I can even feel grief, I realize he's lying beside me.

Only… he's a little different.

He's significantly bigger, his horns shiny silver instead of black. Still has the same blunt nose. His wings are the most noticeable change, looking more like human arms up to the main joint, where a three-fingered clawed hand juts out. The remainder of the wing spar appears to be a separate bone rather than an elongated finger. The Talos I'm used to seeing has more bat-like wings, where the membrane for flight stretches between the fingers of a highly modified hand structure.

Talos emits a breathy wheeze tinged with pain.

I scramble to my feet, unconcerned with not having a stitch of clothing on, and rush to kneel beside his massive head—now nearly the size of my Momvan. I reach out and... touch him. Whoa. This is beyond weird. He doesn't react to me pressing a hand to his face, so I get up and walk around the other side to examine where the demon stabbed him—us. A patch of scales near the base of his long sinuous neck have turned whitish-grey, but they're intact. That looks like the spot where the demon's tail barb caught us. Interestingly, I don't see an actual wound there.

Curiosity nags at me. I pad to the edge of the basin and peer down the side of the mountain to the land far below. It's got to be almost a mile from here to the ground, the rock mostly smooth and featureless except for occasional ridges.

Talos appears to be asleep, curled up on this ledge like an immense, lazy housecat—with wings.

Hands on my hips, I stare out over the bizarre sight in front of me for a while, not quite sure what to make of it. Okay, I'm once again stuck somewhere sans-clothing, with just a bit of demon blood and demonic spider gut slime on me.

"Well, this is an entirely new level of messed up. What the hell happened?" I ask no one in particular.

Talos gives off a pained grunt. The eye on the facing side of his head, slightly larger than the driver door window of my van, opens. "Sam..."

"You're okay!" Overjoyed, I run over and hug him.

Well, hug his head.

Okay, it's more like hugging a wall.

Fine, I lean against him lovingly.

"In a manner of speaking," he says.

Even his attempt to whisper rumbles the ground.

"What happened? I thought you died." Aborted grief catches in my throat. "Where is everyone? Where are we?"

"This is where your body goes when you invite me into your world."

"Wait, I'm in the fourth dimension?"

"Yes, Sam."

I pat myself down. Skin's intact. Nothing hurts. No holes. "I'm not disintegrating."

"Because I've enchanted you, as I always do when you transform, with protection that will last for a short time, but you will need to go back before it wears off."

"Talos…" I move around him, kneel, and press a hand on the damaged white scales. "What is this, exactly? I don't see a noticeable wound."

A low rumble comes out of him reminiscent of a half-hearted chuckle from someone half awake. "When you call me to the third dimension, I create a shadow of myself there in your world. A lesser version of me. That copy of me *did* die. Sadly, I overestimated the speed of the fiend."

"But are you… okay?" I stand and trace a hand over his eye ridge.

"You do not have to pet me like a dog." He chuckles. "Though I do not mind. It is wonderful to be with you again for real, even if it will not last long."

"Umm. Why wouldn't it last long? That sounds ominous. Oh, right, the disintegrating thing."

"Losing my echo self in your world has left me severely weakened. I shall soon fall into a restorative sleep. Forgive me for being unable to guide you home, but it is not my choice. Please, stand in front of me."

I step around by his nose.

His huge eyes light up with a golden glow. Translucent amber energy flows from his nostrils and parted lips and swirls around me. Though I don't notice any discernible sensation, I feel myself growing physically stronger, as if I'd sucked down fresh human blood back in my vampire days. Or siphoned from a whole Starbucks full of hipsters.

"More enchantment?" I ask.

"Indeed. And I'm afraid I've reached the limits of what I can do to protect you, Sam. But the magic should last for a little while."

"How long is that exactly?"

He rocks his head slightly side to side. "It is difficult to say. Some regions of this world are 'stronger' than others and will erode the protection more quickly. It will definitely fade before I am able to wake. You must find a gateway home before this happens."

"Okay. Can you point me to—?"

His eye droops closed. I pat his snout a few times, calling his name, but the big guy is out cold.

"Right. Guess that's a no."

I pace around the ledge, then move to the edge and sit. At least the stone's warm on my bare butt. And wow, I've never felt more alone in all my life.

After all, I'm stranded in the fourth dimension, naked—with a time limit and no idea where to find a gateway. This is obviously a planet of some kind, but how big? Gravity feels Earth normal, so it can't be too different in size. A way back to my home world could be at the bottom of this mountain or tens of thousands of miles away.

Let's try the obviously not-going-to-work idea first. I close my eyes, concentrate on my bedroom at home, and attempt to teleport. The little flame doesn't even appear. Yeah, didn't think so. As a test, I try teleporting twenty feet to my left. The flame starts to appear, but I don't go through with it. No sense wasting energy. Okay, teleporting still works here, but it won't send me across dimensional boundaries. For that, I would need either an artist or writer—a creator—to either paint or write me into the higher or lower dimensions. But with neither Van Gogh nor Charlie Reed present, it looked like I was stuck finding this damn gateway on my own.

So, where do I start? The mountains stretching off in either direction don't hold anything of interest, not even plants, though some of the dark spots in the far distance look like they could be forests. Okay, I know teleporting works. What about my angel wings, since it's beyond obvious that I can't turn into Talos at the moment.

LOST MOON

Panic like ice water down my back paralyzes me at the sudden realization my kids are probably looking at Talos's copy lying there back in the third dimension and thinking I'm dead. Crap! I need to get out of here fast.

Hoping they still work, I try summoning my wings. The expected tingle of energy washes across my shoulders, and the wings appear, unfurling out to either side. Whew. Okay, that's good. They'll let me cover way more ground than walking.

According to what Talos has told me over the years, this world is populated entirely by dragons. Evidently, my soul had somehow reincarnated here at one point due to my deep-seated inner love for flying. At that point, I'd been a dragon as well, half of a mated pair with him. Sounds weird to say that but 'married' doesn't quite describe it accurately. Despite that, we had once been deeply in love, my human form isn't the least bit appealing to him. There is zero chance any dragon is going to get even the slightest puerile thrill from seeing me nude, but that doesn't make being naked any less awkward.

Somehow, I doubt a kindly Civil War era slave is going to offer me clothes here.

For once, I'm grateful to have had a wild upbringing during which clothing had been more of a 'feel like it' thing than a requirement. Of course, I never left our property without something on—unlike my brother Clayton. Still, I'm not a kid anymore and no longer innocent.

Motion catches my eye in the distance along the ground. Small figures moving at the head of a dust plume. It's hard to say from this distance, but they're kinda human-like. Definitely not dragons. Okay, that ups the awkward factor.

Wait. Allison's illusion spell.

Bigger question: will my *magic* work here?

One way to find out.

I focus inward and attempt to invoke magic. My right hand alights in a storm of prickling like it's covered in biting ants too small to really hurt. Transparent energy rushes around me, turns white, and 'solidifies' into a toga-like garment. Ugh. I gotta have angel on the brain to make a garment like this. It might not physically exist, but it *looks* real.

Better than nothing. I take in some alien air, filling my lungs completely.

Time to make contact with the locals. Hope they're friendly.

I leap off the basin-shaped ledge.

Chapter Eleven
The Drajjan

I steer left a bit toward the group of people walking.

In a few minutes, it becomes obvious that they aren't human. They are, however, approximately human sized and bipedal… walking on legs with backward-jointed knees ending in three-toed feet. Long, slender tails hover off the ground behind them. One spots me coming and points. The others, some nine or so individuals, stop walking and all turn toward me. A few of them carry onyx-tipped spears, though they don't brandish them; instead, they hold them like walking staves. That's a good sign.

The crowd tracks me, turning their heads in unison as I swing around and set down on my feet a non-threatening distance away. My toes sink into the pale grey silt, which feels like warm flour.

Sparkles here and there, as well as some black flecks, suggest it's finely eroded stone, worn down to a powdery consistency. Kinda reminds me of the lunar surface, but softer.

Yes, that strange shadow photographed on the moon had been me.

None of these beings wear any sort of clothing, though a few have small bits of jewelry, mostly necklaces, bracelets, tail rings, anklets, and a stud or two in the jaw or eye ridge. Their scales vary in color among white, grey, dark grey, black, and one is sort of an olive-drab. All have the same general shape, flat, muscular chests, and featureless groins… no obvious indicators of sex. Their faces appear to be a combination of human with draconic characteristics, except they lack noses, having two small holes where nostrils would be, and no ears. Three of them are thinner and slightly shorter than the others, without the tiny horns studding their eye ridges. I'm going to guess they're the women… mostly because of their being shorter and more slender, with softer, rounder facial features.

I actually remember the term from my anthropology class in calls: sexual dimorphism, when the male or female of a species have obvious physical differences. Okay, I might have just impressed myself.

Anyway, almond-shaped eyes, in gem hues of bright blue, green, and yellow, regard me with curiosity and a hint of 'what the hell is that thing?' I try really hard to forget I'm wearing nothing but an illusionary toga, which did little to protect me from the elements. Trust me, I feel every blast of wind. That all these creatures are butt naked, too, isn't making it any less uncomfortable, maybe even worse. Whispers pass among them in an indecipherable language composed of harsh sounds, clicks, and even whistles.

"Hello," I say, raising a hand. "You probably don't speak English, but my name is Samantha. Can you help me?"

A pale-grey scaled individual, the tallest of the group at about nine feet, advances toward me, his gold eyes glittering in fascination. We stare at each other for a long moment. He attempts speaking, but the sounds he's making are somewhere between lonely whale and mating call of a jungle bird.

I shake my head, raise my hands. "I'm sorry. I don't understand you."

He cocks his head to the side... then closes his eyes in a moment of concentration. When again he looks at me, he says, "Is this better, Samantha?"

"Wow. Yes. Can you understand me, too?"

"I can."

The clicking from the rest of the group mutates to whispers, mostly things like 'what is it' 'where did it come from' 'look at her beautiful wings' 'is it one of *them*' and so on. My assumption as to what 'them' means is an angel since I'm kinda dressed for the part. Wings out, long robe, yeah... I've become a figure straight out of a Renaissance painting. Speaking of painting, where's Van Gogh when a girl needs him?

"Good." He offers a slight bow. "I am Orounaz. Why have you shown yourself to the Drajjan?"

"The what? And do you mind if I ask *how* you suddenly learned English?"

He turns to the side, gesturing at the other creatures behind him. "My people. We are the Drajjan. Also, we are not using your language. You are merely hearing your language when we speak as we hear ours when you intone vocalizations."

"Right…" Don't have time to dwell on details. Need to get home.

"What message do you bring down to us?" asks Orounaz.

"Oh. I'm not what you think. I'm actually…" Hmm. Can't really say 'human' anymore. "Not from higher up. I came from the third dimension. Actually, that would be down below." Yeah, if that doesn't sound like the title of a cheesy 2:00 a.m. movie, I don't know what does. *It Came from the Third Dimension.*

"Curious." Orounaz rubs his chin. "If that is true, then you are in great danger here."

"Yep. I know. That's why I'm trying to go home. My friend, Talos, is injured. While he'd projected part of himself into the third dimension to help me, a demon attacked us. It struck a fatal blow at the same time as we killed it. With Talos dead in my dimension, I was trapped in this realm."

"His ability to summon his shadow self back is necessary for you to switch places."

"Um, that's exactly right. Oh wow, can you read minds?"

"No, Samantha. I merely understand how the dimensions work."

"Well, this is all new to me."

Ouronaz—and most of the others—bow their heads. "Your friend may not have long to live."

"Wait. He said he only needed to rest."

"I'm afraid he did not wish to alarm you. Severing himself into two parts such as he did is dangerous." Ouronaz walks closer, shaking his head. "He may very well die."

Crap! "Can you help him? Is there anything I can do?" My attempt to peek at his thoughts feels like watching white noise snow on a television. Ugh. Completely different frequencies.

"Show us where he is." Orounaz turns his head to the others. "We shall help this Lumarae."

The group all nod with eagerness.

Wow. What are the odds that the natives would be so friendly? I guess this really is an advanced civilization. Some parts of LA, if I left a dragon lying around for fifteen minutes, I'd return to find his talons and scales missing.

These guys do not look capable of flight, so I walk toward the mountain. "This way."

Orounaz and the others fall in step around me without hesitation. Even the Drajjan who I assume to be women tower over me. Then again, nothing new. I've always been short at five foot three inches.

With little else to do but walk the several miles to the mountain, I find myself studying their motion. Their three toes end in thick velociraptor-style claws that seem more designed for traction on silt than use as weapons. They walk digitigrade, a long swaying tail providing balance. That, plus their highly fluid and graceful stride suggests them capable of traveling much faster than we're going. Basically, I'm slowing them down.

Much the same way I'm studying them, they're observing me. All probably pitying the lowly-evolved monkey. Ha, jokes on them... I've got wings. Some whispering from the outermost individuals confirms they feel like we're crawling along.

"If you want to go faster, I can fly."

Orounaz nods once. "That would be acceptable."

"Okay. No need to run, just go at whatever speed is comfortable for you then." I leap into the air. My already-exposed wings snap taut, catching the slightly heavier air of this alien atmosphere. Then again... was it so alien to me? I mean... I had lived here once, in another lifetime. Maybe that's why I didn't feel too out of sorts here.

So weird.

The Drajjan spring into motion. To me, it looks like they're running, but for all I know, this could be their ordinary walking pace. It's difficult to gauge how fast they're going, but it's kinda obvious a human couldn't keep up with them, especially not on such soft, loose ground.

Flying, I glide along at what feels like a lazy speed they have no trouble keeping up with.

When they reach the base of the mountain, they slow down quite a bit. Their claws offer them stable footing, but they only ascend about as fast as a normal human would walk. Of course, a normal human wouldn't walk straight up a sheer forty-five degree stone ramp. Every so often, one of them springs between outcroppings. Even the Drajjan appear vulnerable to sliding on the wind-worn smooth parts.

I fly up to the basin, landing at the edge so they can see me.

Talos remains curled as he'd been, deep sonorous breaths passing in and out via his wide nostrils.

Eventually, Orounaz and the others reach the basin. Maybe their reptilian anatomy doesn't send off the kind of signals I can pick up on, but despite 'running' for forty minutes nonstop then climbing a mountain, they don't appear tired. They either have freakish endurance or that pace really had been casual for them.

"Ahh, yes. It is as I thought. A Lumarae." Orounaz approaches Talos and puts a hand on the side of his head. "He is quite weak." He steps back and turns to face me, clasping his hands in front of himself. "But we can help him."

Chapter Twelve
Zoxa Duur

Relief lessens the unease that had been boiling in my stomach ever since the true depth of the crap I've stepped in hit me. Yes, my butt needs to get out of here as soon as possible, but I can't leave Talos to die. Not after all the help he's given me over the years.

Orounaz and the other Drajjan surround Talos, raise their arms, and emit a chant consisting of musical trilling interspersed with clicks and the occasional whistle. It sounds similar to a couple of flute players with an army of birds trained to read sheet music singing backup vocals.

I really hope this isn't a funeral rite or something along those lines. Could it be a gesture of respect for a larger dragon? The few things Talos has shared with me about this world over the years never mentioned anything about another civilization of beings like the Drajjan. Perhaps he considers them lesser dragons? It had been naïve of me to think that an entire world could exist with *only* dragons in it. That would be like Earth populated only by cats. We have thousands of species. Stands to reason this place would be similar, flying dragons and lizard-like humanoids aside.

The Drajjan chant louder, their tails stretching, swaying, and undulating along with the intonation like wizards making special hand gestures required for the magic to work right. They raise their arms higher… and Talos floats up to hover a few feet off the ground.

Okay, then. Nothing weird about that.

Orounaz breaks away from the circle and approaches me. "We will take him to Zoxa Duur."

"Is that a place of, um, healing or something?" I ask.

"It is our home. You would call it a city. It is there that we will help this Lumarae." He points to my still-unfurled wings. "Follow in the air if you choose."

Uhh, yeah, as Tammy would say in response to a stupidly obvious question. "Yes, of course."

He returns to the group. They move in formation, pulling Talos along as if towing a hovering barge—only no physical connection links the Drajjan to him. I stand there watching them go by, admittedly awestruck at the strangeness of what could only be called magic. Talos's immense body —never going to get used to seeing him this big—

slips over the edge of the basin and rockets down the mountainside like the ten-ton engine of destruction he is.

Or like the world's biggest toboggan, except this friction-less, monstrous toboggan is gliding on nothing but air.

The Drajjan spill over the edge, too, following behind.

That's my cue to fly.

I jump after them, surprised at the speed the lizard folk are reaching. Although the hurling form of the unconscious Talos leaves them all in the dust, the Drajjan have to be going upwards of eighty MPH on foot. *This* is clearly sprinting, plus they're going downhill. Fortunately, in the air, I can keep up with that speed easily. A short while back, some experimentation with the GPS app in my phone put my flight speed with these wings at around 120 miles per hour during level 'as fast as I can go' flight.

Speaking of as fast as I can go, it's work keeping up with Talos down the slope, even as I power dive after him. Figure at roughly a mile up, the ninety-degree slope's close to a mile and a half before it touches silt. When the big guy reaches the bottom, he kicks up an enormous explosion of grey dust but keeps on zooming off into the desert like an air hockey puck the size of a box truck.

The Drajjan stream down the mountainside, following as fast as they can and still falling behind.

Over the next maybe ten minutes, Talos gradually loses speed to air resistance enough to where they catch up to him and start making a course correction to the left. Still playing the role of human kite, I follow behind.

It's difficult for me to gauge time by eye here. Nothing like a sun hangs in the sky, yet it feels as if there's light. Sure, with my still-sorta-vampiric eyes, I can see in total darkness, so it's possible this realm *is* a lot darker than it appears. Could be why all the Drajjan have gem-eyes that faintly glow. Maybe this world's rotation is matched to its orbit, so it's like the Moon—meaning, the same side always faces the sun… and we're on the dark side.

Or maybe I'm an idiot for attempting to apply real-world astrophysics to a fourth-dimensional world full of dragons and dragon-like humanoids. Yeah, I'll go with that. Nothing here is going to make any sense according to the 'laws of physics' that apply in the third dimension.

Anyway, to the best of my ability to make a totally random guess, we travel over the powdery ground for about three hours before reaching another, smaller mountain ridge. On the way, I spot some occasional tracks that don't look like Drajjan or Talos. Fortunately, they're small. Probably some kind of dog-sized quadrupedal lizard.

A mile or two of scrubland dotted with angry-looking black thorn bushes leads up to a huge square opening in the rock face that's clearly not a natural formation. Patterned engravings surround it, though I can't tell if they're decorative or some kind of writing.

The city of Zoxa Duur is apparently underground. Makes sense considering the barrenness of everything outside. If there are creatures out here that prey on the Drajjan, having the protection of remaining hidden is a good thing.

I land at the back of the formation and walk after them into a yawning tunnel with a ceiling about four stories high. For now, I leave my wings out. Who knows...? I might need them on short notice. Better out than in. And, yes, I could practically hear Kingsley turning that into something sexual.

Damn, I wish I had him by my side right now.

Not far from the opening stands a massive onyx gate, presently open. No guards or anything watch over it. A minute or two after we pass the gate, the tunnel pitches downward at a slight angle for a good ten-plus minutes of walking. Where it levels again, the walls open out into a courtyard full of Drajjan. Some have pushcarts and appear to be selling various items, mostly jewelry, crystals, cooked small reptiles, something that kinda looks like roasted rat, and so on.

Almost all of them stop what they're doing to stare at Talos. A few look at me, but apparently, a human isn't as much of a shock to them. Not like I'm parading naked into their city or anything. Oh… wait. I am. But… illusory toga is still holding strong. Gah, this is so weird to feel the air on my skin but *see* clothes. Clayton would *adore* this, though I have no idea if he's still a nudist. He'd be forty-six now. Wow, that's even weirder to think about than magic clothes. The last I really saw him, he'd been like eighteen. Wonder if he's still living with our parents? Yeah, he's every bit the hippie they were in their prime. If you ask him, a 'day job' is 'the man oppressing the people.'

A few Drajjan who appear to be children check us out, peering nervously around carts or columns. Only their size makes me think of them as kids. The adults don't have facial hair or breasts, so those visual cues as to adulthood don't matter. Pretty sure any Drajjan shorter than me has got to be a juvenile.

One child with dark charcoal-grey scales gawks at me, mouth wide open… the sort of expression a kid might have if one of their favorite superheroes from movies showed up in person. Another kid clutches the edge of a cart, peering at me. It finally occurs to me that they have three fingers on their hands. The awestruck one continues staring, lustrous violet eyes widening.

Curiosity draws the little ones out from their hiding places. They creep along behind me, tails swishing rapidly side to side. None of the juveniles look too different from each other in terms of physique. Adult males appear to be taller and thicker of build, but the kids are all lithe, as if they haven't hit adolescence yet.

The charcoal-scaled one following close to me doesn't have tiny horns above the eyes, so I'll assume her a female. Most of the children have larger eyes in proportion to their faces and soft features like the adult females… but a fair number of them do have rows of small spikes over their eyes. Might be completely off base here, but I'm going with that as a marker. Pointy eye-ridges equals male. No spikes equals female.

Orounaz and the others guide the floating, unconscious Talos past the interior gate—which this time does have a whole bunch of guards. That, plus the seeming primitivism of this place makes me feel like I'm inside one of Anthony's fantasy video games. Honestly though, if a civilization had actual working magic, why would they have developed technology? Who needs electricity and air conditioning when magic can keep your house cool?

Or maybe this world's timeline is closer to medieval Earth? It's a ridiculous thought, but someday, the Drajjan might have cars, airplanes, and television. Though, it's difficult to picture how they'd ride a bike. And riding a bike out in that powder would be truly unpleasant. It kinda sucks to walk on, even. Without my supernatural toughness, I'd have fallen over exhausted in like twenty minutes, my calves ready to mutiny.

We make our way down a street that appears to be a main thoroughfare. Despite there being a stone ceiling at the four-story level, it still feels more like I'm in a city rather than a tunnel system. They've carved façades of buildings out of the rock walls, while other structures are made from brick, mud, and woven leaves. There's no trace of fabric or even wood anywhere.

Every Drajjan we pass stops in place to ogle Talos. More than half radiate contempt or scorn. A few regard me with neutral glances or 'ack what the heck is that' sort of stares. None flinch away when I look at them, putting me on edge. However, what I initially take as a sense of challenge appears to be another difference between males and females. The men have somewhat smaller eyes that I mistook for narrowed, confrontational glares.

The deeper we go into the city, the more our procession feels like hunters returning with a glorious kill than friendly travelers helping a stranger with a hurt friend.

Uh oh. This is not good.

The look on the face of the girl following me starts to make sense. She's watching someone—me—walking straight into a massive screw up and appears concerned enough to try and help me not make an error of epic proportion. I look back at her, trying to ask 'what's wrong' with my expression. Although she's about half the size of an adult, she isn't much shorter than me. In fact, we're probably the same height. Unfortunately, the only response I get from her is a slight shake of the head.

Our destination appears to be a grand four-story building covered in fancy carvings and statuettes of Drajjan. Orounaz leads the group in the front door of what I assume to be a temple of some sort. Only two types of buildings are usually that ornate: a monarch's palace or temples. Either could spell trouble for us.

The Drajjan inside all wear the same type of black medallion, likely onyx—or whatever the mountains here are made of. That has priesthood written all over it. Yeah, this is a temple. I jog ahead, the sound of my bare feet striking the hard stone echoing around the chamber. Some of the priests look at me. Unlike the citizens outside, they gawk at me in... reverence? Ah, I think they're staring at my wings. Hey, if they mistake me for a being from a higher dimension, that could only help, right?

And technically, I've been deputized by Azrael. So in a roundabout stretch of logic, I'm sort of a mini-angel. And yeah, I'm too worried about Talos dying and my kids thinking *I* died to really be caring too much about anything else.

I catch up to the front of the procession by Orounaz. "Umm, you're going to help Talos recover, right?"

Orounaz brings his hands together at his chest. "We, and the servants of Zaa, shall commit him to the higher planes."

"Whoa, hold on there." I blink. "That sounds a whole lot like a euphemism for 'finish him off.'"

"In a manner of speaking, that is accurate. However, with the guidance of Zaa, he will ascend."

"You can't." I keep shaking my head. "He's not dying. There's no reason to kill him. Talos only needs to rest."

Everyone I've been traveling with the past few hours grumbles and scowls. Touched a nerve, I see.

"The winged ones look down on us," says one of the women.

"They regard us as mere animals." A male makes a noise like an angry cat spitting.

A few nod.

Another male pokes Talos in the side with his spear, but doesn't break scales. "This is a rare opportunity for us to give praise to Zaa by sending her one of these arrogant fools."

"The only help we can give this Lumarae is to spare the universe the existence of another of his kind," says Orounaz. "I am afraid he must die."

Chapter Thirteen
The Temple of Zaa

A tall, regal female with jet-black scales and glowing azure eyes approaches to stand beside Orounaz, a temple medallion around her neck. They touch noses, brushing cheek to cheek in a gesture that has to mean they're mates or at least lovers.

Orounaz turns to me. "Being from the third dimension, we are grateful to you for this offering. We ask you to respect our ways."

"I can't let you kill him." I hurl myself against Talos, trying to push him backward, but the big guy doesn't budge. "You can't do this."

"Zaoma, this one does not understand," says Orounaz. "She believes the winged one to be her friend."

The priestess, Zaoma, covers her mouth to stifle a laugh.

"Where did you find this creature?" A jet-black

male, his voice quite a bit deeper than Orounaz, gestures at Talos, then approaches, hand on the hilt of a black-bladed sword hung from a chain belt. He's also some manner of priest as he wears the medallion of the temple-dwellers. Or perhaps a temple guard.

Over a dozen others, all with amulets and swords, appear out of side halls, alcoves, and shadows, converging toward me.

"We owe you an honor for leading us to a defenseless Lumarae," says Orounaz. "But we cannot allow you to interfere with this tribute to Zaa."

Zaoma bows her head in reverence at the utterance of the name.

I run my fingers through my dusty hair, thinking hard. "What if she doesn't want him?"

Orounaz shakes his head. "There could be no greater tribute than a Lumarae."

I focus my psychic feeder on him, intent on siphoning off enough mental energy that he passes out. "If she objects, may she show a sign."

Orounaz sways slightly, but other than his eyes fluttering, he remains upright after I'm too 'full' to drain anything more from him. He doesn't appear to realize the source of his sudden fatigue, and does his damndest not to show any sign of something happening to him. Orounaz shakes his head, says, "Doubtful, for it is she who protects us from the winged menace."

"Menace?" I wipe at my chin, fold my arms, set

my hands on my hips… fidgety from having so much energy. "Talos's kind have evolved beyond violence."

Yes, I know he killed a demon and helps me fight all the damn time, but he's only loaning me his body. Technically, *I'm* the one doing the fighting.

"Talos has saved my life multiple times. There's no way I can stand here and let you kill him." I draw the Devil Killer and hold it out in a ready stance. My alarm sense goes nuts, ringing loud in my ears. Not the worst it's been, but damn unnerving.

Squaring off against the Devil had been probably the scariest thing I've ever had to do. However, twenty-some-odd Drajjan, all easily two heads taller than me, are an altogether different level of 'this is a mistake.' These guys can run over a hundred miles an hour. They're native to the fourth dimension. Me surviving a fight with *one* of them could very well be a tall task.

"Psst," whispers the kid who's been following me.

I glance back at her.

She bids me closer with a wave, shaking her head.

"Do not be foolish," says Orounaz. "Lower your weapon. I will do you the courtesy of asking the High Chanter to seek a sign from our goddess. If it is Zaa's command that we refrain from sending this Lumarae to her, we shall. For now, you should rest."

The child focuses a stare on Zaoma, making a trilling noise and a few rapid clicks as though she's whispering. Somehow, none of the others appear to hear her.

Zaoma's eyes briefly widen, then narrow. "We shall commune. The ceremony is delayed for now."

I should be fast enough to take Orounaz' head off before anyone can react, but where to go from that point? My brain starts plotting an attack route despite the futility of it. Dammit! I know Talos would want me to go home to my kids, but I can't abandon him…

"Psst!" the girl waves more fervently, beckoning me to go to her.

"Please lower your weapon," says Zaoma. "This is a sacred hall, and you are not one of Zaa's chosen. No harm shall befall this winged one until Zaa speaks."

With that, the woman fixes the juvenile with a stare, then nods once at her.

The kid smiles and returns a short bow of agreement.

Okay, what the hell was that all about? Nevermind. Focus, Sam.

Throwing myself into the fray right now is going to get me killed, and won't help Talos. Sounds like I have a little while at least to come up with a better idea. Reluctantly, I put my sword back in its dimensional sheath. The priest-knights, or whatever they are, lower their weapons as well. Orounaz and the others ease Talos past a set of huge double doors into a room that appears to be a ritual space.

The dark-grey juvenile runs over and grasps my arm, wraps her long tail around my waist, and tugs me down another hall, distancing us from the group of armed Drajaan. I'm about to yank away from her, but the urgency in her eyes—as well as concern—makes me hesitate. It's nearly impossible to match her to a human age, but my best guess is around eleven or twelve even though she's my height. Something tells me she wants to help.

And charging that row of guards is not going to end well for me. It is kind of unlikely that they will be able to destroy me—there doesn't appear to be any silver around here—but they could easily do so much damage to my body that I remain unconscious/comatose long enough to disintegrate from being in the fourth dimension. Then they'd kill Talos, anyway.

I glance back seconds before the massive double doors close, blocking my view of Talos. No doubt expecting me to try something, all sixteen or so temple guards stand in front of the now-closed ritual chamber.

"Follow," says the girl in a voice that sounds eerily like that of a child.

What choice do I have?

"Okay." I let her take me by the hand, and do my best to keep up with her ridiculous fast-paced stride.

Chapter Fourteen
The Water Source

The adolescent Drajjan scurries down the street, pulling me along.

What amounts to a brisk walk for her is a breathless jog for me. At least without the full height of an adult, she's a bit slower. She takes a few seemingly random turns before stopping in a sparsely populated alley near an open market square full of vendor carts and other Drajjan going about their day. Except for that temple, the remainder of the architecture down here is quite plain, almost everything is black. It's not an aesthetic choice, though. The stone is black and they haven't bothered to paint or cover it with anything.

"I am Zanjaya," says the girl. "I've always thought it wrong that the chanters wish to kill the winged ones. When you said that the winged one helps someone like you, I *knew* it was wrong."

"Someone like me?" I ask, eyebrow raised.

"You know... a lesser being from a lower place. The chanters say the winged ones are haughty and care only for themselves."

Lesser being? I clench my jaw, but this kid didn't really mean that the way it sounded. Chalk that up to whatever magic is translating language here. This kid had to mean 'being native to a lower dimension.' "Truthfully, Talos is the only one of his kind I've ever met, so I can't vouch for the others." I decide to leave out the fact that I'd likely been one of Talos's kind in the not-so-distant past. "How can we stop the priests from killing him?"

"Hmm." Zanjaya makes a pensive face while tapping a claw on her right foot on the stone floor. "Yes!" She grins. "I know a way."

"Great. What is it?"

For an answer, she again grabs my hand and pulls me up to a run, dashing out of the alley and into the courtyard. We weave among the crowd, dodging around carts and tall-as-hell dragon people to another street at the far end. That one, we follow for a long damn time until the kid turns into another alley. Soon, she skids to a stop where it opens to another passage, seeming confused.

"Are you lost?"

"No. I merely need to consider. I haven't been to this area very often."

She decides to turn left and keeps going, but slow enough that I don't even have to jog to keep up. Yeah, this kid is lost. Seconds before I call her on it, she spots something, squeaks, and dashes over to a square opening in the ground with a stone slab acting as a trapdoor.

When I reach her a few seconds later, I point down. "This is a sewer, isn't it?"

"What's that mean?"

"Underground passage where waste is removed?"

She stares at me with total cluelessness.

"Okay, maybe not. What is this?"

"A secret cave." She lifts the slab with surprising ease. "Go on. I'll jump down after."

This has trap written all over it. "Why don't you go first?"

"Can you lift the cover?" asks Zanjaya.

"Probably."

"Try?"

I squat, grab the slab, and pull it up a little. Not quite as effortlessly as her, but it's not exactly heavy.

"Wow." She blinks. "You're strong for being so small."

"Well, I'm not entirely a normal human anymore. I'm something, ah, a little more."

"Fascinating."

I shrug. "I guess."

"You are humble. Perhaps you will tell me about it another day?"

"Perhaps," I say.

"Very well, let's get moving. Close it after you follow me, okay?"

"Okay."
She smiles and jumps in.

***

All right. So this isn't a trap. Obviously, she wouldn't throw herself into a dungeon.

Anyway, the shaft doesn't have a ladder, just hollows in the wall the right size for Drajjan to step in. Still works for me even if it's a bit awkward. I lower myself in, pull the cover back into place, and climb down about three stories to a natural cave containing multicolored lichen—or something really damn close to lichen—that emits light. Pink, yellow, green, and blue blotches dot the walls in both directions. This part of the cave is flooded, water up to my thighs, the bottom coated with a layer of gooey slime.

My imaginary toga thing doesn't react to the water at all, neither becoming wet nor drifting with the current.

"This is our main water source," says Zanjaya. "But we must be careful because dangerous creatures come here to drink, too."

"Great. So, what good is it doing us to be down here?"

She heads off to my right. "This passage goes under the Temple of Zaa. The water feeds the great fountain. I know of a tunnel that leads to the chamber where the winged one is."

"You're a kid, right?"

"What?"

"Umm. Maybe slang doesn't translate. Child?"

"Oh. Yes."

"How do you know about these passages? Let me guess, you're the king's daughter or something like that?"

She tilts her head. "I do not understand."

"Never mind. Why are you leading me back?"

"To rescue your friend, of course."

I blink. "You are not like the others."

"Yes and no. I am my own person and I know right from wrong. Killing a defenseless creature is wrong. Plus, I see how important he is to you."

I take in some worthless, alien air, marveling at the courage of this juvenile. "Thank you. But how do you know about this passage if you're a child?"

Zanjaya smiles, tail out straight. "Zaa has favored me. I have been gifted a greater attunement with the energy flows than others many times my age. Because of that, my mother gave me to the temple to learn."

Which explains why a child had been hanging out there. But still, her mother gave her up. Ugh, hard to hear. A sense of sadness wells up in me.

She shakes her head, her tail curving as she senses my change in mood. "No, Samantha. I still see her. We are still a family. I merely know the temple intimately."

I smile. "Very well. Lead on then."

We slosh down the water-filled cave, trying to stay quiet. The passage is too narrow for wings, so I pull them back in. My attempt to energetically knock Orounaz on his ass might have failed, but it did amp me up. This isn't a complaint, but overdoing psychic feedings creates a bizarre combination of sensations like downing forty espresso shots plus an entire cake.

So, in flagrant disregard of having spent the past four hours marching across the silt desert, I slosh forward after Zanjaya as fast as the water lets me go. As I do so, streaks of glowing amber burst out from several points along the ceiling up ahead, race along the walls toward us. Holy shit. It looks like magic—in fact, it looks like Allison going full machine gun mode with her attack spell. As the lights head toward us, I instinctively leap in front of the youngling, protecting her.

I'm surprised as hell to see that a staticy force field I'd only just begun to work on with Allison appears around us. Albeit it's spotty as hell, but at least it's something.

Zanjaya laughs behind me.

The sound of rapid pattering goes by overhead. As it does, I peer up at a hundred or so glowing creatures that resemble chameleon-sized dragons, scampering in defiance of gravity.

"Why are you scared, Samantha? These are harmless. You can put your magic away."

I do with a single thought, lowering my hands, then tell her about Allison and her energy bolts.

She goes wide-eyed. "Ooh. I wish to see that. The elders haven't taught me how to do anything like that."

"Not surprised. You're young."

"No, it's not that. Our magic is focused on life. Mending injuries, creating and controlling water, and making light. The High Chanter is concerned that if too many of us learn how to wield magic as a weapon, the winged ones will destroy us. They prefer us weak, or so I'm told."

I shake my head. Never would I have believed such violence and lack of empathy from Talos and his kind. Aren't fourth-dimensional beings supposed to be highly evolved? Would they so wantonly destroy? I doubted it, and Zanjaya sensed my doubt.

"Perhaps it's not true. After all, you perform magic—I just witnessed it—and yet the winged one helps you."

"Talos and I have a special connection. An incredibly long time ago, my soul came to this realm and reincarnated as a dragon. Err, as a winged one. We had been mates, but I died. Maybe because the universe knew my soul didn't really belong in this realm, I returned for another life in the third dimension. Later, Talos found me again, and we were reunited. This time, as friends."

"That's so sweet." She starts to grin at me, but suddenly points behind me. "Danger!"

I spin to the right in time to spot a glop of clear slime flying at my face. "Gah!" It costs me ending up on my butt, neck-deep in freezing water, but I manage to duck fast enough. The ooze that's been squishing between my toes for the past however many hundreds of yards we've been walking makes for a disgusting seat. Anyway, the slime blob hits the water behind us, dense enough that it sounds like a thrown rock going *kerplunk*.

The source of the projectile is a six-foot-tall, bright red growth attached to the wall, studded with similar clear blobs. With its conical shape, it sorta looks like a Christmas tree—one that throws its balls at people.

"Acid," says Zanjaya. "Don't let them hit you."

Since it appears to be a giant fungus, I doubt stabbing it with the Devil Killer is going to help. The kid gets the same idea I do at the same time: we dive underwater and swim. Whatever mechanism that thing has to detect prey evidently doesn't 'see' us below the surface as no more blobs go flying. Upon getting far enough out of its range, we resume walking through the water.

Minutes later, the cave tunnel widens into a vast underground chamber. Numerous columns of varying width and irregular shape suggest they formed naturally. A thin layer of pale blue muck covers almost every bit of stone not underwater. Except for an erosion trench in line with the cave we emerged from, the water filling the chamber is only about a foot deep.

Zanjaya steps out of the center stream, preferring the shallower waters of the chamber floor. Unfortunately, the much slower-moving water in the chamber doesn't erode the muck on the bottom as much. The slime layer is about two-inches deep.

Ugh. Feels nasty, but it's only plant matter, right? God, I hope so.

Strange floating lights dot the distant end of the hundred-yard room in varying sizes and shades of blue and green. At first, I think they're will-o-wisps or something made of energy, but when one drifts near, it turns out to be physical. A kind of airborne jellyfish, luckily without tentacles. They don't react to us at all, drifting wherever the air currents pull them.

My alarm sense goes off, but it's not too loud.

However, rapid sloshing from the left sounds decidedly aggressive. I spin, nearly slipping in the muck. A jet-black creature roughly the size of a large hog charges at us from a cave opening on the left side of the chamber. Six stubby legs propel it along at a startlingly fast speed. The end facing us isn't so much a head as a mass of tubular projections that end in lamprey-like mouths around a shiny, black beak big enough to take my arm off.

At the sight of it, Zanjaya screams pretty much like any kid would scream upon seeing a creature like that. Uh oh. She's been pretty blasé about everything so far. If she's scared of this land squid thing, it must be really nasty.

I'm basically stuck here without armor, claws, fangs, or guns. But I do have a sword. It'll have to do.

And so, seconds before I've got a dozen biting tentacles attached randomly to my anatomy, I sprout wings and leap straight up. This chamber doesn't have tons of room, but it's got just enough for flying.

After rushing past where I'd been standing, the land squid whirls around in a skidding turn and heads for Zanjaya. She sprints away from it, kicking up a spray of water but having little problem staying ahead of the creature. Unfortunately, the tunnel at the far end of the room doesn't have enough room for me to fly, and there's no way I could outrun it on foot like Zanjaya. So...

Sorry, pal. Even if you're just hunting to survive, my kids and Talos need me *not* to become your dinner.

With a flap of my wings, I zoom after it, swerving around two columns. Zanjaya nears the far wall and, rather than plunging into the tunnel and running for her life, she veers around and leads the land squid back toward the side of the room we entered from. Brave kid. She understands my need to fight this thing. Or at least immobilize it.

I swerve left, swooping at the thing halfway through its turn with a raking slash of the Devil Killer that severs a few of the tentacles sticking out of its front end. Not too impressive as they're only as thick as pool noodles. The land squid emits a noise somewhere between terrified pig and furious bird, screeching so loud from the main beak that my ears almost bleed. Leaving the severed tentacles flopping in the water, it bee-lines back to a bigger rough-hewn cave it evidently lairs in, wanting no more part of us.

Zanjaya tries to stop, wipes out in the muck, stands again, and runs to me. "We have to leave. More will have heard."

"There's more of those things?"

"The mother will be furious."

I point the sword at the fleeing creature. "That's a *baby*!?"

She nods.

"How big is the mother?" I swallow hard.

"Much, much bigger."

"Will she fit in there?" I gesture at the cave exit at the far end. It's about the size of an average hallway in an office building. The cave on the left, where the baby squid disappeared into, looks like a subway tunnel. A deep, gurgling screech echoes out of the darkness, loud enough to vibrate the floor.

"Never mind, let's go!"

Zanjaya nods, runs toward a river cave at the far end of the chamber. I stuff the Devil Killer back in its sheath and fly—literally—for the safety of the smaller cave exit.

Once inside, I pull my wings in and land in a dead run. Trying real hard to ignore the earthquakes and deafening roars behind us, I focus on avoiding anything that might trip me up. Adrenaline blurs time, but gradually, the angry mama grows quiet behind us, the noise eventually stopping altogether. How far she pursued us, I don't know, but thank God she gave up. No doubt she has to attend to her injured baby.

Yeah, I kinda feel like shit. But, well... I'm

alive. And so is Zanjaya.

And wow... this planet is damn weird.

But you know what's really, *really* weird? Seeing that thing kinda made me hungry. And no, I'm not in any way actually hungry, still overfull from Orounaz's energy. No, the feeling felt more of an 'I could eat that.' The only possible explanation for that atrocious thought is some manner of ancient soul memory of my life here as a dragon.

Soon, the cave passage abruptly shifts from naturally shaped to square-ish. It also angles down deeper to the point we have to swim. Not far from where the Drajjan evidently dug deliberately into this place to reach the water, the flow goes into a passage flanked on either side by stairs. Zanjaya goes to the left, climbing up out of the water and heading for an open archway.

I follow her into a basic corridor, more of a basement than a cave.

She pauses and looks back at me. "We should be quiet now. There are many openings and someone might hear us."

I nod.

Zanjaya leads me down that corridor to a four-way intersection. She keeps going straight, past two rooms stocked with bags evidently made from woven, narrow leaves. At the end of that corridor, she takes a left, ducks into a doorway and makes a 'shh' gesture.

Again, I nod.

Tail swishing, she presses her hand to the wall

in the corner, closes her eyes, and whispers something that doesn't translate. I'm still not sure what the heck Orounaz did to 'turn on' the translation, but I'm happy he did. Probably used magic on me.

The wall under her hand glows blue. A door-sized panel sinks into the ground, revealing a small chamber with bare walls and a square hatch in the ceiling.

"This is a secret escape route," whispers Zanjaya. "If enemies attack us during a ritual, the chanters can escape down here."

"Enemies?"

She shrugs. "Other Drajjan cities. Sometimes, there is conflict. We are not all one harmonious people. Can you help me up, Sam?"

"Of course."

She points at the wall. "There are no climb-holes to protect the city from enemies sneaking in this way. The passage is only for us to escape down into."

"Gotcha."

After some trial and error, we decide it's best if I grasp her by the waist and lift, which I do. She braces a hand on the wall to steady herself as I push her up to the hatch. It's again easy for her to push it out of the way. The girl grasps the edge, half-pulls herself out, then lets her tail dangle as if encouraging me to grab it.

"Are you sure?" I whisper. "Tails are usually sensitive."

"I am not from your world."

Fair point. I grab hers like a rope. She stands, pulling me up to the edge. As soon as I can reach, I grab the lip and pull myself out. That said, I'm certain I could have jumped out of here on my own... at least I could have back when I was a blood sucking fiend.

Once on my feet, she gives me this victorious little smile, then points behind me. I turn around.

Talos.

He's still curled up asleep in the middle of a pattern on the floor that, while it's not even close to anything Allison ever made, is clearly some manner of arcane ritual circle. In front of him, the entire wall is carved into the bas-relief image of an enormous Drajjan woman. The composition of the statue kinda reminds me of Shiva, only this Zaa has no additional arms. She does, however, look like the sort who'd tend to solve problems with one of those giant swords before talking it out.

Yeah, I'm not waiting around to hope she decides to spare Talos. Assuming, of course, she's more than a myth. My luck, she's real... and I'm about to piss her off.

We do, however, have a slight problem.

Talos—especially the version of him from this world—is *not* fitting down a trapdoor that's three feet on each side. The only other way out of here is the huge door with a small army of Drajjan warriors waiting on the other side.

I stare at the little hole in the floor. This is not gonna work.

LOST MOON

We're screwed.
Poor Talos.

Chapter Fifteen
A Tale of Two Dragons

Zanjaya appears to understand what I'm thinking from looking back and forth between Talos's massive posterior and the tiny opening.

Stifling a laugh, she takes my hand and pulls me across the room. The faint clicking of her toe claws on the stone seems as obvious as gunfire and makes me cringe, staring at the big doors. Those guards are going to hear us.

The child—kinda weird thinking of someone my height as being so young—approaches the bas-relief of Zaa and bows her head in reverence, her tail draped low, the last few feet hovering an inch off the floor. After a moment, she turns to face me, smiling, and rests her left hand against the side of Talos's head. Soft musical sounds come out of her like a songbird attempting to whisper. It has the cadence of a chant, something akin to what Orounaz and the others did when they levitated him.

Just as I'm wondering if this kid is intending to psychically lift and *push* Talos out of here—and if she's strong enough to attempt such a feat—clicks, soft trills, and whistles come from outside in the hall. Not sure why whatever has been translating has stopped working, but I don't have time to ponder it for long. My stomach lurches up into my throat with a sudden sensation like the elevator I'm riding in broke and went into free fall. The temple chamber around us blurs into a smear of green and pink light, then turns dark blue.

In seconds, the blurriness fades to a strange scene. Wind rustles the tops of giant plants covered in cobalt blue leaves. Based on their size and overall shape, they're probably this world's equivalent of trees. Spherical wooden pods of dark grey ranging in size from several feet across to as big as pickup trucks sprout several dozen narrow black branches each. Most have holes that appear to be the homes of various small animals no bigger than rabbits.

Talos has come to rest near the shore of a fairly normal lake. At least, the water seems ordinary. Glowing mushrooms of every conceivable color carpet the bottom, making it look like an enormous bowl of Trix, minus the milk. The sight of a veritable rainbow in a world that has thus far been mostly black and grey captivates me. Why would something so beautiful keep itself hidden? Like this is the only color this world has other than black and grey. Why is it in one little tiny place?

I haven't needed to drink water in a long damn time, but it's tempting. Part of me thinks it would taste like fruit punch.

"Your friend will be safe here… reasonably," says Zanjaya.

"I'll take reasonably. Thank you." I peel my awestruck gaze from the lake and face her. "Hey, wait. I can still understand you."

"Yes."

"But back there…"

She smiles. "The magic allowing you to understand me does not have a way to translate the words I use to call upon Zaa's favor. You did not understand because your language does not have these words."

"Okay. That makes sense." I suppose, anyway. English has no frame of reference for Dragon Latin or whatever it is.

It hits me that this kid basically just teleported us. Wow. Okay. She *did* say she was some kind of prodigy. I'm in another world where nothing says the rules of reality have to be the same as what I'm used to—or even close. Maybe teleporting is child's play here? So far, it seems like every Drajjan has some magical abilities. Wow, we got a bum deal. Human kids get band camp and soccer practice, not magic lessons.

Zanjaya brushes her hand across Talos's eye ridge, affectionately scratching him with her tiny claws. The blue light filtering down from the azure canopy overhead makes her charcoal grey scales even darker, save for a paler strip that starts at her neck and runs down over her front. Not knowing if she's merely being comforting or trying to do something to help him, I stand there in silence.

Eventually, she stops and looks at me with a worried expression. "He is hurt. I fear that he may not survive without additional help. The injury he has suffered far exceeds my magic to mend."

"You have magic? Wait, stupid question. We just teleported. I mean, you can *heal* with magic? Wait. Dumb. You already said most of your magic is for healing and creating water."

"Yes. Mending wounds and making water are the two main duties of the chanters. It almost feels like I've been studying magic even from before fighting my way out from my egg." She giggles like a child—somewhat unsettling considering we're basically the same size—but catches herself with a hand over her mouth. "My apologies. Your friend is gravely hurt. Not even the high chantress can mend a wound like this."

"What do I have to do?" I grasp her hand, hating the helplessness engulfing me from my lack of understanding of Talos' kind, this place, or even how much time remains before my body disintegrates.

I stifle a sob. His last conscious act was to protect me with a spell to keep me alive in the fourth dimension for as long as possible. God, I loved this big flying hairless hairball.

"This type of harm, a fractured soul, is beyond

us. You will need to seek help at the flying city of the winged ones. They will know what to do. They can help." She points up and left. "The Lumarae live within a vast city in the clouds. I cannot go with you there for the winged ones regard my kind as vermin."

I gasp. "How could they?"

She looks down, sighs. "This came to be long before I took my first breath of air. No one knows why. It could merely be that we lack wings and are small. There are writings that the first Drajjan to attempt speaking to the winged ones surprised them. Prior to that, they preyed on us as a food source. We have a writing from the Blind Chanters that mentions the day will come when the winged ones no longer threaten us and we will no longer need to hide underground. But for now, it is dangerous for us to be outside."

Again, I gasp, horrified. "They... *ate* you?"

"When they understood we had minds as sharp as theirs, they no longer ate us, but instead regarded us as abominations. Claimed we had been like them once, but did something bad and were cursed to be small and flightless. I do not believe that. My kind have always been like this." She looks downcast, radiating sorrow for the first time since I'd met her.

"There has to be more to that than what people are saying. At least, if your leaders are anything like the leaders where I come from, someone is lying. When Talos is awake, I will ask him if he knows anything about it."

She forces a smile at me, though I can't help but read a bit of '*if* he wakes up' in her eyes. "Make sure you only go to the flying city. You must avoid following a winged one into the western mountains."

"No western mountains, got it. Anything else I should know?"

Zanjaya nods. "Yes. There are two societies among the winged ones, the Lumarae, enlightened ones, and the Cibalor, the meat-eaters. I am sure your friend is of the Lumarae."

"Wow, so even dragons have vegans?" I blink.

She tilts her head. "I do not understand."

"The Lumarae are enlightened because they don't eat meat?"

"Oh." She laughs. "No. They abhor violence of any kind, including the destruction of plants."

That nearly shorts out my brain. "What the heck do they eat then?"

"They feed on energy. Magical energy, in fact."

"Then he would starve in my world."

"Your world does not have magic?"

"It kinda does now. I fixed it." I hold up my hands in a pinchy gesture. "Little bit more magic floating around than there used to be."

"It is still only the third dimension. Magic is…" She says a few things that come out as clicks and whistles before the translation mechanism comes up with "—stronger than what you are used to. Your world is only getting a taste of it."

"That I can believe. So, Lumarae and Cibalor.

News to me. Never heard those terms before. Orounaz called him a Lumarae…" I glance at the comatose Talos. "How did Orounaz know? Do they look different?"

"Slightly. The most obvious reason is that a Cibalor would have sooner eaten you than befriended you."

I swallow hard. Unless their gullet is lined with silver, being eaten by a dragon would be a truly unpleasant experience. However, strong enough acid or something like falling into a volcano could do the trick even without silver. I'd rather not find out how potent their stomach acid is. "Right. So, avoid the Cibalor at all costs. There's no way to tell the two dragon groups apart?"

"Oh, the Lumarae often have blunter faces and smaller teeth. The Cibalor"—she makes a grasping-and-pulling gesture at where her nose isn't—"have longer snouts and larger teeth. But, it is not a guarantee. They say in times long past both had been one society and are still in the process of evolving apart."

"Right… Okay. So I need to find this flying city?"

She nods, grinning. "Yes. Find your friend's home and the other winged ones there will surely help him. The winged ones hate nothing more than death."

I can sympathize. When you're immortal, even one death is a tragedy. No wonder Talos's grief drove him across dimensions to find me. Head bowed, I lean against his face, the closest thing I can do to hug him. His scaly cheek is warm against my skin, the vibration of his deep, resonant breathing could lull me to sleep if not for everything going on in my head at the moment. "Hold on, okay? I know you told me to get the heck home, but I'm not going to let you die."

My throat catches with the out-of-nowhere thought that maybe he *wanted* to let that demon kill him so he could try to send his soul into the third dimension and reincarnate to be with me? Nah. He likes being a dragon way too much. It would be more likely that he'd have tried to bring my soul here to be reborn as a dragon again, but he can't do that since my soul is kinda stuck permanently inside me now.

And yours truly is in no hurry to reunite with the Creator.

"All right. Seems I've got no better choice at the moment than to look for this flying city."

"Yes." Zanjaya points at the sky again. "Go that way. It is difficult to miss."

"Anything dangerous I should worry about?"

"Possibly, the razekh."

"Gesundheit."

"What?" She tilts her head.

"I mean, what's a razekh?"

"They are beings similar to the winged ones but without the capacity for reason or speech. They hunt the skies for food and will prey upon anything except other razekh."

"Wonderful. Flying mountain lions." I sigh at the treetops.

"What is a 'mountain lion?'" asks Zanjaya.

I explain.

"Perhaps something like that, but they are much larger. The same size as the winged ones."

Yeah. This is gonna suck.

I extend my wings. "Thank you for helping us."

"You are welcome." She clasps her hands in front of her chest and bows.

"Are you going to get in trouble?"

She flashes a cheesy smile, revealing sharp, conical teeth. "There may be some yelling, but the trouble will not be serious."

Wait. That nod…

"Zaoma told you to help us, didn't she?" I ask.

"Yes." She gives me a matter-of-fact stare. "It is the command of Zaa."

Chapter Sixteen
Atonement

The child Drajjan bows once more and disappears in a flicker of dancing blue lights, likely teleporting herself back home.

If I run into one of those razekh things, and they're anywhere near as fast on the wing as Talos, it's going to be a big problem. My angel wings are awesome, but they barely have half the top speed of a dragon. Worse, if the Talos I've gotten used to while shapeshifting is an 'underpowered copy' of the real Talos, that implies they're even faster here.

I'll have to hope that my small size—compared to dragons—makes me uninteresting as a snack. If that fails, the only escape mechanism left for me is teleportation. Pretty sure they can't fly as fast as that. So, my plan is to teleport straight down to the ground and find cover as soon as I see anything vaguely dragon-shaped coming to eat me.

With a disintegration clock stalking me, there isn't time to stand around being nervous or overthinking. Might as well do this.

Once more, I 'hug' the side of Talos' head. "Sit tight, buddy. I'll be back as fast as I can."

Taking a running start, I simultaneously jump up and extend my wings. Flapping hard, I pull up into the air out over the lake. A handful of bird-sized dragons come out of nowhere, screeching and flapping at me—probably trying to chase me away from their nests. I'm not too worried until teeny fireballs start flying past my head.

They're not much bigger than Roman candle fireworks, but those things can still burn. I weave side to side to dodge the hail of little comets. The mini-dragons lose interest in me pretty quick, disappearing again down into the foliage ringing the water. Hmm. Big dragons, dragon-like people… even the birds here look like dragons. I'm sensing a theme.

That gets me wondering if this reality around me is the entire fourth dimension or if each dimension—including mine—houses multiple realities. Meaning, could the whole fourth dimension be this world, or is the world around me now merely one facet of an unknown number of different realities stretching laterally out within the fourth dimension? If so, what the heck else might be in the third dimension?

Talk about ways to melt your brain.

But at least it keeps me from driving myself

crazy with worry over my kids, Talos, and the increasingly real possibility that I'm going to disintegrate before getting out of here. Time to fly faster. To avoid attracting attention from any razekh out hunting for a meal, I stay fairly low to the ground. Flying higher increases the distance at which people—or creatures—on the ground can see me, but it won't hide me if the razekh come sniffing around. However, staying low enough makes it possible for them to lose me in ground clutter and improves my chances of landing and either hiding, fighting, or teleporting my butt out of there.

One really big problem with that, though, is the terrain here consists almost entirely of that grey, powdery dust. Black rocks protrude here and there like islands in a sea of silt, but only a few of them are pointy enough to create cracks and spots for a person to hide in. Most are flat or shaped like tiny mountains.

If one of those dragons comes after me, my best bet for surviving is going to be teleporting back to that forest by Talos. As irritating as it would be to waste time going all the way back there, it beats ending up as a meal.

The light purple hue in the distance suggests it's dawn now. I think. Straight up, the sky remains black, dotted with stars. As I reach a comfortable speed, flying low to the ground and briefly allowing myself to enjoy the cool wind on my face and in my hair, I notice something dark and massive off to my right, far beyond rolling fields of lavender-like flowers.

I angle toward it, suspecting this just might the dragon city in the sky.

Soon, a colossal chunk of earth easily several miles across hangs via mysterious means among the lower reaches of the cloud cover. The bottom resembles upside-down mountains, inverted peaks pointing at the ground below. It looks like some titanic god scooped it out of the ground and hurled it hundreds of feet into the air, where it now drifted. That said, the rippled silt desert under it is as perfectly manicured as a Japanese Zen garden. Did the dragons themselves levitate the land mass to make a city shielded from the dangers of cave-dwelling threats or did such an impossible terrain feature occur naturally in this place?

So much for flying low. I angle up, flapping hard, soon climbing to a level even with the 'surface' of the floating city, which feels pretty damn high up… almost 10,000 feet, at a guess. The closer I get, the bigger it appears. Once I'm near enough to make out individual buildings and dragons, it's obvious my initial estimate of size was way off. This city is far more than 'a couple square miles' in size. The amount of magic necessary to make such a vast amount of rock float is so beyond me to think about—I don't.

Stranger still is how much like an ordinary city it appears. They have buildings and streets, though no cars or vehicles of any kind. The overall look of the place is a mixture of something from a fantasy movie and an alien reality. Dragons much the same as Talos in appearance—wing arms, two legs, long tails, and as big as box trucks, meander about like the citizens of Victorian London. None are wearing anything more than their scales, which makes sense. Who ever heard of dragons wearing clothing? That's as weird as people who put sweaters on their cats.

I fly in to land near a spot that has the look of a town square—and I feel like a freakin' mouse.

The stone is warm under my feet, as is the breeze blowing down the thoroughfare from behind me. My fake toga doesn't rustle in the wind, but it's doing a fair job of tricking me into feeling like I'm wearing something—at least when nothing is touching me.

But yeah, I feel like a mouse, or a two-year-old. The buildings around me are enormous. Dragons walking back and forth shake the ground and force me to make several rapid evasions to avoid being trampled.

When a violet-scaled one nearly steps on me, I zip to the side and yell, "Hey, watch it!"

The dragon stops short, left foot hovering in the air, and peers down. Its eyes widen, and for a moment, I'm expecting an 'eek, a mouse!' reaction, but instead, the dragon shuffles around to face me, lowers its foot, and leans its blunt-nosed head closer.

"Well, what are you doing here?" asks a voice in a distinctly feminine range, without any faint clicking or trills in the background. That tells me she's speaking my language. Boy, Orounaz's language translation magic is working overtime.

"I'm not entirely sure exactly how I ended up here, but something went very wrong. My friend Talos, a dragon like you, is seriously hurt and needs help."

She widens her eyes.

A few other dragons take notice of me—more accurately, they notice another dragon talking to the ground, then spot me.

"There is a human here," says a male with a long, black snout. He sniffs. "No. Not human. Former human. What *are* you?"

For brevity's sake, I say, "Apprentice angel." Don't feel like getting into a two-hour explanation of vampires, dark masters, and everything else. I turn back to the first dragon. "How can I help Talos?"

"You will need to seek the Seven Wisdoms," says the violet female.

"Please tell me that doesn't mean I need to run around and collect seven scrolls from seven ancient temples or something. I don't have that much time." Dammit. I'm trapped in the fourth dimension, not a bad Kung Fu movie.

The dragons exchange confused glances.

"No." The female chuckles. "The Seven Wisdoms are our ruling body." She reaches down with the hand-like structure at the main joint in her wing and picks me up like a Barbie doll. "I shall bring you to them."

Her chitinous fingers close around me in a prison of bones as thick as telephone poles, pinning my arms and legs. Short of teleporting, I'm not getting out of this grip. Mary Lou's son had pet gerbils for a while—or were they hamsters?—anyway, he always picked them up like this. Wonder if they disliked it as much as I do.

Perhaps her intention isn't to 'catch' me and keep me prisoner, but it damn sure feels like it. At least she's not crushing me. This dragon hurries down the street at a brisk walk, which due to her size, covers ground faster than I'd be able to sprint. A few of the others who'd been observing our brief conversation follow. Dragon faces aren't too great at conveying emotions in ways humans can pick up on, but my guess is they're curious. Most whisper amongst themselves, wondering how an angel feels like a 'mere' third-dimensional creature.

Guess they missed that 'apprentice' part.

A short while later, my escort-slash-captor enters another town square type area, only this one is three times the size of the one I landed in, with a fountain depicting several dragons in flight, spewing water instead of fire from their mouths. I'd ask where the heck water is coming from on a floating island, but yeah. Magic.

One entire edge of the courtyard is the façade of a massive, ornate building. Again, my thoughts start toward 'temple,' but based on what this dragon said about the seven wisdoms being their ruling body, it's probably their city hall.

She walks right in the front door, no guard or anyone challenging her, then heads down a wide corridor with a curved arch for a ceiling. The other dragons follow in single file. About midway down the hall on the left, she ducks through an archway into a big chamber with the look of something between courtroom and auditorium. The innermost wall has a huge edifice that resembles a judge's bench, only it's big enough for seven dragons to sit behind.

Presently, it's empty.

My purple Uber stops in the middle of the chamber and simply sits there.

I squirm, trying to wriggle out of her grip, but I may as well be encased in cement from shoulder to shin. If the dragon even notices me trying to escape her grasp, she doesn't react. Great, I'm the mouse some kid found and desperately wants to show her father. The others gather up behind us, all keeping silent.

My patience wears pretty thin. I'm inches from shouting something to the effect of 'get the eff off me' when tromping and scraping echo from a passageway behind the bench. Between worry, curiosity, and doubting my yelling will get this dragon to let go of me, I keep my mouth shut—but continue squirming.

A black-scaled dragon with brilliant golden eyes emerges from the hallway and takes a position at the center of the judicial bench. "Vixana, welcome to the Seat of Seven."

The purple dragon bows her head. "Great Baxxus, I am honored to seek your wisdom."

"In what matter do you desire counsel?"

Vixana reaches up and deposits me atop the judicial bench, *finally* letting go. She's gentle enough that I don't fall over… and find myself standing there feeling like a Barbie doll on a desk looking up at a person. Baxxus has a long, classical snout, though his teeth are smallish. Two metallic silver horns stick up from either side of his head, curving sharply like those of a ram. He's not *too* massive. His head is only about the size of a Ford cargo van. Modestly larger than Talos.

"Ahh. A being from a lower realm. Know that I am Baxxus, Keeper of Law, principal of the Seven Wisdoms." He turns his head to the left, leaning his right eye closer to me. "More than a simple human. You should not be here. It is unsafe for you."

"Yeah. I know. Not my idea. Some bad stuff happened. I've come here to ask for your help, mostly because my friend Talos is gravely ill."

Baxxus leans back, reacting to the name. "You know of Talos?"

"Yes. Why? Is he like famous or something?"

"Not particularly. He is one of us. How is it you are aware of his name?"

"Long story. The short version is… he's kind of like my spirit animal and he's going to die. Can you help?"

At me saying 'die,' all the assembled dragons

gasp.

"Surely there is time enough for understanding," says Baxxus. "Please, elaborate."

Fine. Whatever. I take a deep breath and explain about calling the flame, shapeshifting into what I believed to be Talos—turns out it's a secondary version of him he projects into the third dimension—and the fight with the demon that ultimately led to his duplicate self suffering a fatal wound and disrupting whatever mechanism that allows me to shapeshift, thus stranding my butt here in the fourth dimension.

"Hmm." Baxxus regards me with a contemplative stare for a minute or two.

Whispers among the dragons in audience behind me sound alarmed at the 'most unusual' situation. More shuffling and scraping echoes in the passageway behind Baxxus. Near-total silence falls over the chamber while six more dragons shuffle in, going to the left or right behind the judge's bench, three to either side. Two are black-scaled, one white, one violet, and two dark grey. The last one to enter is somewhat smaller than the others and seems a bit younger. In human terms, I'd say he's the newly appointed forty-year-old jurist among a bunch of old men.

"I have convened the Seven Wisdoms to discuss this matter," says Baxxus, before looking side to side at the others behind the bench. "This being from the third dimension claims that one of our own, Talos, has routinely made contact with her and subsequently breached via symbiotic projection into that dimension."

The other Wisdoms emit varying degrees of shocked gasps.

Uh oh. That doesn't sound very promising. Did I just get the big fella in trouble?

"On a recent breach, Talos' projection was destroyed during a fight with an izoreth, though he took the foul creature down as well."

The Wisdoms all cringe at that word. The smallest one does, however, nod at me in a way that makes me think he's happy the demon died, too. I'm assuming 'izoreth' is their word for demon. No idea what dimension they're native to, but apparently, they've shown up here, since the mere mention of them elicited such a strong negative reaction.

For the next few minutes, the seven dragons look back and forth at each other, making subtle eye motions. Somehow, I get the feeling a conversation is going on, perhaps telepathically or via sounds beyond the range of my hearing. Attempting to read the Drajjan's thoughts was a wall of static to me like trying to pick up television signals with a transistor radio. These dragons are on high-def. Way out of my reach.

"Regretfully," says Baxxus, "interaction with the third dimension is prohibited by our laws and customs. We are unable to provide any assistance to Talos until he atones. Part of that atonement would need to include his connection to you being severed forever."

My turn to gasp. Breaking our connection would crush him. I know this without a doubt. Hell, it would crush me too. Still, better that than he loses his life, though. Talos might not agree, but dammit, I can't let him perish.

"You can't just sit back and let him die," I say. "Don't your kind treasure each dragon's life beyond measure? How can you do nothing? And how exactly is he supposed to atone? He's in no shape to do anything but sleep. His projection in my dimension *died*. He can't even open his eyes now, let alone speak."

The Seven Wisdoms collectively lean back, their expressions grim. Even a non-dragon like me can read the look on their mostly inflexible faces. They clearly didn't realize he'd gone into a coma or whatever, and hearing that has made them all look guilty as hell. This worries me even more as it appears they expect him to die. Okay, so they don't *want* him dead. They probably saw a chance to be prigs and make things difficult for him over the 'don't talk to the lesser beings' law.

"I'm sure Talos respects your laws, but exigent circumstances were in play. A long time ago, my soul incarnated in this realm as one of you. I lived for quite a long time as a dragon, Talos' mate, in fact—until I died. No idea what pulled me here for one lifetime, but my soul went back to the third dimension. His need to be with me never stopped. He did it out of love."

Baxxus again exchanges looks with the other Wisdoms. One by one, they nod at him.

"Very well," says Baxxus. "There is another option. You may atone in his place."

"I'm sorry?"

Six of the Wisdoms chuckle. Can't say for sure, but the way they're looking at me suggests they don't expect me capable of surviving this atonement.

Baxxus appears amused as well, but remains stoic. "We recognize that as a being from a lower dimension, your capabilities are not the same as ours. To provide atonement for Talos' breach of law, we ask that you journey to the Vale of Torment."

The others stop chuckling.

"Oh, that sounds lovely." I bite my lip. "Couldn't you guys just like torture me here or something?"

He bows his head. "My dear…"

"Samantha."

"Samantha," echoes Baxxus, "it is not our desire to inflict suffering. Our notion of atonement differs from yours. To correct the breach of trust that Talos committed, we would ask that you provide us aid with a task we are incapable of. The Vale of Torment is our name for a place where the third dimension intrudes upon this world. It is a dangerous place to us, filled with poisons like envy, greed, bloodlust, and misery."

"Wow." I whistle. "Didn't realize they held the

NFL draft here."

The dragons again exchange confused looks.

"Okay. So this place is like being in the third dimension?" I ask, eyebrow up.

"That is correct. You should not inherently suffer any discomfort or pain from being there. In fact, you may find it natural. Our kind cannot enter this realm as it assaults our mind and causes great suffering. We are certain *you* can enter without ill effect as this energy is matched to your being. If you are able to discover what has caused this invasion, we shall consider that atonement for Talos. By some chance, if you are able to seal this breach, banishing the third dimension back to where it belongs, we would be well in your debt."

If they owe me a favor, I can ask them to permit Talos to keep his connection with me. Probably would be smarter of me to use that favor to go home, but one thing at a time. First and foremost, the big guy needed help. Like stat.

Baxxus leans down and does something strange... he breathes glowing gold fumes all over me.

Tingles sweep throughout my body like a mass of tiny electrified spiders. In seconds, it feels as though I've been driving around this world for years and know exactly where things are. The Vale of Torment sits approximately 800 miles northeast from here. My memory also now contains knowledge of areas where razekh are in large numbers and even the location of the Cibalor nation—

roughly 1,200 miles to the west in another mountain range. Both of those facts are tinged with strong feelings of aversion and fear. Even the Vale of Torment feels like a place I'd rather avoid: tornadoes ripping up the land, various faceless monsters ready to flay the scales off any dragon who ventures too close, constant lightning, earthquakes, and vast swamps of black, sticky tar with giant blood-sucking insects big enough to be a danger to even dragons.

Yikes. Well, maybe that's just Baxxus's interpretation of the place. Hopefully, it's overstated.

"How much time does Talos have left?" I ask.

Baxxus debates this for a moment. "Hours, perhaps a day or two. If he has already succumbed to sleep, it is grim indeed."

"Any chance someone could give me a ride to at least the edge of the Vale? It's going to take me six or seven hours to fly there. These wings"—I flap them—"aren't all that fast compared to you guys."

"I will," says Vixana. "Come, there isn't time to waste."

So help me, if this woman grabs me like a hamster again…

Baxxus nods once.

Vixana motions for me to jump on her back. That, I can handle. She does have some rather sharp horn-like projections sticking up along the ridge of her spine, but they're spaced wide enough that I can sit between two of them near the base of her neck. The one in front of me is taller than my face when

I'm sitting down. Eep.

She waddle-walks out from the chamber, hurries down the hall, and goes outside, leaping into the air from the grand courtyard. Soon after we level off above the clouds, she asks me about my former life as a dragon.

Unfortunately, I really don't remember anything beyond the few tidbits that Talos shared with me. Those little stories appear to sate her curiosity, and we fly mostly without conversation to the northwest.

Yeah, I'm flying on the back of a dragon, on another world in the fourth dimension, breathing air that would probably kill me a hundred times over had I not been immortal.

Life is weird... but kind of fun, too.

I hang on, staring down, watching the strange, swirling cloud formation and stranger landscape slip by, wondering what I had just agreed to... and if I would survive.

We'll see...

Chapter Seventeen
The Heart of the World

The trip to the Vale of Torment—or at least as far as Vixana is willing to go—takes about two hours. Of course, I'm purely guessing there as I kinda forgot my cell phone back in my homeworld. I don't even have pants.

"I can feel the effect of the reality tear affecting me already, small one," says Vixana, hovering in place. "This is as near as my body and mind are able to withstand. Please, do whatever you can to help Talos."

"You know him?"

"Only in the sense that he is one of us. I regret that the Wisdoms cannot help him without atonement. I shall wait for you here to hasten your return."

"Thank you, but that isn't necessary. I can actually get back to the city in an instant."

"How is that possible?"

I explain my teleportation. Unfortunately, Baxxus hadn't ever been to the Vale of Torment. He only imparted me an idea of which way to go to get there, no actual memory of being there, so I couldn't use that information to aim a teleport.

"Ahh. Yes. I see that within you now. Very well. Please hurry."

"I'm all about hurry right now." I examine my fingers—no sign of disintegration yet. Good. "Thanks again."

I stand on her back, extend my angel wings, and leap off to the side. There's a pretty good reason people generally don't go skydiving naked. Stuff flaps around. Fortunately, I don't need my arms to steer in the air so I can hold my swinging bits in place while diving. The first twenty seconds or so is blank nothingness as clouds surround me, blocking all vision. When I burst out the bottom, the sight on the ground below is exactly the opposite of my expectations.

Amid an endless ocean of grey silt and black mountains sits an oasis of verdant green. A highly unnatural ring of mountains encloses an area that looks like a pastoral valley straight out of the Swiss Alps. Walls of opaque vapors sit atop said mountains, which suffer a constant pounding of lightning as well as random explosions of magical energy. Similar flashes of lightning and racing plasma clouds arc through the air, suggesting the presence of an invisible bubble over the otherwise peaceful interior.

Hate to say it, but this looks like an enormous snow globe... a self-contained picture-perfect little diorama dropped in the middle of mind-numbing desolation.

A dark vortex of energy swirls in a tornado-shaped funnel at the midpoint of the dome, extending down to touch the top of a structure that resembles a medieval castle tower. At first, I think it's surrounded by moss, but no... those are trees. That tower is ridiculously big. It's got to be 500 stories tall or more.

Really hope that 'dome' is merely an illusion created by the clash of dimensional energies and I'm not about to feel like a bird flying into a window at full speed. Going slow isn't an option due to my severe allergy to lightning strikes. Pretty good chance those racing plasma sheets are hot enough to turn me to cinders in an instant, too.

I keep diving toward the idyllic little world-in-a-world. If this is a true third-dimensional pocket, it should at least function as an oasis to shield me from disintegration. While plummeting head-first toward the raging torrent below, I try to get a feel for any patterns in the lightning indicating a clear spot to aim for.

Wait. Why am I being dumb?

There's no need for me to play chicken with lightning—or globs of plasma the size of buses.

Wings flared, I 'slam on the brakes' about four hundred feet above the maelstrom and focus on a spot of ground inside. The instant I start concentrating on the flame to teleport, the ground leaps up to meet me. Whoa. I stare up at placid skies—no trace of chaos. The teleportation worked, but much faster than usual.

There is something *very* funky about this place.

Ordinary earth-like meadow grass as tall as my hips tickles my legs. Warm sun—yes, it's apparently here, too—chases away the chill I hadn't realized existed everywhere else in this realm. It would be easy to pretend that whole 'dragon world' thing had been a dream and rather than being catapulted across dimensions, I'd merely landed somewhere in the highlands of like Germany and slid face-first into a grove of magic mushrooms.

A fat honeybee checks me out, loses interest, and buzzes off over the meadow. My illusory toga is still here, proof that I hadn't dreamed everything. Also, the tower of ridiculous size still stands in front of me. At a guess, I figure I'm about three miles away, and there is roughly two-and-a-half miles of dense forest between me and it. The tower is so damn big it appears to be standing on top of the forest, not jutting out of it. Frighteningly enough judging by the size of its windows, it only has ten stories.

Bright day, nice clouds, green grass, light breeze… this Vale of Torment is far from 'torment.' Either Baxxus lied to me or he's been woefully misinformed. Maybe dragons have tried to get in here and this place acted like a huge bug-zapper, killing any that tried to fly past the 'dome.' It's mesmerizing to watch the maelstrom from below. That violent clash of energies must be caused by the interference of different dimensions touching.

I fly up for a better look around. Grass and trees everywhere, along with a single river running southeast from the ring of mountains. There's no sign of any life here capable of speaking. Sheep or goats, bugs, birds, animals, yes. People, not so much. If there is anything to be done here, it's in the tower.

This entire scene is a total hippie dream. There's nothing between my skin and miles of untarnished nature. All that's missing is the patchouli oil. I can't enjoy it though. While my body might not disintegrate here, my kids and Allison are no doubt losing their minds thinking me dead... oh, and Talos' life is completely in my hands.

It doesn't take long to cover the few miles to the tower by air. The ridiculousness of its scale defies words. Downtown Los Angeles skyscrapers could fit in the windows of this thing. I'd thought the dragon city made me feel like a gerbil in terms of size, but wow. If something human-shaped lives here, Talos—even his bigger form—would be about as big as a squirrel to them.

Scratching and murmuring emanate from the topmost floor. Worth a shot, right? Worst-case scenario if it's something mean, I'll be so damn tiny they won't notice me.

I fly to the windowsill—a stone opening the size of a city block—and land near the inside edge. The massive room inside looks pretty close to my imagined vision of what a fantasy wizard would use for a home, except the center table doesn't have any chairs around it, and rather than a bed, the far corner has a massive low-lying bird-like nest.

The reason for this becomes apparent as soon as another scraping noise makes me look to my right—at a huge red dragon. Unlike Talos' brethren, this one has four legs plus wings, a long neck, bright green eyes as big as cars, and an extended snout lined with teeth as tall as I am. Take the most classical image of 'fantasy red dragon' and that's what I'm looking at.

I know the universe has a tendency to make real those things that a large enough number of people believe in, but in this case… it's more likely the reverse happened. I suspect this thing had been around for ages. And at some point, someone saw it, painted it, and everyone thought it was make believe.

And yeah, I'm super tiny here, basically a three-inch tall faerie sneaking into a human's house.

"Hello, little one," says a voice on the deeper end of feminine. "Please, enter. You are in no danger."

I can believe that. I mean, who eats *one* raisin? Against my better judgment, I fly up off the windowsill and glide over to the giant dragon. She's perched sejant by a podium holding a massive book covered in florid (or floral?) writing that's so intricate my brain interprets it as a meaningless pattern rather than individual letters. For no particular reason, I decide to sit along the top edge of the book. Each page is over an inch thick and feels coarse, like canvas.

It's kind of a weird feeling to be sitting here looking up at a red dragon with a head the size of a small house and *not* being terrified. While naked, to boot. Anyway, something about her makes me think she's sad. Perhaps lonely if she's living here all alone.

"Greetings, tiny one. I am Poendraz."

"Pen-draz?" I ask.

"No. There's an o. P-o-e-n-d-r-a-z. The o is silent."

"Pendraz."

"Not exactly. There's an o."

"How do you know I'm not saying the o? It sounds the same. What, do you have subtitles on?"

The dragon chuckles.

"So, umm... I'm guessing this isn't really a Vale of Torment, and you're not a dark force."

"No, tiny one."

"Samantha. The 'tiny one' is silent."

She laughs, nearly blowing me off the book.

"You are partially correct, Samantha. I am not sad though; I am heartbroken because my creations are quarreling."

"It always tore me up inside when my kids fought. Sorry."

Poendraz nods.

I decide to dive in. "What's the deal with this

dimensional breach? Are the third and fourth dimensions crashing into each other here? Can I fix it?"

The dragon chuckles at me as though I said something cute, like when four-year-old Anthony asked me if it rained because the clouds are crying. "This is quite normal, merely the natural bridge between realms."

"So it's not invading?"

"No. This window into the third is neither growing nor shrinking. At the other end, a pocket of fourth-dimensionality exists in the third dimension."

"We've pretty thoroughly mapped the Earth and haven't seen anything like this."

"My dear, that's because it is not *in* your Earth. It's in another, similar realm a few steps sideways. One where magic remains dominant."

"Oh. Does that mean I can't use this bridge to go home?"

"You could use it to return to the third dimension and avoid the danger of your physical form breaking apart, but you would still be stuck in a world not your own and in need of finding a way to move laterally."

Grr. That's not going to help. If I'm on the verge of disintegration, there might not be a choice, but that moment isn't here yet. "Is it true that the other dragons can't go here?"

"It is. They could not withstand my presence."

"But I can?"

Poendraz smiles—the last few inches of her mouth curling up. "Yes."

"Why?"

"Because I did not create you."

Realization hits me over the head like a dead fish, leaving my mouth hanging open. "You're a creator?"

"Indeed. But, my creations have run wild, quarreling with each other and dividing themselves into two groups."

"Yes, Zanjaya said there's like the Cibalor who are warlike, hunt, eat meat, and such, and the Lumarae who subsist on magical energy and abhor violence."

Poendraz sighs, shaking her massive head. "My children have taken to the extremes. Those you call Lumarae have elevated the notion of pacifism to an unwieldy degree. They have constructed an artificial floating city so they do not disrupt the natural world. Some even regard leaving footprints as regrettable 'damage.' It is true that they ceased hunting animals for food, refusing to consume even plant life. For the past several centuries, they have altered themselves through arcane means to subsist on the absorption of energy from crystals they harvest."

That makes me chuckle mentally, thinking of how I went from drinking blood to absorbing mental energy from people harmlessly. Good change. Also, my change means it's possible for me to feed here. The fangs I no longer have—and mostly forgot about—wouldn't have pierced dragon scales. Might have been able to punch a hole in a

Drajjan's neck, but it's possible their blood wouldn't have worked for vampire food—and I'm sure they wouldn't appreciate being bitten.

"Wow. And the Cibalor are trying to kill them?"

"There exists the drive within them to overrun the Lumarae, yes. None have yet acted on it, but several prominent individuals attempt to sway the rest of their society into believing that other dimensions, specifically yours, are a threat to their existence. They prepare for war not only with humans and other creatures living within the various iterations of third-dimensional worlds, but with their brethren the Lumarae. They see them as weak, a hindrance when the inevitable invasion occurs. My children you call Cibalor desire to invade lower, and even upper dimensions to spread their influence."

Poendraz goes on to compare her creations to spoiled siblings who won't speak to each other.

I ponder this, and ask, "But what of the Drajjan? Is their goddess Zaa real?"

"They were a spontaneous idea of mine. I believed it would add some variety to this place. The individual they revere as Zaa is an entity comparable to your Devil, though I mean that in terms of how she came into existence, not her function. Zaa is neither, as you would say, 'good' nor 'evil.'"

"Enough Drajjan believed she existed, so the universe made her."

"Precisely. They view her as a creator-mother

goddess, defender of their kind, and a great warrior. I am despondent because all of my creations hate each other. Perhaps as an outsider, you might be able to convince a leader from both sides to journey here so that I may speak with them?"

"Just both sides? What about the Drajjan?"

"Oh, they're merely small creatures I made as a bit of decoration."

I blink. "I'm pretty sure they hate being thought of as trivial."

Poendraz gives me this 'well, they are sort of trivial' sort of look, but emits a clipped sigh from her nostrils. "Perhaps they, too have evolved beyond my expectation."

"Most people would be shocked if they came home from work one day to discover their pet white mice developed a society with a full political system and tribes. Why did you give them sentience if you only wanted decoration?"

"A fair point. You are quite intelligent for a creature with such a small brain."

I stare at her. Okay, so her brain is literally the size of a swimming pool, but still. "What about them not being able to withstand your presence?"

"Creations often cannot meet their creator. It is not the natural way of things, at least not without the creations transcending the flesh and becoming beings of energy. An intermediary vessel is needed. I will create an avatar to stand in my stead, through which I can speak… hopefully convincing the Lumarae and Cibalor that they are one society."

This is so bizarre. I'm a faerie sitting on top of a book. Even got the wings and clothes made of pure light. Speaking of brains, mine is about at the upper limit for weird. This is a creator. She might be a gargantuan dragon, but she's still a creator. Which gets me thinking...

If Van Gogh can paint me into different dimensions, Poendraz can send me home. But... I can't abandon Talos. If I go home now, he's dead.

Also, this dragon appears to know what's going on in my head. I'm sure she knows of my need to go home, hence asking me to invite the leaders of the two dragon groups here for a meeting. No doubt there's a bit of quid pro quo going on there. Right. So I've got my way home, just need to save Talos' life and broker peace between two rival factions of dragons who've been warring for a millennia or so.

Should be easy.

"I'll do my best."

Poendraz dips a claw in an ink well the size of a hot tub, and scrawls more ornate writing on the massive book. Ah, it's her Book of Creation. What she writes, comes to be. "The disturbance above this place will no longer be able to harm you. Do not fear the boundary between dimensions."

"Thank you." I float up on my wings. "Gonna go get started."

"Fly well, tiny one." The big dragon offers a grateful smile, then resumes writing.

More determined than ever, I head for the window.

Chapter Eighteen
A Little Snag

Soon after leaving the tower, my wings begin emitting trails of golden light that hang in the air for a few seconds after I pass. At first, it seems Poendraz sensed my self-comparison to faeries and wanted to make the illusion more complete, but the ground is going by way faster than it should be, closer to the speed at which Vixana flew.

Guess she decided to throw me a small bone and give me the ability to fly faster. I don't feel any different, so it's more likely she altered this world to enhance my flight rather than changed me.

Time is precious, I'm not about to complain.

But what to do? Okay, so I've discovered the nature of the dimensional 'invasion' is not an invasion at all. That should be enough for 'atonement.' Trying to convince Baxxus that his creator wants to talk to him, though might be rough. Say something like that to the average person on the street, they'll laugh—or the opposite direction.

Bigger question is the Cibalor. How do I approach a violent, warlike race of dragons and talk them into sending their leader to speak with Poendraz? Good question. Suppose it's 'play it by ear' time.

Thanks to Baxxus giving me a memory map, I've got an idea where to go to meet the Cibalor. Two things are in my favor: size and teleportation. If it turns out that they're super dangerous, I can hide in a place they can't fit in… or go poof. It's unlike Poendraz is going to hold it against me if the Cibalor won't even talk to me. She's not asking me to die for her cause. Then again, she did seem kind of ambivalent to the Drajjan, so who knows?

After orienting myself toward the Cibalor region, I accelerate and fly at whatever my new top speed is. The place is roughly 1,200 miles away from the Lumarae floating city, but I've already gone some distance northwest to reach the Vale of Torment—really, that place needs a different name. Anyway, mysterious knowledge tells me the Cibalor territory is only about 700 more miles away.

Worry dogs me for the next hour and a half or so. All this racing around is burning up time. I force myself to not think about it now.

Vast oceans of grey silt give way to craggy terrain with canyons and valleys nestled between black stone ridges. Large swaths of rock glitter from thousands of diamond-like crystals catching the mysterious light in this place, not from any sun. I spot a few packs of those weird 'land squid' creatures congregating by streams, as well as other, smaller animals reminiscent of iguanas or some such medium-sized lizard.

Fast motion high and to my left draws my attention to a pair of brick-red colored dragons. They appear to be on the smaller side, closer to the version of Talos that goes to my world when I shapeshift, only they have longer snouts. The pair have already seen me and are racing closer.

Uh oh. Looks like they've decided they want a Sam-nom. Grr. There are a whole bunch of fat six-legged, undoubtedly delicious land squids down there, but these two are in the mood to chase something scrawny with wings. Go figure.

With whatever boost to my flight speed Poendraz has evidently written into her book for me, I'm no longer panicking at the idea of having to fight these creatures. Sure, the Devil Killer will do a number on them, but it's only a broadsword's length. Using it on flying dragons, even the smaller 'Earth-Talos' sized ones, requires getting far too close to claws and teeth for my comfort.

So, I dive to the right, both razekh on my tail. Flying straight and level gives me a slight speed advantage over them. They beat me in climbs and we hold even on dives. A minute or three of wild zig-zagging doesn't dissuade them, making the thought of fighting them closer to reality. I can't afford to get messed up here. The time it takes me to heal could mean disintegrating alone in the barren wastes of this world.

That's a little pessimistic of me, but it feels that for every step forward here, I'm sliding back three. Really need to lose these damn things. Heading low, I dive into a canyon, hoping to use the narrow confines to exploit our size difference to my advantage. Huge tangles of black roots that kinda look like tumbleweeds jut out from the rock walls, turning it into more of a maze than I expected. Looks like decent cover, so I angle toward them, soon weaving between the twenty-foot wide vine balls.

Some of the bushes unfurl and start trying to grab me with thorny vines. Oh, hell no.

"Gah!" I yell, pulling away.

A flailing root snags my right ankle, yanking me to a halt by a half dozen one-inch thorns embedded in my skin. Before I can even yell in pain, it yanks me back into a birds' nest of grabby vines. Tiny daggers stab into me all over as the giant plant pulls me deep inside. I struggle as much as I can tolerate, grabbing the pencil-thin strands and snapping them away from my arms and torso while shielding my face so I don't end up losing my eyes.

Both razekh fly up to hover nearby, raking at the bush with their talons. I'd say they're trying to help save me from this carnivorous weed but, no, it's more like a hyena just stole their dinner.

More vines encircle me, each thorn that enters

my flesh makes me gasp or yelp depending on where it punctures. As fast as I'm breaking them off, more appear. A thorn pierces the front of my throat causing blood to bubble up into my mouth.

Dammit. I've got a murderous rosebush all around me and a pair of voracious dragons hovering mere feet away…

Yeah, this ain't good.

Chapter Nineteen
Freely Given

If offered a choice between death via dragons devouring me or bleeding out while the digestive juices of an enormous bramble liquefy me... I'd probably give whoever asked that question the finger.

Both razekh continue ripping at the vines. One emits a startled squeal when a thorn punctures it somewhere. The startled quasi-dragon backs off with a demeanor like a dog that just tried to lick an electric fence. A lucky whip strike from the bush catches the other one in the side of the head, drawing blood. That one, too, whines and decides to stop messing with the plant.

Great, I'm in a world where the damn weeds are more dangerous than dragons. I need to do something *now*.

Allison suggested my ability to feed on psychic

energy might extend to plants—but I'm too rattled to calmly search for any trace of sentience in this thing. Especially with the branches formerly engaging the dragons returning to help pin me down.

One option left.

I summon the dancing flame, focus on a spot in midair a safe distance away, and invoke a teleport.

The pain of forty or so thorns wiggling around inside me shifts to the shock of cold air on open puncture wounds. Down below, the sphere of writhing black vines erupts in a furious frenzy of flailing, whipping at the air and surrounding mountainside. Can a weed be pissed and throw a tantrum? Sure looks like it. I give it a double middle finger.

"You're damn lucky I don't have a lighter on me!"

And... ouch!

I hang there for a moment, wings flapping idly, waiting for the wounds to close. They hurt quite a bit, but they're pretty shallow and not too big around, so it only takes about five minutes for them to heal. I'm bloodied, but intact. And my toga is still pristine white. Yeah, now it's obvious I've been here too long. I no longer feel naked. Well, I do, but it seems normal now. I'm close to going full Clayton. Wearing nothing but an illusion is starting to feel routine, even comfortable.

Granted, I'm experiencing the multi-dimensional equivalent of being stranded alone on a desert island. If other people were around (besides Allison or Kingsley), no doubt I'd be mortified. In fact, I'm pretty sure if the big hairy oaf could dream, his dreams would frequently involve me being stranded on an island somewhere without clothes. Horn dog.

That helps me laugh away the last bit of pain.

Before the razekh realize the plant no longer has me, I resume flying fast to the west, toward larger mountains. The sense of 'where stuff is' that Baxxus shot into my mind angles me to the right. When I spot a mountain stream, it tempts me in for a quick bath to rid myself of blood. The water is so cold it feels like falling into a bathtub full of icy needles and triggers an involuntary gasp. Needless to say, my bath is rushed.

Since there's still no guarantee the Cibalor won't want to eat me, going in there smelling like fresh blood is probably a bad idea. Fortunately, my sense of smell is way sharper than a normal human's. Once I can no longer detect any unusual scents on me, I leave the damnably frigid stream behind and head into the air again.

A couple miles up the mountain range, the surface is dotted with hundreds of holes that remind me of some ancient sites where humans had carved dwellings into mountainsides—the Pueblos, if I recall. Nothing even close to trails or walkways connects them. No surprise since the dragons can fly. Several large open areas resemble courtyards populated with dragons much like the ones in the

Lumarae's floating city.

The biggest such plaza has an imposing fortress-like façade at the innermost end. It's not overly decorated, having a highly utilitarian aesthetic more akin to a military command center than a king's palace. Of everything here, it is the most grandiose thing but that isn't saying much. However, it's as good a place as any to start.

Now, here's hoping the Cibalor won't try to eat me.

Hmm. It occurs to be me that playing up the 'angel from a higher dimension' angle is probably a good idea.

So I land near the grand entrance, gaining instant notice by about fifteen dragons. Most are black-scaled, a few dark red. One blue. All but two have the longer snouts and straight horns. Like the Lumarae, they're bipedal, with wings and arms sharing a common limb and a weird three-fingered hand at the joint. I'm so used to the projection Talos made in my world with more bat-like wings that seeing a hand jutting out from the wing looks beyond weird. Come to think of it, what I turn into back home is closer to a razekh, only smaller.

Anyway, under the gazes of a whole bunch of carnivorous dragons, I walk into the doorway like I've got every right to be here. A short hallway goes past a space just big enough to hold whatever gears open and close a likely massive door over the entrance and brings me to a large, rectangular chamber that contains a scene simultaneously normal and weird.

An empty 'throne' is positioned against the wall on the far left. However, rather than a chair, it's more of a bowl-shaped nest with a fancy backing upon a raised dais. At the middle of the chamber, four dragons sit by what appears to be a war map of unfamiliar terrain, complete with little figurines of dragons and humanoids.

The largest one, with brick-red scales, wears an ornate headdress made of gold and gems. It's not so much a crown per se as a pair of small bead curtains hanging from his horns. Either way, it likely indicates he's the big cheese around here. At least these dragons aren't anywhere near the size of Poendraz. I don't feel like a faerie in here, more a human walking around between tractor-trailer cabs.

"What is this?" asks the 'king' in a raising tone that belies genuine curiosity rather than disdain or concern.

The other three dragons look up from the map at him, confused, then follow his gaze to me.

"Rather too small to munch on," says one of the black-scaled ones I'm going to think of as an advisor.

"Quite," replies advisor two.

"It appears to be from a higher realm but smells of lower places." The last advisor, pale grey in color, leans closer, sniffing at me.

"I am Samantha. I've come to speak with, um... whoever's in charge here."

The 'advisors' all bow deferentially to the one

with the fancy adornments on his horns.

He beckons me closer with a curl of his right hand. "I am Aoshandre."

"The Wise One," echo the advisors together.

"You are from the world of humans," says Aoshandre.

"A spy!" hisses advisor one. "They've learned of our plan!"

I shake my head, although 'the plan' sounds a bit alarming. "I'm not here to spy on you or figure out what your plans are. I have a message for you from Poendraz."

The four dragons in front of me as well as the ones who followed me inside from the courtyard all break up in titters and chuckles as if I'd told a bunch of people back home that I was speaking on behalf of Santa Claus.

"She lives in the place you know of as the Vale of Torment, and—"

"Yes, yes. We know the fables," says Aoshandre, waving his winged-hand dismissively. "The creation myth is an old story."

"This one sounds like the Lumarae," says advisor three. "Next you know, she'll plead with us not to extend our empire into the third dimension."

"I'm not here to do that, but you probably should reconsider that idea. The third dimension isn't all it's cracked up to be. There's taxes, dark masters on the loose, and the Kardashians."

The dragons look at each other, then at me.

"What is a Kardashian?" asks Aoshandre.

"I'm not really sure. We're still trying to understand that last one." I step up onto the war table among the little figurines they've been using, most as tall as my knees. "As I'm sure you know, my time here is limited, so I'm not going to waste it attempting to convince you that Poendraz is real. Sure, I'm human—mostly—but I've been to dimensions and places very few of my kind have. I understand some of the nature of creators and how things function, in general. So, the reason—"

"Enlighten us," says advisor one in a patronizing tone. "How do things work?"

My eyebrows knit into a flat line of annoyance.

Aoshandre chuckles, apparently agreeing with me, but gestures at me to humor his advisor.

"Forgive my ignorance," I say, "but your kind have stories, right? Made up tales purely for amusement?"

They nod.

"Creators are similar to that, only the beings and places they make up come into existence for real. The entities within that story world aren't aware that they are entities within a world created at the whim of another being."

The advisors find this funny, though Aoshandre tilts his head, his luminous emerald eyes widening and narrowing, studying me.

I continue. "Poendraz is a creator. She wrote about your people and thus you came to be. However, she's become quite sad over you and the Lumarae breaking apart into two separate societies."

"They are insufferable," snaps advisor two in a sort of effete tone that reeks of snobbery. "Refusing to hunt? To eat meat—or even plants? How ridiculous."

"Not only that, but they object to us exercising our power over weaker civilizations. Why should we not take advantage of our strength?" asks advisor one. "Large beings eat small beings. It is the natural order."

"Aren't you above the natural order?" I ask, eyebrow up. "You have the capacity to reason, to contemplate the future, to consider matters of philosophy and theory. Animals react on instinct."

"She does sound like a Lumarae," whispers advisor three behind his hand, making the others snicker.

Aoshandre gestures at them to be silent. "What is it you have come to ask of me?"

"Poendraz wishes to speak directly—well, through an avatar—to the leaders of the Cibalor and the Lumarae. According to her, you belong as one society."

All the dragons except Aoshandre laugh uproariously at that.

"Look… you guys don't have to take my word for it. All I'm asking here is that you go to the prearranged location, talk to the avatar, and see whatever it has to say. If I'm making this up, there won't be anything there and all you lose is the time it takes you to fly there and back."

"Small one," says Aoshandre, "if what you say is true, why would this great Poendraz need the help of a being from the third dimension? Could she not simply 'create' us back to one people? Or send that avatar here? And, how are you even in this world?"

All good questions. I take in some air and sort through the answers, and let it out again. "Okay, no idea why she doesn't 'create' you back together. She asked me to talk to you because she hasn't made an avatar yet. No clue why she didn't. Maybe she's been so heartbroken she's stopped thinking of ways to fix it and just wallowed in sadness." I shrug. "You'd be better off asking those questions to the avatar when you go talk to it. Why am I here? Well…" I give them a summary explanation of the Talos situation. When I get to the point of explaining Talos' present dire circumstances, Aoshandre grunts, sitting back on his great haunches.

After he seemingly digests this, he leans his head out over the table and exhales a wisp of golden light. It coalesces in front of my feet, forming into a dark ruby about as big as a softball. He says something, but I'm too stunned at seeing a gemstone that size to process it.

"Samantha?" asks Aoshandre.

I snap out of my 'holy crap that's worth a billion dollars' trance and look up at his truck-sized face. "Yes?"

"Take this to your friend Talos immediately. Feed it to him. This will prevent his death."

I blink, staring at him. Wait, that's it? Just gives

me the thing? No hoops to jump through? No atonement? Aren't these supposed to be the bloodthirsty savages? Wow. Things have really gotten twisted here. The Lumarae's opinion of these guys is perhaps a little harsh.

Aoshandre gestures at it. "You should not waste time."

I open my mouth to speak, but haven't found the right words yet.

"Why do you appear confused, little one?" asks the ruler.

The question snaps me out of it. "Well, since Talos came from there, I went to see Baxxus first and they wouldn't help him without some atonement for his breaking the rule about contacting my dimension."

Advisor two rolls his eyes. "So much for the great pacifists respecting life. They'd let a dragon die rather than admit their rules are less important."

The other advisors cluck their tongues.

"It is reprehensible for them to withhold aid based on asking you to perform a task near to impossible for a dragon, much less one such as yourself." Aoshandre nudges the ruby closer with the tip of his nose. "Take this and go. Be quick. Return to discuss the matter of Poendraz if you so choose after."

I crouch and start to pick up the big ruby with both hands—but stop short, gawking at my mostly transparent fingers. Itchy tingles spread up my arms. The same feeling is in my toes as well, and ears... the tip of my nose. Extremities go first.

Shit. This is *not* good. The huge ruby beckons me with a pulsating energy at its core. I've still got no idea whatsoever how to get back to my world, and... likely minutes left to live. No choice really. If it kills me to save Talos, so be it. It's my fault he's hurt.

Head bowed, I grasp the enormous gemstone, my skin prickling from the vast amount of energy held within. "Thank you."

Aoshandre emits a low noise in his throat and nods. I sense his great concern for me.

Hang on. Nothing is ever free. Staring into the ruby's depths reveals only dark red crystal and a faint glow at its core. This could do just about anything to Talos. How can I trust it? Or am I being too 'human' in thinking it impossible for anyone to freely offer help without strings being attached? For all these dragons supposedly value the life of other dragons above everything, Baxxus still insisted on that atonement deal. He could've helped Talos and *then* sent us off to do something. But no, he left my friend's life dangling in the balance, perhaps as motivation for me to do his task.

The bloodthirsty Cibalor that the Lumarae look down on for consuming the flesh of animals don't know me or Talos from a hole in the ground and yet he gives me this crystal that could theoretically save his life? It could also be a cruel joke, merely something to make the weak little human run around and waste time. I peer up at the "Wise One."

Aoshandre's large emerald eyes brim with a sort of grandfatherly urging as if to say, *Go, child. Make haste.*

I'm desperate, but can't see any deception there. Granted, Quantico didn't have any training classes on reading a dragon's body language. Even the sarcastic advisors are giving me the same look. Behind me, the crowd of curious Cibalor dragons also nod at me. A few appear perplexed at my hesitation as if the very idea I'd not immediately run off to help Talos is mind boggling to them.

Right. Guess I'm being too human here, even when death is on the line. And speaking of death being on the line, my ass is disintegrating. Well, not literally. It's just my hands and feet at the moment.

"Thank you." I bow to the dragons, stand, and call the dancing flame, picturing the small wooded area by the lake where Zanjaya took us, and where Talos presently rests.

***

My surroundings change in an instant to the azure forest, a short distance from where Talos remains curled up asleep by the lake lined with rainbow mushrooms. Not sure what unsettles me more, seeing him from the outside or that he's much larger than he 'should' be.

I hold the volleyball-sized gem up to look at it. "Please work…"

Talos doesn't react to my approach. I kneel by

his mouth, set the ruby on the ground, and attempt to get a grip on his jaw. My old partner at HUD, Chad Helling, used to have a dog. When it got older, he had to force-feed the poor animal its medicine twice a day. This resulted in story after story of how epic a challenge it had been for him to make this maybe thirty-pound dog take a pill.

If I ever get home, I should call him and apologize for laughing at him.

The first few minutes go nowhere as my fingers keep slipping off Talos' jaw. Not sure if he's slippery or my body is becoming insubstantial. I finally manage to wedge my hand in deep enough to get a decent grip. Did I mention in this world, his head's only a little bit smaller than my Momvan? Sure, I'm strong enough to shove cars around, but the average Toyota isn't drooling all over me.

Hot breath blasts out of his mouth, blowing my hair back. At least it doesn't stink too much. Guess a diet of magical energy and crystals is pretty healthy for teeth. I strain to lift the upper part of his head, but the lower jaw moves with it. After much contortionism—and some involuntary yoga lessons—I end up bracing his lower jaw down with my left knee, shoving the upper part of his head upward, and stuffing the faux ruby between his teeth onto a tongue big enough to use as a surfboard.

"Hah!" I shout in victory, then ease his head down so his mouth closes. "I've successfully pilled a dragon."

My urge to laugh at that plummets into a need to

cry. I end up doing neither and sit on the ground beside his head, leaning against him. Not sure exactly what to expect, but after like ten minutes with no obvious effect, the worry that the Cibalor might have tricked me begins to orbit my thoughts.

At faint tingling in my forearms, I glance down and gasp—my hands are entirely gone. Shit! My body's breaking apart. I can't bear to even look at my legs. My ears and nose have stopped prickling, probably because they've vanished. Good thing this place has no mirrors. Talos isn't moving and I'm fading out, still with zero clue how to go home.

Oh well… I suppose it's only fitting that we die together.

Resigned to my fate, I curl up against Talos' cheek and, with tears flowing, concentrate all my energy on trying to tell Tammy and Anthony I'm sorry for leaving them, and how much I love them...

Chapter Twenty
The Canyon of Rifts

The vanishing crawls up my arms, though not quite fast enough for me to see it move.

Time drags on, seeming an eternity. Soon after my arms stop existing below the elbow and my knees disappear, red smoke begins wafting up from Talos' nostrils. Too weak to do anything but sit there watching, I wait. Talos emits a low moan, then something akin to a cough. This gets me moving, giving him some space. Next, he convulses, leaps upright into a sitting position and gags, likely choking down the ruby that had been sitting on his tongue.

His tremendously deep cough startles the tiny dragons out of their nests, but—much to the benefit of their health I'm sure—they don't assail him with tiny fireballs. The coughing fit subsides in a minute or two and Talos once again reclines on the ground, breathing hard.

"This, I was not expecting," says Talos.

"It worked," I whisper, overcome with joy.

I try to caress his face, but my arm is gone below the bicep.

He stares, eyes wide in alarm. Still coughing like Jacky my boxing trainer getting whiskey down the wrong pipe, he draws in a long, gurgling breath. That posture from a dragon, even Talos, makes me brace for a blast of flames. Instead, he hacks out a hot glob of phlegm all over me... followed by a blast of magical energy that surrounds me, nearly lifting me off my feet.

Dripping with goop, I cringe, giving him a 'was that really necessary' sort of stare for a second. Meanwhile, the fear in his expression fades as he watches me. In fact, he looks downright relieved. Hmm. When I go to wipe my eyes, it occurs to me that I have hands again. I stare at them, wiggling my fingers. That's why the fear in his eyes left! I'm not disappearing anymore! I doubted the phlegm had done much, but that magical exhalation had done wonders.

"Humans sometimes say that one can lose themselves in a journey. I do not think they mean it to be literal," says Talos. "You cut that a bit too close, Sam."

Too happy for words, I jump up and 'hug' the side of his face.

"I'm so, so sorry…" Guilt shivers shake my body. "I should've been more careful taking on that demon."

"It is not your fault. The demon had the upper hand. Another few runs at each other and he would've defeated us. That moment he and I collided presented the only opportunity to destroy it. So, I took it... and hoped for the best."

"Except, we didn't destroy it," I say. "My body was sucked backward through the inner workings of the dimensional machinery—or whatever—before I had a chance to finish it off with the sword. The demon's still out there somewhere."

"Yes, but it won't be able to re-enter your world for many years, decades in fact."

"Why not?"

He exhales hard, sounding tired. "That is how demons work. If they are killed there, in your third dimension, they return to a place humans call 'Hell.' Time varies based on a set of circumstances and conditions I am not privy to understanding, but it will be multiple decades before he can escape and set foot on Earth."

"He was killed but not destroyed," I say, knowing the Devil Killer sends the entity back to the Origin.

"Exactly."

"Does that apply to anything killed in the third dimension or just demons? Are you banned, too?"

"No. *I* didn't physically go there. A lesser copy of me did."

"Sneaky. Kinda sounds like something Danny would come up with to exploit a technicality in the rules."

"You married him, Sam."

I chuckle at that, knowing that in a different lifetime, I had "married" the giant creature presently crouched next to me. Being coated in dragon snot is highly unpleasant, so I head into the lake to rinse off. The rainbow-colored mushrooms all over the lakebed feel like they're made out of Jell-O. This is seriously funky to walk on, but could be worse. I'm tempted to take a sip of this water just because my brain really wants it to taste like Trix cereal or something fruity… but I resist. No idea if this is safe or not, plus I don't need water. The snot rinses off with surprising ease. And another upside to wearing an illusion—my clothes don't get wet.

"So, what have I missed?" he asks, rolling his head and stretching his massive, elongated neck. "You are still here, obviously. Why haven't you gone home?"

"Oh, a couple reasons. Not the least of which was trying to stop you from dying." I rub the side of his head. "I met Baxxus."

Talos groans.

"Yeah, sorry." I look down, shrug. "We got in trouble. They're not happy you and I have a… thing."

"Their displeasure is not my concern. You've managed to mend my essence without their intercession so they have nothing to hold over me. However, I likely will not be returning to the city for a while."

The loneliness in his voice is painful to hear. I almost want to tell him to be with his people and not worry about being able to lend me a dragon form anymore... but I know he'd never go for that. His feelings for my soul run far too deep.

"Indeed. Our connection means more to me than anything. A moment without your soul in contact with mine is worse than an eternity absent the presence of dragons."

"You say the sweetest things."

He chuckles.

"We need to get you home." He stretches, then stands.

"But you're injured, right?"

"Not so much now. I've had rest."

His face is too high to reach, so I lean against his leg. "Don't be like that. Why is it men never want to admit they need a doctor?"

"Sometimes, a doctor is not actually needed. I have had plenty of rest, Samantha. The wound I sustained here was not a physical one. The crystal has restored the part of me lost when the projection died."

"I'm still not sure how to process Aoshandre just giving me something like that without asking anything in return."

"Nothing is as precious to my kind as another dragon's life."

"So, any of you could've made such a crystal?"

"Any past a certain age, yes. Aoshandre is quite old. As is Baxxus. Most of the Seven Wisdoms are of sufficient age."

"Grr." I scowl. "So it's not even that big a deal and they *still* wouldn't do it without demanding atonement?"

He stretches again. "Look at it from their perspective. Creating an essence crystal is a small task. Contacting the third dimension is a small misstep. They likely did not realize the severity of my situation."

"They did." I fold my arms. "Showed clear in their eyes. Got the feeling he wanted to help but had so much red tape tied around his brain he couldn't bring himself to break the rules. He would've let you die because of some stupid, inflexible interpretation of law. Why not help you *then* ask for atonement?"

"That is not how the law is written."

Before I can even shout 'Screw the law,' Talos picks up the thought in my head and starts laughing. Wow, if my 'down with The Man' Dad could see me now ready to shout something like that, he'd be so proud of me. You know… it's half tempting to show up at their new place in Las Vegas just like this—Toga and wings—to mess with my dad. Tell him it's an LSD flashback, then teleport out.

Nah.

I'm more mature than that. Well, a little more mature than that.

We sit there for a while as Talos regains his strength. I spend the time explaining what happened with Aoshandre and Baxxus. When I tell him the

Cibalor and Lumarae used to be one society, he laughs.

"Don't be silly. That's quite impossible."

"Well, it's not that difficult for me to believe," I say. "You take a large group of people, divide them into two smaller groups and isolate them from each other for hundreds of years... and yeah, the odds of them remaining the same are pretty low. Heck, look at Earth. Countries hundreds of miles apart have vastly different cultures, and yet we're all the same species."

"Yes, but... you're humans. I expect you—well, them—to be..."

"Less than dragons?"

He does the best 'sheepish grin' his mouth is capable of. "Something like that. Perhaps you are right and hubris *is* the Lumarae's greatest flaw."

"You know Poendraz?"

"All my kind know of the mythology."

I face-palm. "It's not mythology. I met her."

Talos sits back on his haunches, eyes wide. He's looking into my thoughts and I think it broke him. The idea of the draconic creator being real leaves him gawking. He'd heard rumors that the Lumarae and Cibalor had diverged from a common society a long time ago, but he'd never considered it possible due to the severe differences in ideology.

"Samantha, this is... this will change everything."

"If we can convince both sides to talk to the avatar."

He shifts his jaw side to side. "Hmm. That will be difficult. I'm still not sure I truly believe you experienced what you think you did. It might be an illusion or a hallucination."

"How would I imagine seeing a legend I had no idea ever existed before meeting her?"

Twice, he starts to say something and merely ends up staring at me, wordless.

"I don't think the Cibalor are as savage as your leader believes them to be, Talos. Yes, they are considering ways to invade the third dimension, but it doesn't seem likely they'll attack your kind on sight. It *is* possible to talk. I should return to Baxxus and tell him about Poendraz."

"They won't believe you. Especially not the Seven Wisdoms. The notion that something greater than them, a creator even, exists, would be unfathomable to their egos. Without our link that allowed me to see your thoughts, I would not have accepted that as truth either. This is not your burden to carry. I will deal with Baxxus once you are safe."

"But… they want to sever our connection. If you go back to them, what will happen?"

"Samantha, our connection is already severed. That happened when your soul was drawn back across our link after the death of my projection. Within hours of you no longer being in the third dimension, the pinhole I had been using to connect across the barrier sealed."

"No…" Despite it making no sense to feel like a dear friend died, hearing that our link is gone already hits me hard.

"Do not worry." He tries to pat me on the back with his hand, but it's sorta like being bumped by a car door. "It works in our favor. There is no link for Baxxus to sense and demand to be abolished. Remember, I created the link once so it can be done again."

"All right. Whew!" Okay, so that link hadn't always existed. He made it once; he can do it again —provided he isn't caught. Nothing to be sad about. In fact, I felt overjoyed. "So, what's our next step?"

"Getting you home. There is a place we used to fly together long ago, back in your dragon form. The fabric between this world and other worlds is thin there. I've come to believe this is where you once came through when you incarnated as a Lumarae. It is also the place where, long after losing you, I found a way to project my consciousness into your realm. If anywhere exists on my world to open a gateway back to Earth, it would be there."

"What of Poendraz' tower? That place is an entire pocket of third-dimensionality. She even said it's a bridge… but not to my world."

"Yes. Within each dimensional layer, third, fourth, fifth, and so on, an infinite number of side-by-side realities may exist. Crossing laterally between them is somewhat more difficult than going up or down between dimensional layers. However, sideways motion does not run the risk of disintegration."

I examine my hands. Fingers are still solid. "Seems like I'm holding on."

"For now. My magic isn't a fix-all. Climb aboard, Sam. It's time to take you home."

"There's a problem. I can't leave yet."

"Oh? Why not?" he asks, his voice unusually placid. Playing coy?

"I gave Poendraz my word I'd get the Cibalor and Lumarae to speak with her avatar. That's not finished yet. Barely started even."

"It is not your concern. You belong on the third dimension."

"Talos…" I brush my hand down the side of his massive head. "I'm already here. You can keep me from disintegrating, and she asked me to do this for her. I can't simply abandon that promise."

He emits a resigned sigh, head bowed. The big guy's protective of me, but he also knows me well enough to realize I'm going to see this through. "Climb on. We will figure something out."

A little wing-assisted leap is much easier than literally climbing him.

Talos doesn't have the same tall spines as Vixana. His back has a ridge of broad, bony armor-like plates. The low spots between them kinda feel a bit like a motorcycle seat, but there's nothing to hang on to. Rough maneuvering is going to send me careening off into the sky. No big deal though. Just means I need to fly on my own. Since Poendraz boosted my flight speed, the only real difference is that riding Talos (or some other dragon) doesn't tire me out. And I still think he's a bit faster.

He launches into the air, cruising out over the lake. The tiny dragons in the trees behind us screech and chatter in annoyance, but they don't attack. Definitely don't blame them. That's about as silly as me trying to kill Poendraz with a sword. Even if I managed to penetrate her scales, a broadsword to me is an irritating splinter to a dragon that big.

Unless, of course, we're talking about the Devil Killer—then all bets are off.

Of all the morbid things to talk about, I bring up a conversation about medieval Europe and the stories of knights slaying dragons. According to those legends, the dragons involved had been more like Poendraz than Talos, having four legs and being quite large indeed—though none came close to the creator-dragon's massiveness.

Talos nods his great head. "It is more than possible that a reality exists somewhere, perhaps even another third-dimensional world where such dragons exist. One may have slipped sideways into your world for a brief time, enough to be seen and birth legends, before going back to where it belonged. Or maybe some humans stumbled into a realm where dragons existed. The energies that maintain the separation of things are fickle. Occasionally, creatures migrate randomly without intention to do so, but in those cases, they almost always return where they belong once the universe corrects the error."

"Hmm. Sounds like *Final Countdown* type

stuff."

"I'm not familiar…"

"Old movie. Basically, a modern aircraft carrier goes back in time to World War II, but before they can make a real difference… stopping Pearl Harbor I think, they get sent back to their own time. Like the universe realized it made a mistake and fixed it."

"Ahh. Yes. That does sound similar in concept. And familiar."

"Ugh. Time travel." I cringe. "Don't remind me. If I never see another Civil War soldier again in my lifetime, it will be too soon."

"With that, I agree," says Talos… who had, of course, traveled back in time with me.

"We lead an interesting existence, Talos," I say.

"Hey, you're the vampire. I'm just being me."

I shake my head, chuckling. "Oh. Idea."

"Hmm?" asks Talos.

"You know how the Seven Wisdoms wanted me to perform an atonement for you breaking their stupid rule? I went to see Poendraz because they think the Vale of Torment is a dimensional instability."

"Correct. The Lumarae do not believe Poendraz is real. If you try to tell them she is, they will react much the same way as humans if you attempted to convince them to believe in unicorns."

Sighing, I nod. "Yeah, I know. My idea is that we convince Baxxus to either come with me or maybe send the new guy on the council because I met another dragon who will only speak with one of your kind that has standing. We don't mention anything about Poendraz or avatars."

"This plan of yours may potentially work," says Talos while steering for home. "Let us hope they do not belabor the issue of my transgression."

"Yeah, well. At least you can keep me from falling to pieces now." I pat him on the neck.

Like five minutes later, the Devil Killer appears out of its dimensional sheath by itself, flies into my hand, and begins thrumming. Bright golden-orange fire licks up the blade. No idea how I know this, but I know the sword wants like hell to go to the southwest, and it's giving off some serious urgency.

I've found something true to the nature of working as a private investigator. When jobs are scarce, they're really scarce. But when clients appear, they all seem to want me at the same time. Azrael is one of my VIPs. Heck, after my kids, he's the top of the list. If *he's* paging me, that means it's serious. Sorry, Poendraz, but I need to take this call.

Chapter Twenty-One
Disturbance

According to the information Baxxus gave me about the area, my Earth-adjusted brain considers the direction the sword wants to go as south.

Meanwhile, this place has no visible sun. And I still have no idea if it's a legit planet or merely a flat plane, or even a ring. The three moons hovering in the sky suggests this is a planet. What if there isn't any real concept of compass directions here at all? There'd have to be if this is a planet, but the dragons might not use magnetic fields. Maybe they navigate based on the three moons?

While our flight takes us across another vast swath of grey silt to the same range of black mountains where I first appeared, Talos tries to explain about their cognizant sense of spatial existence simultaneously in four dimensions, but it melts my brain. These peaks are noticeably taller than the ones where the Cibalor dwell. Pretty to look at, but nothing for us there, so we continue past it.

Soon, we come across verdant deep-grey grassland crisscrossed with glittering rivers and streams. Ink-black creatures somewhere between stags and elk, as big as garbage trucks, scatter as soon as we come into sight. More than their enormous size, the sight of something here that is *not* reptilian in nature surprises me.

"The old legends that mention Poendraz explain this," says Talos. "Back when all of my kind dwelled as one, we had individuals you would refer to as priests. Many of us revered Poendraz in a way similar to human religion. The teachings of the time stated that all creatures bearing scales had been made in Poendraz's image."

"Gee, where have I heard that before?"

He chuckles. "I'm talking about enormous four-legged dragons. It is possible that the legends are incorrect or Poendraz never got around to making larger dragons like herself. Or they could simply dwell so far away from here that we have never encountered them. Quite obviously, she created multiple types of dragon-kind as well as other creatures, the ones you refer to as 'land squid,' those beasts fleeing below us now. Those with fur or soft skin—that is, devoid of scale—were placed upon the land by Poendraz for our sustenance. In fact, the old laws forbid the consumption of any creature with scales."

"Makes sense, I suppose. Kind of like how most humans cringe at the idea of eating dogs or cats."

"Something like that."

A vast array of valleys, ridges, and deep trench-like ruts appears up ahead in the distance, awash in a dazzling array of flickering lights and dancing plasma pillows similar to the ones by the Vale of Torment.

"You talk of the priests as though they died out?"

"Poendraz is now regarded as little more than a myth, I'm afraid. It surprises me less to discover she exists than my kind ceased holding her in reverence. Tens of thousands of years elapsed with no sign of her. My kind overcame their fear of invoking her wrath, and gradually, many considered it pointless to hold reverence for a being who appeared disinterested in our existence... or to have never existed at all."

"Well, she exists, but I don't think she wants to be worshiped. She said only that it pains her to see the Lumarae and Cibalor separated and at odds with each other."

"That is something for the Seven Wisdoms to debate. Certainly not a quandary for Samantha Moon, ace detective." He grins, though I more feel it mentally than see it from my position on his back.

Something flashes below. Whoa, what was that? I lean out over Talos and look down as web-like lightning skitters across the surface terrain, jumping from silver rock to silver rock with an electrical crackle like a downed power line, but ten times as loud. Silver rocks? Yeah, we can stay away from those damn things, thank you very much. Meanwhile, pulsating thunder follows, reaching us in near-physical sound waves. Truly an odd sensation to have such sights and sound coming from beneath me.

"Is that real silver, Talos?"

"There is no word for that mineral in your language. But it is not silver. The rocks will not harm you."

"Okay, that's a relief. And I hereby name it... Talosite."

My friend laughs at my silliness. Not for the first time, I get a sense that I can do no wrong in his eyes.

Breathtaking bursts of light occur seemingly everywhere over the ground and down into the many canyons. As we fly, hanging curtains of energy fade in and out all around us, wavering in an ephemeral breeze not made of air. The powerful web-lighting below worries me, especially since I've never seen ground-running lightning before. Whatever the 'talosite' is really made of, it evidently conducts electricity.

I'm lost to the beauty below me for a while, though Talos appears focused on going to a particular spot. A short while later, his sudden descent snaps me out of my touristy reverie. We dive into a valley where a section of canyon widens around an oval-shaped lake with a mound-shaped island of black dirt in the center—his apparent destination.

The air here has so much energy it feels like I'm moving through cobwebs. Random static appears in my hair, more tickling than painful.

The Devil Killer pulses again, radiating dire warning.

"What is this place?" I ask, as we swoop down a little lower.

Talos emits a troubled sigh. "We would come here together and spend hours watching the lights. After your passing, I would visit this island to remember you and search for the moment your soul returned to Earth."

"Sorry."

It's odd hearing a dragon this big sniffle. He contains his sorrow, clears his throat, and advances a few paces. "This is also the spot where I first poked my sight across into your world upon sensing you had reincarnated. There is a natural breach here, one that connects our worlds. However, creating a gateway wide enough for your physical body is not something I've done before, but the process should be within reach."

"We can revisit that idea soon enough, Talos—once my mission here is completed."

"It will be no easy task to get the Lumarae and Cibalor to talk to each other, Sam."

"I gave Poendraz my word I would try, and I intend to keep it. She seems to think there is a way. She is, after all, a creator. Perhaps she will create an opportunity for the talks to happen."

"That sounds like it could be dangerous."

"Heh, she's your creator—not mine."

Talos grunts, and I sense he really, *really* wishes I would abandon my mission. Ha! Guess he doesn't know me as well as he thinks. I say, "Why do you think the Devil Killer is pulling us here now?"

"A good question," says Talos. "When I first suggested trying to send you home, this is the place from which I would do it. The non-space between the third and fourth dimensions is thin here."

No sooner does he say that than I notice black goop bubbling up from the ground. It looks like crude oil. And it's not just bubbling... it's taking shape... forming a sort of living, dripping tentacled mass. "Umm. What's that?"

Talos banks to port, angling lower for a closer look. "I'm afraid something is coming through the breach."

"Through the breach? You mean, from my world?"

"Yes, Sam. And it brims with negative energy."

The closer we get, the stronger the vibration within the Devil Killer becomes. "It's demonic!"

"I would assume so. I believe your sword can sense some entities."

"Wait, the portal is in the ground?"

"Temporarily. The opening can shift."

"Lordy, who makes up these rules? Never mind, we should seriously try to plug that hole."

Of course, I could try to slice and dice it, except

the thing is barely a solid.

Talos swoops down and comes in for a landing a short distance from the disgusting well of black ooze.

Bleh. It stinks like rotting eggs here.

At his mental direction, I leap off his back, glide a short distance, and land in the gritty black soil that crunches under my feet. Ugh. I feel like I'm standing in a cat box. I note I'm a safe distance away.

"It is only a crack in the dimensional fabric. Perhaps I can seal it and send it back through." Talos spreads his 'arms' wide. Soon, faint bluish light begins collecting in bright clouds under his massive wing membranes.

Meanwhile, the Devil Killer wants to hit something. I need to hold it in both hands to control it. Seems to be trying to pull me *away* from the spout of black liquid that's now gushing at least twenty feet into the sky.

Talos continues focusing, faint twitches in the muscles of his face and around his eyes give away an extreme level of concentration that isn't coming over our mental link. The air behind me takes on a strange solidity, a mass of gelatin against my back. Wait, why against my back? Why isn't he trying to stop that thing from escaping from the ground? What's happening behind me?

Oh, crap. Is he trying to send me home because he's a giant overprotective doofus?

"No, Sam. Well, yes, I am protective of you. But what you're experiencing is your third-dimensional world. You are naturally attracted to it. The pull is undeniable."

"But I don't want to be pulled back in. At least not yet."

"I'm... trying to seal it... but... something else has a hold on it."

With a faint *pop*, a small hole opens behind my head. The voices of Tammy and Allison shouting leak through, too far away to make out exactly what they're saying beyond that they sound freaked out. Anthony's quiet. Hope that just means he's still the Fire Warrior and not hurt.

Soft ripping, like a knife scoring down a bedsheet, comes from behind me. My shoulders begin to slip backward past the inter-dimensional boundary. Tammy's mind link reconnects. A rapid blast of grief, surprise, and joy follow.

Mom! You're back!

Tammy!

Hearing my daughter's voice, even if just inside my head, is enough for me to abandon the entire mission to help Poendraz and all these damned dragons. Really, they are higher evolved beings; they should work out their own problems. My daughter. Ah, my sweet daughter. She needs me. I need her.

I'm just about to allow myself to be sucked back into my own world—when a loud explosion goes off behind me. Something akin to a speeding bus hits me, launching me up and out of whatever space between dimensions I'd been occupying.

LOST MOON

I flip head over ass and land face first in the granular sand, where I lay for a second or two, hands outstretched, wondering if anything is broken, let alone what world I'm in.

Wow, that hurt like a bitch.

And what the heck made me want to race home to Tammy like that out of nowhere? Where did that come from? As I lift my head and turn it—I catch a glimpse of something huge and black, an amorphous shape part way between human and dragon, with humungous wings. It's gloopy around the edges—like a statue sculpted from liquid tar. It races up and hovers over us, glaring down. Okay, what the hell is that thing? Amazingly, its distorted, shifting, slightly human countenance smiles. As it does so, it raises its clawed hands a bit like how a maestro might. Except it's not commanding an orchestra.

It's commanding those living, oily, black tentacles.

The next thing I know, I'm picked up into the air and slammed face-down again into the gritty dirt. Electric jolts ripple along my arms and legs as the rubbery appendages slither over me. Talos—also attacked—staggers nearby, fighting the damn things. His massive foot smashes into the ground close to me, nearly burying me under a wave of coarse granules. It feels like someone's mummified me in living snakes, pinning my arms to my sides and my legs together. I can't sit up, but thrashing side to side works, flinging dirt away enough for me to turn my head out of the fine gravel and look at Talos. Slick black tentacles have wrapped themselves around his body, too, anchoring him to the ground.

Whatever that *thing* was that went flying into the air apparently did not want us following it. And somehow it controlled these tentacles.

"Not quite, Sam," grunts Talos nearby. "They are a part of it."

"But... how?"

"It shed its third-dimensional body, which, as you can see, couldn't make the transition into the fourth dimension."

"But that thing in the sky is a humanoid/dragon. Not a giant kraken."

"My guess is... the demon adopted the look and feel of our native species here."

As I process Talos's words, I'm all too aware that I'm basically tied down with snot-coated eels. Disgusting. However, this is reasonably pleasant compared to that stupid thorn bush that tried to eat me before. Slime I can deal with more easily than punctures. Nothing a bath won't fix.

Growling, I brace my hands on the ground and push. The tentacles slip down my body, slithering around in an effort to regain their hold on me. Oh, hell no. Never in my life did I sign up to be food for a monster with tentacles. Absolutely freakin' not.

Panic gives me strength, but the stupid squirmy things are fast. I manage to roll over onto my side and end up essentially lashed to Talos' leg, the tentacles crushing me into him with enough force to probably kill—or at least seriously injure—a normal human.

This position gives me a nice clear view of something I really didn't want to see. And no, I'm not talking about a remake of *Howard the Duck*. The demon is flapping away into the distance, only it doesn't look like a person made out of dripping, oily slime anymore. It's taken on the solid form of a 747-sized dragon with massive, tattered wings. It's pretty skinny though, more bony than anything. Kind of like a giant dragon's skeleton brought to life, still with scraps of flesh stuck to it here and there. A long neck of exposed vertebra, also shiny and black, ends with a human-like skull bedecked in a ring of vertical horns like a crown. The monster's forelegs resemble human arms, the rear legs those of a giant dragon. Three tails tipped in barbed onyx flap behind it.

Talos impresses a thought on me. He thinks the demon is the same one that was inside Mindy Hogan. Only… it's gotten way bigger and way more, uhh, dragony. Maybe since everything about this world is up to its eyeballs in dragons, the very nature of this realm affected the demon, changing it as it absorbed power to make itself stronger.

"Good to know," I grunt. "Except it doesn't mean diddly squat unless we can get the hell out of here."

"Fair point, Sam."

That son of a bitch wanted to zombie-apocalypse my world to death... so I'm gonna assume it's planning to do the same thing here. It must have sniffed out the trail I left behind when my soul got sucked back across dimensions to my body here, and kept digging at it like an overly curious dog smelling a buried treat. Don't know if it being here is technically my fault. But damn... I just might be responsible for the imminent annihilation of every living thing in this world.

Okay, this just got awkward.

"As much my fault, I'm afraid," said Talos. "My meddling in the third dimension established a connection, a weakness the demon undoubtedly exploited."

"Don't be so hard on yourself. You ain't the only one messing with dimensions," I say, thinking of Dracula and his own dragon. Then again, the dark prince's alter-ego could easily come from another third-dimension dragon-like world.

"Likely a third-dimensional creature. I am unaware of any others in my world contacting the third dimension with any type of regularity."

"That you know of. And enough chit-chat. We have to get out of here and stop that damn thing."

I thrash, grunting, doing what I can to wriggle out of the rubbery things holding me in place. One tentacle around my neck proceeds to squeeze the life out of me... except I don't need air, so the joke is on it. Ha! Others close around me like ropes. Slime dribbles from the tentacles, running down my shoulders, side and legs. Ick.

The bleak reality of our situation finally sinks in—I'm stuck here. Heavy, pervasive hopelessness devours my thoughts. Talos doesn't seem to be in much of a mood to struggle against the tentacles either. Eventually, I become aware of the distant sizzle of lightning along the canyon ridge and the resultant thunder. The sound is distant and oddly forlorn. I'm losing hope.

"Talos?"

He emits a belabored sigh. "Yes, Sam?"

"I think we're screwed."

Chapter Twenty-Two
Blood and Dragon Fire

There's no point in doing anything other than laying here and waiting to disintegrate. I suppose Talos could keep protecting me with his magic... but, yeah, what's the point? Death is inevitable... even for an immortal.

I sigh. Not even Tammy or Anthony cuddling up to me would make me feel better.

I'm sure that's wrong—cuddling with my kids damn well makes everything right. Except I don't care enough to debate it. Not anymore. Maybe never again.

A sad smile comes with me thinking of them.

They're back on Earth, safe. Sadly, I'll never see them again.

Oh well.

They'll be okay without me. Hell, maybe they'll be better off.

I bow my head, staring past the bulbous crisscross of black rubbery strands over my body.

Wait. Hold on. Did I really just think 'oh well' about the idea of never seeing my kids again? Son of a bitch. These tentacles are *making* me feel hopeless. Considering Talos is merely lying there like a sad, giant, dragon-shaped throw pillow, they're probably having the same effect on him.

"Talos."

"I am here."

"No kidding. We're a little tied up right now."

"I detect dark humor."

"Since when have you become Mr. Literal?"

"Does it matter?"

"Yes, dammit, it matters! The defeated apathy is coming from the tentacles. It's not real."

Talos shifts. His attempt to tug at them crushes me into the slimy bands holding me tight to his foot. For an instant, it feels like I'm about to experience what it's like for a potato to go through a French fry cutter, but he stops pushing before I split open.

"Gimme a minute," I rasp. "Let me teleport out of here before you squish me."

"I wouldn't do that," says Talos.

"Umm. Why not?"

He again tries briefly to break loose, leaning the other way. "This region is awash in unpredictable planar energies. If you attempt to teleport anywhere here, it may work… or you may wind up randomly dropping into any one of an infinite number of destinations."

"That's a pretty good reason not to risk it." I sigh. Of course, teleporting others isn't too difficult, but it does take some degree of concentration that I can't quite find here in this moment. Then again, I'd never tried to teleport something as big as Talos, either. That said, it remained an option. In fact, we could always return to that pretty rainbow lake. No need to stick around here.

Again, a strong sense of 'we're totally screwed and what's the point?' starts to infiltrate my brain. Before it gets its hooks too deep, I force myself to think about Danny hanging up the phone on me, denying my fifteen minutes of talk time with the kids. Even so many years ago, that moment sets off a rage inside me that burns away the external influence. As it does, a certainty hits me.

"Since it's Mindy's demon," I say, my voice mostly a growl, "it's going to destroy everything here instead."

"Doubtful, Sam. Let's not worry about it. Let's just... sleep."

"No, dammit. It wanted to create an apocalypse on earth, and we stopped it. Who's to say it won't try to do the same in this world? We can't just sit here, Talos. We have to stop it. Damn these tentacles."

"It would be unwise for us to do so, at least not without quite a bit of help."

"Whoa. Why? We kicked his ass once... well, sorta."

"It will be more powerful here. *Much* more."

I look down at the writhing ooze-covered tentacles holding us. The worst part about this, other than being immobilized, is the slime. It makes them slippery and requires they keep moving to recover their hold and reminding me that they're alive somehow. This is *beyond* nasty. However, if they're demonic in nature, they have one big weakness. Taking advantage of the slipperiness, I start working just my right arm out from under them. "Why would it be more powerful here?"

"The higher up in dimensions a demon goes, the stronger they become. It's an exponential curve."

"Wait. This thing has become a fourth-dimensional demon?"

"It appears so."

Grunting, I force my arm across to my left hip, sliding it under the tentacles wrapped around my mid-section... and into the interdimensional sheath I keep the Devil Killer in. Although I don't have room to maneuver it out, the sword materializes as soon as I grab hold of it. We'll call that angel magic. Touching it to a tentacle around my leg burns the black flesh off, sorta like 'encouraging' a tick to let go with a lit match. Strand by strand, I burn or slice the things away until I drop free.

Another tentacle lets go of Talos to grab for me.

I hold my ground and slash the thing out of midair. The severed length of rubbery horror flops around for a few seconds before going still and melting into a puddle of ichor. No longer wrapped up in tendrils of pure apathy, my mood explodes into vengeful anger that almost launches me into the air after the giant dragon-demon thing.

But, no. Must contain rage.

It takes me about five minutes to completely cut Talos free… and another five or so swinging at flailing black serpents until nothing is moving anymore.

"We have to stop it, Talos" I say, wiping my face and arms clean of the muck.

"Sam, this is beyond us. Whatever I have unleashed on this realm is my burden."

"You can't take all the credit, big guy. We're sort of in this together. Besides, I have the Devil Killer, remember? You saw what it did to that weird, tentacle-thing it left behind."

He shakes his massive head. "I cannot allow you to stay. We are so close to sending you home. It would be so easy for me to—"

"No, I'm staying and helping. And I still need to honor Poendraz's request… that is, if there's still anyone left to meet that avatar of hers when we're done with the demon."

He sighs. "Very well."

"Let's find that damn thing, Talos."

I leap up onto his back with a little help from my wings.

Talos launches us skyward, climbing fast.

A few minutes into flying, I say, "What about the Cibalor? They gave me the crystal for you without hesitation. Maybe Aoshandre can help us?"

"Doubtful. Remember, if they had the ability to

open a portal to your world, they would surely have invaded it by now and tried to dominate the lesser beings there. That is their way."

"No, not with me going home. I mean helping us fight that demon. The Cibalor didn't talk down to me or mistreat me when I visited them. Talos, what if your people have the Cibalor all wrong? Sure it might be due to something that happened thousands of years ago, but is it still true? The Cibalor supposedly want to wipe the Lumarae out. But if that's true, why would they give me a crystal to save you?"

"A fair point."

"Look. Nothing matters at the moment except for dealing with that demon. If we're lucky, it might still be weak. But the longer we wait, the worse this is going to be. Any idea where it went?"

"Based on its current course... it's heading toward the Floating City."

"And you know this how?"

"I'm following its trail of sulfurous stink."

'Of course you are. Let's haul ass for the city."

Talos flaps harder and faster, increasing our speed.

Yes, the more I think about it, the more certain I am that creature is a threat to this whole damn world, Lumina, Cibalor and Drajjan alike. I think of the sweet and plucky Zanjaya who risked herself to help Talos. Damn, I hope she didn't get in trouble for defying her elders.

Worries about what the Seven Wisdoms will

think or decide regarding Talos having a link to me don't seem like such a big deal in comparison. Whether or not we can make any difference in the situation here remains to be seen, but I'd never forgive myself for not at least attempting something. After all, Azrael charged me with helping him destroy demons.

And this is one helluva demon.

Talos flies us toward the Lumarae city, not saying much. It's difficult to tell if he's worried, guilty, angry, or hesitant out of his desire to protect me. It's obvious he wants me to leave and go home, be safe, stay alive—or whatever I am.

But we've just unleashed a devourer of worlds into his home plane.

No damn way can I abandon him to that thing.

Chapter Twenty-Three
War of Attrition

Talos slams on the metaphorical brakes.

His rapid deceleration causes me to lurch forward and wrap my arms around his neck, narrowly avoiding having my nose bounce off a hard armor plate. I sit back, peering around his neck in a futile attempt to make eye contact with him.

"What's wr—?"

There's no need for me to finish asking.

The sky ahead of us teems with winged shadowy figures both small and large. There have to be thousands of dragons engaging in an aerial battle with each other as well as with smaller, winged humanoid figures. The majority appear to be either Lumarae or Cibalor—impossible to tell by looking at them as they're the same species. However, it's pretty clear by formation that two different groups of dragons have assembled for war.

As we get closer, I can see that the smaller creatures are dragon-like in shape but these appear skeletal, their wings more bat-shaped than anything. Like the enormous thing that came out of the portal, they're entirely black. My assumption is they're demons whose bodies have changed into a draconic image, perhaps due to the nature of this world. My other assumption is they're offshoots of that main demon. Like its hideous offspring or something. That said, other combatants resemble the demons I'm used to seeing, winged humanoids with pointy ears, fangs, and skin either crimson or black. They look tiny compared to the Lumarae or Cibalor, and appear to be harassing the dragons more than presenting a serious danger.

Every minute or so, a handful of black holes open up in the air, spitting out dozens of demons. Ugh. Mindy's demon is up to his old tricks, calling in help. I definitely liked the chest-mouths and goat kin demons more in my world, assuming what I'm seeing in front of me is what the fourth dimension does to them. Grr. One irritating thing about demons is their tendency to keep summoning more help.

Meanwhile, the two dragon armies have already engaged each other in a vast, chaotic sky-brawl spanning an area several miles across and hundreds of meters tall. The demon-dragons are attacking both armies and suffering attacks from both in return. Smaller demons also annoy dragons apparently at random with no regard for teams. Pure chaos. Near the approximate center of the fray, a dense mass of fighting dragons forms a sphere, almost as if they're defending something inside that space.

"What is going on, Talos?"

A low rumble resonates within Talos, something akin to the noise I might make after returning to my world and seeing a nuclear mushroom cloud devouring LA—a nuclear cloud I was responsible for.

"He's here because we failed to kill it, Sam."

"We did our best to stop it. Hell, a part of you *died* trying to stop it."

To my surprise, Talos snarls. Wow. Kind of badass. Good. Anger is better than surrender. He's pissed off that he sacrificed his—well his projection's—life for nothing. At least we got the bastard out of Mindy. But... crap! Are my kids okay? Allison? What sort of damage did the fiend do in Canelo before it found its way here?"

"So we finish it then," I say, reaching for the Devil Killer.

"It may already be too late. Look at them." He gestures with his leg since his wings are occupied by hovering. "My kind do not even fight back, merely raising shields or pushing the meat-eaters away. The Cibalor have made war for time beyond your ability to comprehend. We have focused our energies on intellectual pursuits, greater knowledge, empathy... yes, we have magic but only for defense. My people will tire, and then the Cibalor will strike them down one by one. When the last Lumarae falls, the Cibalor, exhausted from the battle, are likely to fall to the demons. Like you, the vile ones do not tire."

"Of course I get tired."

"Sam, you've been continuously awake for six days."

I blink. "What?"

"This realm does not have a sun as you have already realized. The equivalent of nearly six full earth days has elapsed since your arrival."

Wow. Apparently, I *don't* need to sleep as often as I thought after all. Learn something new every day, especially one long ass day here on Talos's world.

"Rest assured, big guy, we will figure something out. Now, pick yourself up. You're being a real downer."

He chuckles miserably. "This will be dangerous."

"Yeah, well, what else is new? And I'm the one with the Devil Killer. So maybe the demons should be the ones scared."

As light flashes in glints off scales of various color, a brilliant purple blast draws my attention to Vixana (that big purple dragon with a fondness for carrying me around like a little girl with a hamster) creating a huge energy shield to protect herself from two red dragons raking at her with their talons. She makes no move to attack, but also doesn't retreat. They must be defending the city from a Cibalor invasion. Wow, Talos is right. Time *does* flow differently here. It didn't seem like we'd been stuck in those tentacles that long, but... for this battle to be so large suggests a different truth.

A loud explosion near the center of the hornets' nest of combat accompanies a huge fireball. The flames dissipate in seconds, revealing that the dense sphere of dragons has dispersed somewhat. At the center, Aoshandre reels away from Baxxus—the apparent source of the blast, which I suspect was magical in nature. The old wise one's eyes glow with dark red light, his face awash in pure rage. He lunges in, trying to clamp his teeth around Aoshandre's sinuous neck, but the Cibalor warrior feigned his degree of injury from the fireball. He rolls away from the bite, grasping Baxxus about the throat with his talons and squeezing, trying to crush the life from his rival.

Baxxus rakes both legs at the other leader's belly, forcing him to let go and retreat lest he be disemboweled. The two elders circle around, eyeing each other.

The Devil Killer in my hand emits a pulse of energy as well as a faint tug toward the two dragons. Now, why the hell would the Devil Killer direct me to two dragons?

My alarm sense begins ringing a warning tone. It's mild but persistent. Not a 'you're going to die' as much as a 'be freakin' careful.'

Then it hits me. "Talos, the dragon elders are under the influence of the demon." I point. "We have to get to Baxxus and Aoshandre before they kill each other."

Talos nods, angles up toward the fighting above us. The big fella is quite nimble despite his considerable size here, but nowhere near as agile as the version of him that appears in my world during my transformation. He flies harder, picking up speed. An air battle that looked like an epic mural from a distance soon becomes pure chaos as we cease observing and enter the outer edges of warfare. Humanoid demons dive bomb us, coming after me with scythes, claws, or barbed tail-blades. Talos does his best to avoid as much as he can; however, he can't duck, bite, or ram all of them.

A demon lances at me from the right. I limbo under its passing scythe while swinging the Devil Killer one-handed. The speed of our flight adds power to my strike, allowing my blade to cut that demon in half through the chest. The next one, coming in from straight ahead, lines me up for a tackle—but never makes it past Talos' mouth. He snaps at it like a cobra, devouring its head and most of the torso in one bite.

Damn… if he'd been this big back on Earth, he'd have completely humiliated Mindy's demon in a fight. Maybe my world has the opposite effect on Talos that this one did on the demon, and makes him weaker? Sounds logical. Wait. Nothing about any of this is logical.

I duck the flailing mess of dead demon-flesh and look back up in time to block a wicked curved sword coming for my face. A resounding *clang* happens inches from my nose. The flying humanoid demon nearly crashes into me and ends up standing on Talos's shoulders while trying to overpower my block, pushing his sword down on me. Black-forged Hell steel squeals and sparks against the Devil Killer's angelic edge. Snarling, the demon keeps trying to overpower me and slice my head off. In seconds, magmatic cracks appear in the demon's blade. The creature barely has time to make an 'oh crap' face before my blade breaks through its disintegrating sword. All the tension of us pushing our weapons against each other releases in an instant, driving the Devil Killer forward and slicing open the fiend's gut. Gasping from the pain of boiling demon blood spraying on my chest, I ram my weapon upward into the demon's chin.

Talos dives hard, swerving under another dragon trying to claw the hell out of us. Yes, dragon, not a demon. I honestly have no idea how they can recognize each other—Cibalor or Lumarae—on sight. We pull up out of that dive, looping around in a tight circle, looking for Baxxus and Aoshandre. Even to my relatively untrained eyes, it's pretty clear the Lumarae dragons are losing this war. They are ill-equipped for battle, and many have already fallen from the sky, too exhausted to keep going. According to Talos, magical defenses take much more out of them than actually physically fighting would. Another reason the Cibalor could decimate them. Indeed, this is not so much a war as a one-sided beating producing a slow, painful loss of attrition. The Lumarae refuse to give up, but their rare counterattacks are feeble and easily deflected. No matter how well they defend themselves, punching bags never win battles.

"We gotta stop this, Talos!"

"I'm open to suggestions."

My gaze stalls on a large mass of darkness to the north, on the opposite side of the battle from where we entered. What I initially took for the peak of a mountain… moves. An immense, dragon-shaped creature perches catlike atop a small floating island, one of hundreds that exist in the air around the Lumarae city. Its tattered wings folded close to its body, the massive demon turns its enormous humanoid skull side to side, watching the goings on. Dark crimson light glows from within hollow sockets beneath its crown of tall horns. Fibrous tubes along a neck of exposed onyx vertebrae pulsate with infernal blood. The greater demon— the same son of a bitch that attacked Mindy— observes the bedlam he initiated like a kid who pulled the fire alarm at school and sits there laughing while people fall down the stairs.

Okay, he's not *too* big. 747s are bigger. Somewhat.

I raise the sword and point at him, but Talos spots Baxxus at that moment and heads for him. We weave in a corkscrew pattern, dodging dragons and demons alike, no interest in engaging any of them if we don't have to. Evidently, word got around among the small demons about the sword I'm carrying, since they've decided to leave us alone. Either that or we're only getting lucky since nothing tries to stick a blade up my nose in the forty seconds or so it takes us to make it to the heart of the battle.

Talos briefly hovers outside the ball of dragon bodies tearing at each other, a living barrier around the two leaders fighting. Many of the 'dragons' in the fray near the center appear to be demonic—as in they look kinda like the big demon watching from his little floating throne, only they're about half the size of Talos.

It seems some of the demons are trying to prevent other Cibalor or Lumarae from interfering to help either Baxxus or Aoshandre, forcing the two of them to fight each other alone.

Meanwhile, the two leaders fly in close figure-eights, making strafing passes at each other much the way I remember dueling the big demon back on Earth not so long ago. It's surprising to see the supposed pacifist ruler holding his own. Both he and Aoshandre are riddled with superficial claw wounds, missing multiple scales, and covered in scorch marks. Baxxus moves like a warrior long retired, rusty but remembering. Aoshandre's in his prime.

The only sense it makes for the demons to keep other dragons away from the leaders is that it amuses the greater demon to watch… or maybe he's using them as a conduit for controlling other dragons. My alarm sense, which has been ringing continuously since we reached the battle, spikes loud seconds before leathery fluttering approaches from behind.

I leap upward on my wings, whirling around and thrusting the Devil Killer at the entity I hear approaching. My feet touch Talos' neck at the same time my sword plunges into the eerily human head of a demon-dragon coming to bite me. The blade pierces the open nasal hole, filling the interior with fire, which spits out from the eye sockets an instant later. Glowing red flames consume the skull and race down the spine like a fuse into an explosive charge. The remainder of the demon bursts into a shower of black ashes and a few small bones that wash over me with the stink of charred meat and bad eggs.

Embers whorl around my legs. I face forward and drop again to sit on Talos' back.

"I guess this is what they mean by 'all hell breaking loose.'"

Talos hovers, studying the wall of demons and dragons between us and the two leaders. "I find it odd how humans sometimes find humor in situations like this."

"It's a coping mechanism," I say. "This situation is very much *not* good."

"What is your plan, little one?"

"Still working on it."

Two more demon dragons come at us, one from above, one from the right.

"Then I suggest you work faster," says Talos—right before he dives straight down.

Chapter Twenty-Four
A Place for Violence

The sudden, hard evasive maneuver throws me off Talos's back.

This is not necessarily a problem, since I can fly. However, being a human-sized, non-scaly, non-armored snack bite in the midst of several thousand pissed off dragons is not my idea of a good time. Most of the Cibalor could inhale me in one bite. Sitting on Talos' back had basically been like me wearing armor since his bulk acted as a shield.

My toga looks nice, but it's not going to stop dragon teeth. It doesn't even protect me from the wind.

While I fall pretty much straight down, one of the dragon-demons that attacked us from the side crashes into Talos, and like some strange version of Judo, he wraps himself around the creature and eviscerates it, biting the neck while shredding at the belly with both legs.

The second demon coming in from overhead completely misses him, doesn't notice me, and circles back around to go after Talos. Maybe there *is* an advantage to being tiny. Truth is, I kinda feel like a housecat surrounded by Civil War reenactors using live ammo.

Idea.

I stare at Aoshandre and Baxxus—and call the dancing flame.

A quick teleport straight forward about 150 meters puts me right next to them, inside the sphere of bloodshed surrounding them. The two elder dragons still go at each other in a continuous series of 'jousting' passes. I've done some dumb freakin' things in my life, but putting myself between a pair of tractor-trailers playing chicken hasn't been one of them—until now.

I zip up to eye level with them as they charge toward each other, and shout, "Wait!"

The elders abort their attack, managing to stop themselves only a few feet away from me on either side. Compared to the last time I saw them, nearly all the reason and clarity that had been in their expressions is gone. At the moment, their eyes radiate little more than the feral rage of two wild dogs having a fight in an alley. Hell, they're even growling at each other. Neither seems to recognize me as anything more than a strange object in their way.

I shout, "The demon—"

Aoshandre swats me aside with one of his wings.

As I tumble through the air, Baxxus lunges at him, biting the edge of that wing, teeth crunching into bone. I regain my balance and dash back in, landing atop his head and stomping on the flat space between his eyes. Not that my bare foot is going to inflict any serious damage here, but kicking as hard as I can is hopefully at least going to be comparable to slapping some sense into a crazy person.

"Hey!" I shout. "Baxxus! Aoshandre! Stop fighting!"

A demon-dragon, having taken notice of my attempted interference, dives out of the sphere toward me. With Baxxus still chewing on Aoshandre's wing and Aoshandre trying to return the favor, both elders kicking at each other, I stare upward at the approaching demon, watching it swoop in to grab me. Seconds before impact, I teleport about a hundred feet straight up.

The demon crashes into the two dragon leaders, knocking them away from each other, and ends up mostly wrapped around Baxxus, dragging him down to the left while Aoshandre recovers. With Baxxus preoccupied, I've got seconds for a one-on-one with Aoshandre here. Hate to say it, but the 'warlike' dragon strikes me as the more reasonable of the two.

I zip into Aoshandre's face and yell, "What are you doing?"

The next thing I know, I'm inside his mouth. By

some miracle, none of his teeth pierce me. And yeah, lying face-down on a slimy, hot tongue with nothing but an illusion between my skin and ick is *extremely* disgusting.

Well, that didn't work.

I grab a telephone-pole sized tooth, holding on when he tries to swallow me. Absolute panic can sometimes have the paradoxical effect of bringing calm. It doesn't even occur to me to ask what form of muck is squishing between my fingers—dragons evidently don't have dental floss—but I do manage enough focus to teleport again, reappearing a short distance outside and above him.

Perhaps believing he swallowed me, Aoshandre pounces on Baxxus, who's made short work of the demon-dragon that collided with him. Talos's grunts and roars come from a ways off to my left. I can't tell which one of the fast-moving winged blobs is him amid the chaos, but our mental connection gives me the sense he's focusing on attacking demons and doing everything he can to avoid getting into a duel with another dragon. Apparently, his time watching me use his body for occasionally violent purposes has allowed him to set aside his abhorrence of combat... at least against demonic problems.

Not far below, the two huge elders keep trying to tear each other's throats out.

And, crap. What the heck can I possibly do except hover here dripping with dragon drool?

Both Baxxus and Aoshandre are beyond

listening to reason. The demon has affected their minds somehow. My mental powers don't work on dragons. Ugh. How the heck am I going to 'exorcise' a demon out of a freakin' dragon?

The Devil Killer throbs.

I glance down at the blade and a wash of orange light runs up the edge—kinda like sun glare, but this place doesn't have a sun. That's a message. Thank you, Azrael… or maybe the sword's got a mind of its own. It surely hungers for demons.

Hmm. Perhaps my idea to 'slap some sense' into these two has merit, only it's going to take a much firmer slap than my heel between the eyes. Worth a shot, right? Another demon-dragon screech comes from behind me. I whirl around to face it the same instant its taloned hand closes around me. Miraculously, I manage to avoid being impaled by its giant claws, and even keep my arms free. Then it hits me: this critter is clearly trying to catch me alive—probably to bring me to the master demon.

Yeah, not happening, pal.

My hasty upswing slices the Devil Killer into the side of its neck, leaving a wound that gushes black blood and fire. Howling in agony, the demon-dragon throws me aside and tries to flee. After recovering myself upright from its toss, I chase after it, drawing as much speed as possible from my little wings, my blade in both hands. Two seconds before our paths cross, I pull up, gaining some altitude. It tries to swerve down and right, but the sharp dive gives me even more speed, and I deliver a slash that severs the long, serpentine neck at about the halfway point between head and body. The demon breaks apart into black dust.

Another idea.

I steer around in a turn, then race for the two leaders, who have again resumed making jousting passes at each other. Baxxus seems like the less dangerous one in terms of fighting ability, so I veer toward him on an intercept at the outside of his figure-eight pattern. With as much ninja-like sneakiness as is possible for me to muster, I streak like a missile into his left flank from behind. He's so focused on the approaching Aoshandre, he doesn't even react to me.

The tip of the Devil Killer bounces over a few scales before catching on a seam and going under one, sinking straight to the hilt. Oops. I did *not* intend to stick all forty-something inches of blade into him. At least the angle's shallow. He roars in pain, cringing into an abrupt leftward roll. Aoshandre mistimes his bite, having expected his foe to commit to an attack, and hits nothing.

Baxxus tumbles as if unconscious for a second or two before he flares his wings out and catches himself in a hover. His giant head appears upside down past his belly, staring at me much the same way a person might give the evil eye to a burr they stepped on while barefoot hiking. The flat-eyed 'highly unamused' stare tells me my attack didn't cause significant damage, even if I'm still hanging on the blade which remains up to the hilt in his hindquarters.

"Do you mind, human?" growls Baxxus.

"Baxxus!"

"Indeed. What has possessed you to impale me with that splinter?"

"Sorry. This might hurt." I yank it out—he doesn't flinch at all. "You should be asking what possessed you."

"Possessed me?"

Aoshandre, roaring, dives at us.

"Look out!" I yell, pointing.

Baxxus whips his head out from under himself to stare up at the diving Cibalor leader. His eyes widen for a split second, then he hurls himself to the side half a breath before impact. Aoshandre's jaws slam shut on air—but he crashes straight into me. I bounce off his face like a tennis ball thrown at a speeding car, probably breaking a rib or three in the process, and go spinning off to the side.

Aoshandre diverts, tempted by another demon-dragon coming after me. He pounces on it in a rather catlike way, falling into a wild, out-of-control tumble while savaging it. It suffers the wrath of his frustration at missing Baxxus yet again. While that shredding goes on, Baxxus wings over to me.

"Small one, what is happening?" asks Baxxus. "Why is there war? Oh, by Poendraz, what have they done!?"

"Hold that thought." I point at him. "Quick version. The demon that tried to destroy my world is now in your world. And because of some freaky fourth-dimensional thing, it's bigger and more powerful than ever. Talos and I tried to stop it, and failed miserably. Oh, and it's made your armies start fighting each other, and to spice it up, it sent some demon offspring to randomly attack anyone and everyone. Finally, Poendraz is real and she wants you and the Cibalor to talk to her. But that's kind of a moot point until we can stop this demon and its horde."

Baxxus blinks. "For what reason did you attack me?"

I hold up the sword. "Demons don't like this thing. I hoped drawing blood from you might break the fiend's control. Didn't mean to ram the whole thing in. Sorry. Mistimed the speed. This is my first dragon war. Anyway, it worked. You have your mind back. Gotta do it to Aoshandre now. But he kinda swallowed me last time. Can you distract him?"

Baxxus tilts his head. He opens his mouth to ask something, but instead thrusts his wings out to either side and conjures a big energy shield. Aoshandre, in a full dive, crashes into it with a tremendous *boom*. Holy crap, I didn't even see him climb again after shredding that demon.

Snarling, Aoshandre rears back and breathes a torrent of fire, but the shield holds. Some heat—too much for me to withstand—gets past it. I hastily fly around behind Baxxus to take cover. Being between these two is *not* smart.

"Aoshandre, you fool. What are you doing?"

bellows Baxxus. "Have you lost your mind?"

"Yes!" I yell in the Lumarae leader's ear. "He has!"

The Cibalor merely growls and keeps raking at the shield, which dissipates after only three passes from his talons. Baxxus pounces at him, an attack quite sudden and unexpected from a Lumarae. It successfully catches Aoshandre off guard, and he fails to avoid a kick to the face that knocks him spinning. Pretty obvious that Baxxus *could* have clawed the hell out of him but didn't, merely booting him away. Passive to the bitter end.

Aoshandre rolls out of the tumble and rushes back in with a furious barrage of biting and clawing. He and Baxxus go at it like a pair of twenty-ton alley cats with wings. My alarm sense starts going completely nuts. I look back over my shoulder at more than a dozen demon-dragons all pulling away from the defensive sphere around the leaders' battle, every last one of them looking at me.

Uh oh. Papa demon's a wee bit peeved at me for breaking Baxxus free from his control, I bet.

I've got maybe eight seconds. Aoshandre and Baxxus still tumble around in a ball of hate and claws. Screw it. I've got to make this work. At least with Baxxus keeping the warrior dragon occupied, I'm not going to get nommed on again. I beat my wings with a hard flap, throwing myself toward the brawling generals. Or kings. Or whatever the hell dragons call their leaders.

Even after pushing my supernatural reflexes to

their upper limit, the two dragons still appear to be spinning quite fast. Accidentally stabbing Baxxus again won't really do anything *too* bad, so I take the chance, diving in before the army of demonic faux-dragons can tear me to bits.

With a swerve worthy of Vin Diesel in one of those *Furious* movies, I slide under Baxxus' wing, dive over Aoshandre's raking talons, twist upside down, and stab the Devil Killer into the Cibalor's ruler's belly, up through thinner, smaller scales. About a third of the blade disappears into his flesh, releasing free in under a second from the speed with which I'm cruising past him.

The mass of demonic dragons swarm around the two leaders, chasing me with such desperation they start clawing and grabbing at each other, fighting to be first to eat me. Unlike Aoshandre, however, these human-headed dragon-shaped abominations don't have terribly large mouths. Being devoured by them would be kinda painful. One at a time, I can take them fairly easily, thanks to the Devil Killer, but there's a pack of about twenty closing in.

That's a big 'nope' from me.

My wings practically scream in protest at the speed I'm trying to eke out of them. If I ever see Poendraz again, remind me to kiss her talon or something for whatever she did to let me fly faster. The writhing mass of false dragons chases me around in circles. Having no better ideas, I race for the dense mass of scaly bodies forming the 'sphere' around the leaders' duel.

Being a—comparatively—minuscule winged human gives me the illusion of chance that I can slip unnoticed past a bunch of dragons. Two of them, however, whip their heads around and stare at me mere seconds before I'd have flown through a gap between them. Gotta be the light trails my wings are leaving now. Yeah, they're drawing a nice glowing line in the air telling everyone where I'm going.

Much to my surprise, neither dragon bites me, merely watches me go by.

As I do so, the crowd of demonic dragons crashes into the Cibalor and Lumarae hanging there, in an explosion of violence and twisted limbs worthy of New York City rush hour. Wait no, this is more brutal. Maybe Walmart on Black Friday? And… holy crap! The dragons aren't fighting each other anymore! No, they seemed to have teamed up against the demons. Smart move.

I swing around and look past the mass of dragons at the two leaders. They're hanging in midair while staring at each other like Old West gunslingers who have gotten old to the point where they're not quite sure if they should draw their pistols or just drink together and complain about young people.

Perfect.

I teleport again, appearing beside them at head level. Strangely enough, all this teleporting isn't making me feel tired. Must be subconsciously feeding from all the dragons. Yeah, that's like a single flea taking a drink from a cow. They don't even notice.

"—has happened. The tiny one says she can explain," says Baxxus.

Both dragons turn at my sudden presence.

"Small one." Aoshandre swings his head toward me. "Explain."

Since the dragons—at least the ones nearby—have apparently stopped fighting each other, my assumption is they have some manner of telepathic mass communication. Or, the demon's influence over the other dragons had spread from the leaders into their Lumarae and Cibalor brethren. And once I stopped the possession, the mass control stopped too.

Wow, that is one powerful demon. No wonder why we couldn't kill it on Earth.

And poor Mindy, what a nightmare it must have been having *that* possess you. Hell, I'd take Elizabeth any day of the week!

Speaking of… the big demon in the distance doesn't look at all happy with me. It's already stretching its wings out in preparation for takeoff.

I give them as quick an explanation of the demon, the portal, it slipping through, and influencing their minds as is possible to cram into about twenty seconds. "It drove both of you, and all the rest of the dragons who follow you, mad, making you fight each other."

"Why?" Baxxus rubs at a claw gash on his side. "Violence is always purposeless."

"Not so, old friend." Aoshandre bows his head apologetically. "It has its place, but such a place is not here."

"What drives this creature?" asks Baxxus. "Why is it causing such atrocity?"

The distant demon leaps from its perch on the small, hovering island.

"Why?" I ask. "Well, it's a demon, for one. It's doing it because it can. They adore chaos. I'm afraid I have to agree with Aoshandre here. There *is* a place for violence, and this *is* it. No, not between the Lumarae and the Cibalor, but between all of us and the demons."

Aoshandre nods once in my direction. "Agreed."

"Umm." Baxxus cringes, seeming as though he wants to run off and convene the Seven Wisdoms to have a deliberation about a temporary suspension of the rule against violence. Fortunately, even he seems to appreciate we have no time for belabored decision making. "Yes. You are right. We have not raised tooth or claw in anger, or even in hunger in many years. I am afraid we are unskilled in the art of war."

I point the sword at him. "Then have your people magically protect the Cibalor while they engage the demons. Attack if absolutely necessary. The survival of your world as you've come to know it depends on every last one of those demons being destroyed."

"So many thousands of years it took us in our

advancement, yet we are reduced to mere savages in moments," says Baxxus with a sigh. "Regrettable, but also unavoidable."

"Speaking of unavoidable…" I gesture at the approaching greater demon.

Wow, he's really got some compensation issues. Damn thing's the size of a passenger jetliner. This magic toga of mine is nice and all, but I could really go for a Kevlar vest right about now. Preferably one infused with holy water or some potion Max whips up to ward off demons. This freakin' creature is so damn big, I should have no trouble outmaneuvering him. Problem being, his hands are the size of a Ford Crown Victoria. If one of them *does* connect, it's going to likely break every bone in my body.

As the giant demon's mouth opens, I see a dark crimson glow welling up deep in his throat.

Oh, crap. He's gonna breathe hellfire.

Chapter Twenty-Five
Natural Law

A fireball the size of a house comes flying at us amid a deep roar.

I zip straight up. Aoshandre goes one way, Baxxus the other. The inferno catches a few dragons too slow to avoid it as well as a handful of demons, ashing them all. Relative stillness among the dragons in the 'sphere' erupts into a chaotic mess of roaring and the rushing whoosh from hundreds of much smaller flaming breaths. All the living dragons nearby focus their attacks on the demonic parodies mimicking their shape. The scene around me is absolute chaos, a locust swarm… with locusts the size of trucks.

Talos, slightly scorched and bearing a few claw wounds, emerges from the fray and races over to me. Grateful to have some protection, I waste no time hopping on his back again.

"You're hurt," I say, patting his neck.

"Mere scratches. When Aoshandre swallowed you, I almost lost my shit."

I duck a fast-moving demon running away from a big violet... oh, that's Vixana. "He didn't swallow me. Just trapped me in his mouth for the few seconds it took me to remember I can teleport."

He continues hovering at the upper reaches of the battle. "I thought I lost you again, Sam."

"But you didn't. It's okay. I'm okay. Now, can we go kick some demon ass?"

He shakes his head. "You are serving a more important role."

"Um. We're just sitting here."

"Concentrate on Aoshandre and Baxxus," says Talos. "It is your will shielding them from the demon."

"My will?"

"I am certain you are what is protecting them. Keep doing it."

I doubted it was me, per se. Maybe the will of Azrael, or even this crazy sword. In the end, I shrug and do what is asked... focusing my thoughts on shielding the two dragon leaders. It's much easier when they are near each other. As they separate, my intent and focus diffuses. Still, something seems to be working. Maybe Talos is right?

So... we kinda hang there like generals overseeing the battle.

The fighting is brutal and quick. Even the Lumarae rip the demonic fake dragons apart with ease. The sight is awesome to behold but not too surprising. If I can kill one of those fake helldragons with a single sweep of the blade, they *should* be a triviality to dragons.

Though, admittedly, this sword gives me a bit of an advantage against the fiends.

The greater demon we exiled from Mindy tried this trick back on Earth, too—summoning a ton of help. However, unlike me, my kids, and Allison, the combined might of the Lumarae and Cibalor slaughters them faster than the big guy can pull reinforcements in through dimensional gateways… and we don't have Millicent running around closing those portals for us here like she did back in Arizona

In maybe fifteen minutes, most of the demons have been destroyed. Wow, that was impressive.

Next, all 1,500 or so remaining dragons converge on the big demon. Despite them being so much smaller, the sheer number of them—including the handful that keep breaking away to deal with the nonstop arrivals of lesser demons from the constant stream of tiny black holes that keep appearing and closing—appear to be worrying the big bastard.

It roars and swats at them, killing one every so often when they make an error and mistime a maneuver. I do *not* like seeing that thing able to slay a dragon as big as Talos in one hit. That doesn't bode well for me at all.

"My kin are not immortal," says Talos, a note of heartbreak in his voice.

LOST MOON

Watching dragons, even Cibalor, die has to be torment for him.

Frustrated at being overrun, the greater demon emits a roar. It grows even larger, changing shape. The human-like skull elongates into a head more like that of a dragon's. Bony exposed vertebra erupt with black veins and fleshy strands, growing out into a solid neck covered in glossy black scales. Its tail grows as well, the three spears at the end merging together to form one bony, spiked mass, reminiscent of a medieval mace. Getting caught with that tail would be like someone hitting me over the head with a small house.

Now it's about the size of a 747. Maybe bigger. Cripes. This just keeps getting better and better.

More Cibalor descend on him, going for his belly and ripping at the membranes of the wings. The greater demon roars again, a cry of incredible frustration more than pain. Another wave of lesser demons appears from a scattering of temporary red, swirling portals.

"Go. Get me closer. He's too distracted to control the dragons now. That's probably why he was perched on that island, watching. The bastard can't concentrate with claws all over him. Go. Please. Before more die."

Talos hesitates only briefly, then pitches forward into a dive. From above, it looks like we're chasing a giant bomber besieged by teeny fighter planes. Except, this bomber has arms and is screeching ... grabbing dragons off itself wherever it can reach and hurling them away. The Lumarae hang back somewhat, projecting energy shields around the Cibalor while they attempt strafing runs at the colossal demon. Those magical barriers make the difference between a wrathful smash from the demon's claws causing a dragon to go splat in midair, or simply careening to the ground with broken wings and too many crushed bones inside to keep fighting.

Still, severely injured probably beats dead, right?

A few Lumarae, Baxxus among them, do something magical that changes their fire breath from orangey-red to white. Though the blasts don't appear to cause visible damage to the demon-dragon, each hit draws forth roars of increasing anger.

The nagging worry that Talos is going to pull another sacrifice dive like the one in Canelo hits me as soon as I realize we're coming in at what's possibly a blind angle to the big bastard. Instinct, even for an evolved being like my friend, is a difficult burden to cast aside. If he can end this thing to save others, even at the cost of his own life, he will. He's going for its neck again, but in the demon's present form, pumped up beyond ridiculous from the exponential increase in energy that comes with hopping up a dimension, its neck is way too big for Talos to bite off.

No. I'm not going to let him sacrifice himself again.

I can't stop Talos from attacking, but I can hopefully distract the demon away from retaliating.

Plummeting almost straight down on top of an enormous dragon-shaped monster covered in hundreds of angry dragons would give me nightmares if I could dream.

But jump is exactly what I do.

Three seconds before Talos will crash into the demon's neck, I leap away from him, wings stretched wide, Devil Killer high over my head in both hands, swooping down onto the demon's head as silent as death herself, and drive my sword down as hard as I can.

Clang!

The tip bounces off the black chitin between the demon's glowing red eyes—which promptly focus upward at me.

Next, Talos slams into its neck, biting and hanging on. The demon either doesn't notice him or doesn't care, still staring at me. Oh, he sees the sword and knows exactly what it is.

I drive it down, again and again, looking for a weakness between the scales and plates, but finding none. Meanwhile, the tip is leaving little more than scratches.

As I raise the blade again—no doubt futilely— the demon whips its head to the side, throwing me into the air. I'm still tumbling head over ass when it swerves after me, mouth open. Something smacks into me from below, punting me up out of the way. Nothing visible hit me, so it had to be a magical assist from a Lumarae.

Part of my plan worked. The demon *is* ignoring Talos. Unfortunately, he's also ignoring the other dragons, too. Meaning, he wants *me*. Or more accurately, he probably wants the Devil Killer out of this fight. Which means he wants me out of the fight. Gonna go out on a limb here and assume he's become power drunk with what this dimension did to him, and my sword is the only thing he probably has left to fear.

Except I can't punch it through those damned scales. Hmm. Maybe I can get under him like I did with Baxxus?

The demon rolls side to side, throwing fifty or sixty dragons off like fleas, as it turns and orientates on me again. I hold my ground, sword up as if I'm going to 'parry' its giant mouth or something stupid like that. I wait. I have to time this just right.

When he's fifteen feet away, mouth wide open, I dive, trying to get under his chin. My left shoulder bumps into a horned spur sticking out from his jawline, breaking my bone with a loud *crack*. Gritting my teeth in pain, I bounce along the side of his neck and slam into the leading edge of his wing where it meets his side. Ouch. Pretty sure my spine would've shattered from that hit if not for my being an immortal.

He's flying so fast, speed pins me against the wing, but that's fine. Close to him is where I want to be.

The scales to my right are as big as card tables.

And yeah, they're like two inches thick. I poke the Devil Killer at the seam of the nearest one, trying to wedge it up and under the scale like a crowbar.

Surprisingly, it slips in fairly easily, causing the demon to emit a roar of anguish.

Alas, all it does is roar.

Damn. I'm being an idiot. Devil Killer or not, I still have to hit the heart. This sword would need to be like ten times bigger. As it is, only a few inches of blade are in flesh. I'm going to have to somehow burrow through its eye or something.

My alarm sense screams louder than ever.

Eek!

I notice the huge hand coming for me with maybe three seconds to spare. Reacting purely by instinct, I leap to the side, power-flapping my wings. Swear its hand brushes my toes before a resounding *slap* shakes the air below me.

Great. It tried to swat me like a damn mosquito.

Evidently having lost sight of me, the demon spends a few seconds grabbing at dragons and throwing them off. Maybe I should teleport to the Vale of Torment and beg Poendraz to come out here in person and slap this thing around. She's only a little bit bigger than this demon. The two of them going at it would be a fair fight in terms of size. Tempting… but before I can convince myself she'd do anything but ignore my request, the demon's head comes at me like a cobra strike, mouth open.

With only a second to think, I do the absolute dumbest thing that comes to mind on the spur of the moment—and dive straight down its throat on purpose.

LOST MOON

Chapter Twenty-Six
Under the Skin

My sudden, unexpected, acceleration *at* the demon gets me in past its teeth before its jaw crashes closed.

This thing's mouth is so damn big, I'm hovering inside it without even touching the tongue. Gotta stab it in the damn heart—and I have to do it before the next time this thing breathes fire. Against every instinct imaginable, my alarm sense screaming in my ears, I fly deeper into the subway-tunnel sized throat. When the passage narrows, I land, running on scalding hot slimy flesh. For no reason other than how pissed off I am, I slash willy nilly at the insides of its throat on the way down, slicing long gashes in the tender crimson flesh.

This damn thing breathes fireballs large enough to incinerate a dozen dragons at once. I must force my way to where I need to be before this freakin' demon gets the bright idea to burp up another mini-nuke.

As I run and slide and slash, the walls of its throat contract, squeezing me down its gullet. After a few seconds of disorienting—and disgusting—sliding, I fall through an opening and land waist deep in syrupy brown liquid.

Great. A stomach the size of an Olympic swimming pool. And this isn't water.

There's no point trying to fight the urge to scream in pain. The acid raises blisters all over my body in seconds. I jump up out of the deadly pool, stabbing and slashing at the crenelated flesh above my head. My overly sensitive ears hone in on the deep thudding of a heart bigger than I am. The pulsing guides me as I burrow deeper and deeper into its flesh. Blood gushes all over me, a rain of boiling hot suffering, many times more painful than it should be on my acid-tenderized skin. So much pain engulfs me that my capacity for rational thought starts to diminish. The primal, cavewoman 'get the hell out of here' urge drives me onward into the flesh-tunnel I'm carving, barely able to care about direction.

Now I know how a dumpling dropped into a kettle of boiling soup feels.

And I can't even scream. If I open my mouth, demon blood will go down my throat and burn me from the inside out. Can't even tell if any of my skin remains. That white stuff on my hand might be my bones showing through, or ooze from the demon. I don't know, and I don't want to know.

The only good thing at the moment is that my broken left shoulder no longer even registers as painful.

Slurping fills my ears; I can't see a damn thing. My sense of touch is gone. Somewhere the thrub-dub-dub of a massive heart looms closer... I think. My body is wedged headfirst in a passage of organ meat. The heart must be close; the beating vibrates in the tissues surrounding me. Screaming agony lights up all my muscles. They're starting to fail, to not respond. My body is about to quit. Can't stop fighting. Surrender means I slip back into its stomach acid, and that's a one-way ticket to the Creator for me.

Despite the horror waiting outside my clenched lips, it's impossible not to scream. Everything turns white. Pain has become euphoric. Still, I keep pushing the Devil Killer forward, slicing, stabbing, thrusting anywhere I can. Heartbeat vibrations become stronger. Soon, it's the only sensory input I'm aware of.

Must... push... deeper...

I slash, knowing the heart is nearby.

Slashing, pushing forward, weeping.

Where is it? Where is it?

The pounding fills my head. The flesh around me moves in time with it.

My next thrust hits something particularly dense. Blindly, I reverse grip on the handle and, screaming, drive it into whatever is before me...

praying like hell it's the heart.

And just like that, the beating stops

***

In an instant, the slimy gore around me bursts into a rain of black goo and ash particles.

A powerful 'electrical' spirit jolt rockets through me. I know it to be the vast amounts of energy released when a demon suffers a true death. But after going for a swim in acid, I don't even notice it beyond a faint coppery taste in my mouth.

I'm distantly aware of a tremendous, agonized scream… somewhere.

Outside air feels like I've gone skinny dipping in the Arctic Ocean.

It takes a second or two for my brain to resume processing things. I blink, but nothing happens. Guess my eyelids melted off. My skin's bright red. At least the blisters are gone. Oh, wait. That's exposed muscle, not skin.

But hey, the toga is pristine.

I whimper in my head at how much this hurts. Also, thank Azrael my wings are made of magic and not flesh. Otherwise, my butt would be in free fall. Didn't even lose a single feather.

Hundreds of dragons hover around me, all dripping with viscous black goo. Some wipe at their eyes, most simply shudder.

Something gooey and warm drips down my body and falls off my toes. Really hope that's demon slime and not parts of me still melting due to acid.

Vixana and Talos glide over at roughly the same time. She breathes at me, but rather than spit flames, it's water. Or at least something that feels a whole lot like water. The scalding pain all over stops in an instant to a nice, soothing coolness.

"That will stop the burning and help with the pain," says Vixana. "Talos tells me you heal yourself much more rapidly than most humans."

Don't try to talk, says Talos in my head. *I can see straight through to your vocal cords.*

I shudder, then nod at Vixana.

That was… brave, says Talos. *But so, so foolish.*

Worked, didn't it?

He smirks—as much as a mostly-inflexible dragon mouth can smirk.

Yes. I kinda regret doing that. Probably won't ever do anything like that again. Yeah, I definitely will never throw myself down the throat of an enormous demonic dragon ever again.

Good.

I also hope I never, ever, *see* an enormous demonic dragon ever again.

That is a good hope. 'Tis mine as well.

In a few minutes, I have skin again—and eyelids. Even my hair grows back rapidly to the length it had been before. It's good to be an immortal. The dragons are ever so generous in providing me nutrition, even if only Talos is aware they're feeding me. Most of the damage I suffered had been superficial, skin deep. Lost eyelids, a couple fingers, most of my toes, but nothing critical. The acid hadn't attacked any of my internal organs yet.

By the time my body has restored itself—except for the broken shoulder, that's going to take about twenty more minutes—all the dragons hover around me in a mass of flapping wings, doing what they can to rid themselves of the black goop.

"Talos?" I ask. "Why must every damn demon always die in an explosion of disgusting slime?"

He shrugs one shoulder. "Perhaps it is, what is the phrase your kind use? 'It is what it is, and it ain't nothin' else."

Overcome with genuine laughter and relief, I land seated on Talos' back and come damn close to passing out for a nap.

Chapter Twenty-Seven
A Not Small Undertaking

Cibalor and Lumarae dragons hovering around us linger in place, keeping vigilant in case any additional demons show up.

Other groups of dragons from both sides descend to ground level in search of wounded. Vixana goes with them as her magic is evidently of the healing variety. Bits of conversation drift over from the nearer dragons, mostly about the battle, though a few Cibalor both apologize for the violence and compliment the Lumarae on their courage for standing their proverbial ground despite having little ability at combat and no expectation of victory.

The general tone suggests both sides understand the war had come about as a result of demonic influence. It's remarkable to watch them forgive each other so freely and without hesitation. I doubt humans would get over something like this as fast. People, even if shown clear evidence of possession making them act against their will, would harbor resentment and anger.

For my part, I'm perfectly happy to sit here and do nothing but rest for a while. It's tempting to ask Tammy—if or when I get home—to try erasing my memory of being inside a demonic dragon. Unfortunately, doing that would mean she sees and feels what I did, so… nah. Coping it is. Then again, she's probably going to stumble across it anyway as she's quite free with eavesdropping on my head.

My hope is that she'll see the start of that memory and decide *not* to watch it.

Eventually, the dragons become secure in their belief that the demon is banished back to where it came from and no additional smaller ones will appear. I don't bother mentioning that demons destroyed by this sword are gone for keeps. Way too tired for *that* conversation now.

The flight to the Lumarae city doesn't take too long as the massive sky battle happened a few miles from it. According to Talos, only juveniles and the very old remained within the city. The approximately 1,400 Lumarae who had participated in the battle represented what humans would call 'all able-bodied individuals.' And every one of them had been prepared to fight to the death to protect the young. Not sure how many dragons died today, though the death toll is easily a couple hundred on both sides.

It's heartbreaking to see so many dragons all so somber and quiet.

There had been only one other time in our history where so many of our kind perished so quickly. You once knew the story. It happened long before either of us existed here, says Talos over our mind link. *I believe it even predates the presence of humans on your world.*

Both Talos and I struggle with our guilt at potentially being responsible for this. But it's not like Talos opened a pinhole to my world expecting a demon to exploit it. We tried to protect my world from a zombie apocalypse and weren't quite able to defeat such a strong demon. Losing a fight we threw everything into shouldn't be a cause of guilt. And dammit, for all I know, this entire thing happened because Poendraz wanted it to. She wanted me to get the Lumarae and Cibalor together to talk to her avatar. What if that avatar had been the transformed dragon-demon? Naturally, I'd assumed she'd make some monk-like creature of wisdom to sedately talk to each side and try to convince them.

But that's thinking like a human. A human with an overdeveloped sense of nice.

One doesn't shrug off millennia of prejudice purely from having a talk with the wise elder on the mountaintop. Maybe she needed to slap them back to reality? I mean, she's a creator after all. This is her world. Can anything happen here she doesn't want to happen—or set in motion?

So, yeah… it's plausible. And now I feel like a

little cog in a much bigger machine. We didn't kill all those dragons who perished—we saved the ones who are still alive.

As we cruise over the barren grey landscape, he tells me about a time when dragons did not dwell in cities or identify themselves as Lumarae or Cibalor. Hundreds of groups existed then, though they behaved more like roving prides of lions than an organized society. Aside from the occasional fight over territory and hunting grounds, the dragons didn't harm each other often.

Aoshandre must be eavesdropping on us, since his voice fills our minds. *You speak of a time long since passed. The days of scattered clans ended when a group of larger dragons, ones similar in appearance to Poendraz with four legs plus wings, began attacking them. Those ancient ones regarded our kind as inferiors, hunting us for food and sport. Our peoples' small clans came together to fight a great war that saw the deaths of many of my ancestors, and the extinction of the ancients.*

Talos radiates astonishment at the idea even bigger, four-legged dragons really had existed.

Maybe Poendraz regretted making the bigger dragons? Kind of ironic though. I let that thought trail off, and I think both Talos and Aoshandre catch my drift.

Ah, yes, says Aoshandre via telepathy. *You wonder how my kind could detest being treated as lessers yet do the same to the Drajjan down below?*

Something like that, yeah.

It was not mistreatment my kind objected to, merely that they were the ones suffering it. Aoshandre's mental voice has a hint of contrition in tone. No secret his kind attack the Drajjan. Hopefully, he reconsiders that in light of what just happened here.

I sigh. Maybe you guys aren't quite as evolved as you think?

The Lumarae do not harm them, thinks Talos. *We never have, as far as I am aware.*

That's all well and good, but don't you look down your noses at them?

I do not. My nose is not long enough for me to even see.

Heh.

Alas, I will admit a degree of condescension, yes. Talos emits a mental sigh. *My kind regard them as unfortunate for being so small.*

I bop my fist into his armor plate. Hey, now. I'm even smaller than they are.

Yes, but you are human. It is not the same. They are of dragon blood, and many of my kind feel they have been mistreated by fate, that they should be grander.

Right… like they have a choice in the matter?

Talos follows a group led by Baxxus and Aoshandre to an immense courtyard near the center of the city upon the floating island. Five of the Seven Wisdoms wait for us on the ground. The seventh and youngest of them is with our returning group. He appears distressed, his head bowed, tears as big as melons sliding down the angular sides of his cobalt blue face. Despite convincing myself that everything happened as Poendraz intended, it is difficult for me not to feel guilt over his pain. If we hadn't kicked that demon out of Mindy, none of the death that happened here would have occurred.

But there would have been as much or more death in your world. Our actions did not cause this evil, merely changed the where of it. Nalamoz weeps for two others who shielded him when he should have died.

What? I look over at Talos. What do you mean *should* have died?

He is the youngest of the Seven Wisdoms. Young enough that he could not in good conscience remain here in the city while others fought, despite his station. However, due to that station, two other dragons sacrificed themselves to protect his life.

Oh. I bow my head. If he stayed behind, they might not have died but he would have felt like a coward.

Yes.

"Tiny one?" calls Baxxus. "Are you here?"

Standing up on Talos' back, I gaze over the courtyard, searching for him. The area's packed with dragons, many of whom lay wounded, awaiting help from the few others who possess the type of magic capable of healing them. Baxxus is perched at the north end of the courtyard, near a wall. Light glimmers from his scales, making him resemble a statue made of black diamonds. Beside him sits Aoshandre, the slightly larger red Cibalor dragon.

As soon as Baxxus sees me, he beckons for me to approach.

I hop down from Talos and make my way through the crowd, mostly holding my breath to ward off the stink of blood and brimstone. If any of the Lumarae in the area have feelings one way or the other about Cibalor being in their city, none show it. Trade humans for dragons and musket wounds for slashes and it's eerie how similar this scene of mass triage is to what I remember of being stuck briefly in the past during the American Civil War.

Mercifully, no one is amputating limbs with saws here.

"Tiny one," says Baxxus, when I arrive, "please explain what has happened."

There's no accusation in his tone, even though this does kind of feel like I'm facing a judge. Still, I take a deep breath and relay the entire story going all the way back to Mindy Hogan. They don't need too many details about her, merely that a demon had possessed her. My assumption was that the dark masters—meaning Elizabeth and company—wanted to sow chaos and death in the form of a zombie apocalypse to weaken society, making it easier for them to reestablish a foothold of power on Earth. But, with a demon being inside her instead of a dark master… that raises more questions than I have answers for. My old investigator's hunch paints a scary picture: somehow, the demons are working with—or for—Elizabeth.

Aoshandre and Baxxus listen patiently to everything about the exorcism, trying to kill the demon on Earth, believing we'd done so at the cost of Talos sacrificing his projection—which would have killed him here without the help of Aoshandre.

"It astounds me you didn't simply help the one called Talos," says Aoshandre. "The life of a dragon is—"

"Yes, yes. I know." Baxxus bows his head. "It pained me to follow the traditions, but—"

"But nothing." Aoshandre puts his hand on Baxxus' wing. "Inflexible laws cause as much harm as they seek to prevent. Is any rule worth a dragon's life?"

Baxxus stares into nowhere for a moment, then sighs. "No, my friend. You are correct. It has been thus for many thousands—"

"It was not always thus, hence it does not need to remain so." Aoshandre smiles.

"The Wisdoms shall discuss the matter."

"Always discussion." Aoshandre rolls his great green eyes. "Do you seek the input of a committee when deciding how to scratch your chin?"

Baxxus emits this odd noise that's either a gurgle of irritation or a chuckle. "Perhaps when one gets too accustomed to flight, we forget how to walk."

"Indeed."

"Thank you, Tiny One." Baxxus nods at me.

"Rest, for now. You are welcome to stay here for a time. I realize you wish to return to your world soon, but there are matters we must discuss."

"Always with the discussion," says Aoshandre in a sighing voice.

No point protesting, so I offer a respectful bow and back away, turning to face the courtyard of injured dragons. While I no longer consume blood, my nose still picks it up quite well. Quite a few of these creatures look like they're not going to make it. The Lumarae are not used to dealing with severe injuries since they are usually pacifistic beyond reason. The Cibalor apparently lacked the temperament to pursue magic despite being dragons, and thus capable of using it.

Hmm.

I have an idea.

Chapter Twenty-Eight
Little Help

A teleport brings me to the courtyard square in Zoxa Duur, the Drajjan city, right in front of the temple where they almost killed Talos. This is kind of a long-shot thing, but it might just help everyone involved.

Considering I am the only human in this entire world, the Drajjan recognize me right away. Most merely comment that the naked one is back. This makes me blush like mad and reflexively look down to make sure my illusion is still there. Yep. I still look like an angel from an old Renaissance painting. Still, I'm embarrassed until I realize they have no concept of clothing whatsoever and are referring to my lack of scales. Evidently, their word for a creature with no scales gets translated to 'naked'.

Whew.

At the temple entrance, a pair of male Drajjan

glower at me.

"Have you not done enough here, creature?" asks the one on the left.

"Actually, I haven't. I need to speak with Zaoma."

The other one hisses at me. "You stole the offering to Zaa! The high chantress will not speak with you."

"This is regarding a matter of utmost importance to your people. Please, I need to speak to Zaoma."

After a brief—and—heated discussion, the one on the left waves for me to follow and goes inside. At least the Drajjan buildings aren't significantly larger than human construction. I don't feel *so* much like a tiny creature here.

We find Zaoma and Zanjaya in a square room, sitting in a circle with nine other women, six men, and one other child who is a little older than Zanjaya. At the center of their group stands a shiny black statue of a female Drajjan, most likely a depiction of their goddess, Zaa.

"Sam!" Zanjaya leaps to her feet and runs over, bowing at me. "It is good to see you. I didn't expect you would return."

"It's good to see you too." I give her a wink of thanks, then look at Zaoma. "Please forgive me for barging in here without notice, but it's really urgent. I realize your people and the winged ones are not on terribly good terms, but right now, there is a great opportunity to change that."

All the chanters shift around to look at me.

"It is true," whispers Zanjaya to Zaoma. "It has come to be. Zaa's words made real."

Zaoma's eyes widen with unusual eagerness and trepidation. She speaks in a cadence like she's reciting old scripture memorized ages ago. "Wings of torn shadows stretch to the horizon, covering all in darkness."

"The exalted shall lose themselves," adds Zanjaya.

A male bows his head reverently. "And the blood of dragons falls like rain upon the sands."

"The mind and claw unite as one," says a green-scaled female.

"Is this of what you speak?" Zaoma steps up to me. "Has this come to pass?"

At my confused look, Zanjaya smiles and says, "Zaa has told us of our salvation, many generations ago. We spoke the words she gave us as our hope."

"Have you seen this?" Zaoma takes my hand gently.

"Wings of torn shadows? That does kind of sound like what I saw. That enormous demon-dragon."

Zaoma squeezes my hand. "Please tell us what happened, Samantha."

"There isn't time, but here's the short version: Talos and I tried to destroy a demon back in my world. We didn't quite do it and it followed us here. In this world, it grew in power, brought forth thousands of smaller demons, and made the Lumarae and Cibalor fight each other. There was a big, messy war"—I wave my arms around as if to illustrate—"which ultimately included the giant demon himself."

All the chanters gasp. Even the guard who led me in here stops scowling.

"Needless to say, the dragons won in the end. But there are hundreds of injured winged ones at the floating city. Many will die since they do not have enough dragons who can help them. If I remember right, your order can heal? Zanjaya said the 'soul' injury Talos suffered was beyond her ability, but what about ordinary claw and bite wounds?"

Most of the Drajjan break into nervous laughter. Several think Zaa would condemn them for *helping* the creatures who have for so long hunted and killed them. Zaoma appears torn. Okay, maybe this isn't going to be as easy as I thought considering they wanted to kill Talos as a sacrifice. Dead and dying 'winged ones' are probably an occasion of joy for them.

"Do you want to continue being looked down on?" I say, my voice raised over the arguing. "This is a chance to change everything."

"Let them die," says Orounaz. "They have visited nothing upon us but death. They do not deserve any mercy, least of all from Zaa." One or two others agree, but they are not the majority.

Zanjaya steps forward. "I will help."

Zaoma puts a hand on the girl's shoulder. "From the mouths of babes, we know the truth. We cannot forget the words of Zaa. The mind and claw unite as one. We will help. Allow us a few minutes to gather ourselves. We will arrive as soon as we can. It is but a short journey for us."

I nod. "Thank you."

Now let's hope the Lumarae and Cibalor don't eat them when they appear.

***

I teleport back to the courtyard at the floating city.

Baxxus and Aoshandre are gone, though nothing else appears obviously different. Many wounded and dying dragons remain. Talos, still standing where I'd left him, shrouds me with his left wing.

"The Seven Wisdoms speak with Aoshandre now. I explained your plan to them while you were gone. They will accept any aid that prevents more death. The Drajjan will not be harmed."

Music to my ears.

With Seven Wisdoms convening and the Drajjan still hours away, I have some time to finally relax. Truth is, my shoulder could use some rest. "Say, is there some place I can sneak in a nap?"

***

I awake on a grassy nook just off to the side of the courtyard. Talos is sitting with me.

I also awake to far less wailing and groaning. Perhaps a third of the dragons have gone. Forty or so Drajjan move about the remaining injured, including Zaoma and the child Zanjaya, using their magic to tend to the injured along with Vixana and the six or so dragons capable of it.

"How long was I out?" I rasp.

"Only a few hours." Talos points to the left with his head. "Baxxus has asked that you see him as soon as you are able."

"I'm able." I stand. "Faster I talk to him, faster I go home."

We make our way out of the courtyard and down the street, a little over a mile or so to the council chambers—or whatever they call it. Baxxus and Aoshandre sit down below in front of the judicial bench, chatting away like old friends who haven't seen each other in years. At our arrival, they pause, watching expectantly as Talos and I approach.

"Talos tells us you were exhausted," says Baxxus, nodding to my friend. "We are surprised to see you awake so soon."

I offer a blasé shrug. "My sleep schedule is kinda unusual. What's up?"

"Aoshandre and I have come to an agreement. Neither the Lumarae nor the Cibalor have been perfectly correct. It saddens us beyond measure that it required so much death for us to realize how far astray we had both gone from Poendraz's vision. We do not expect it to be easy, but we are going to work on reintegrating our societies into one whole that is a blend of both ideologies."

"Whoa." I blink. "That's… awesome. Poendraz will be thrilled."

"We owe you and Talos a great debt." Aoshandre bows at me.

"Thank you, but I would feel too awkward accepting anything but your thanks. That demon would never have even been here if we hadn't done the job right the first time."

Both leaders nod once.

"We are referring more to you illustrating the folly of our refusal to see any way but our own as the correct one." Baxxus tilts his head side to side. "Though we would have preferred not having a demon slip into this world, there is a human phrase that Talos shared with us I believe is appropriate here."

Aoshandre chuckles. "We required a 'slap upside the head.'"

I can't help but laugh at hearing a dragon say that.

"Something less drastic may well have failed to force us to look inside ourselves," says Baxxus. "I have gained wisdom. There are indeed times to fight for what one believes in."

"And violence cannot solve everything." Aoshandre wags his eyebrows. "Merely most things."

Baxxus gives him side eye, then both of them laugh.

"If it's not overstepping my position in all this, can I make one small request? The Drajjan feel shunned and belittled by the Lumarae… and they're preyed on by the Cibalor. Would it be possible for you not to look down on them so much and maybe stop eating them? Perhaps even initiate trading relations? I mean, their healers are out there even now saving dragons lives."

Aoshandre raises one finger. "It has been quite some time since we actively pursued them as a source of sustenance. Though the teachings of Poendraz forbade consuming creatures of scale, during a time we faced a severe food shortage, it is true that we preyed upon the Drajjan. It seemed to us less an affront to feed upon them than to starve."

"But they are dragon-life too," says Baxxus. "If a lesser form."

"There you go again." I gesture at him. "They're small and wingless, yes, but no less intelligent than you. There is no reason to pity them for being different."

Baxxus sighs. "It will take us time to adjust, but I give you my word we shall try. One cannot change tens of thousands of years of opinion in days. However, all in this city have witnessed what they have done to help us."

They are understating things, says Talos in my mind. *Nothing is as valuable to us as our lives. That the Drajjan would risk the journey here to offer help to our dying is a gesture that will not be forgotten.*

"We are in the midst of determining the best way to send you home." Aoshandre leans in to sniff me. "My people have had little success with dimensional gateways. And while the Lumarae are capable, they make such little use of it, there are issues of accuracy. At least we do not need to worry about the demon escaping into a demi-plane this time."

"Can you repeat that in English?" I ask.

"We *did* kill the demon at the moment my projection was also slain." Talos rubs his side where the spear tail got him; a few scales there are still white. "However, as you know, demons killed by means other than your sword merely return to Hell. The Seven Wisdoms think that this demon refused to go back down easily, and managed to catch himself on an intermediary world between yours and Hell, still on the third dimension. Think of it like falling off a cliff, and getting hold of a small ledge part way down."

"And it somehow sensed the path my soul took when it got punted back here… and followed. So, how is that relevant to me going home?"

Talos sighs. "The place I once used to connect with you has become dimensionally weak. Re-establishing a bridge there would leave both of our worlds susceptible to unwanted excursions."

"So what do I do?" I clench my hands into fists, trying not to give off as much frustration as is boiling inside me. Worry over what's going through my kids' heads is almost enough to make me scream.

"For now, you wait," says Aoshandre kindly. "The Seven Wisdoms are already attempting to calculate a new bridge."

Damn. Well, at least they're trying. "Am I going to disintegrate?"

"No." Talos pats me on the... well, pats me on the *everything* since his clawed hand is so big. "As I do when you borrow my projected body, I shall keep you safe from the dissonant energies."

"All right. Guess we wait then." Not sure if I should simply walk away, so I stand there waiting.

"Oh, one more thing," says Baxxus. "The Seven Wisdoms and I have come to an agreement on another matter. While contact with the Third Dimension is still regarded as highly restricted, it is our decision that we will not interfere with Talos should he decide to reestablish his link with you across dimensional boundaries."

Talos is so stunned he just sits there, mouth agape.

"That's great!" I jump to hug Talos... or at least his leg.

Considering that several hundred dragons died today, I can't quite call this a perfect resolution. Yeah, they're a little on the arrogant side and think that *one* dead dragon is more tragic than all of Earth being wiped out... but still. It's what Poendraz wanted.

Poendraz the creator.

Well, not *the* creator, just *a* creator.

Hmm. How much of what happened had she written into her gargantuan book? It didn't seem completely right for me to think of a creator wielding such vile entities as that demon. But, then again, the World of Dur had all sorts of bad guys and monsters for the characters to deal with. Creators make more than nice things. So… maybe. Still, though, if she could've fixed the rift between Cibalor and Lumarae with a snap of her giant fingers—or few swipes of ink from her claw—wouldn't she have done that ages ago?

Ugh. I'm too exhausted and worried to think about that sort of thing. Wait. Creator. Van Gogh.

"Oh, crap."

All three dragons look at me with alarm.

"Crap? As in defecate?" says Baxxus. "Does the little one need privacy?"

"No, I—"

"No, my friend," says Aoshandre. "I believe she means something is wrong. Am I correct, Samantha?"

I shake my head, smirking. "In this case, it means I forgot something… and also that I got an idea." Here I go again with the 'getting an idea' thing. Hopefully, this one won't bite me in the ass.

The Cibalor ruler sits back, nods. "A useful, and rather far-ranging word."

Okay, now I chuckle. "I guess so. On a more serious note, maybe your people *don't* need to figure out how to open portals."

"Why wouldn't we?" asks Baxxus. "Do you not

wish to go home?"

"Very much so. More than anything else right now. But…" I look up at Talos. "When I hopped around dimensions before, Van Gogh painted me into them. Poendraz is a creator. *She* can definitely send me back."

Baxxus and Aoshandre exchange a look, almost touching snouts.

"I will take you." Talos regards me with sad eyes, though he is smiling. "Your place is with your family."

Chapter Twenty-Nine
Farewell

The Drajjan are still tending to the wounded when we fly over the city square.

Sensing what's on my mind, Talos circles back and lands near where Zanjaya and Zaoma are both examining an injured dragon. Even though she said her mother gave her to the temple, the two of them working together seem so damn much like mother and daughter that… oh, wow. Tricky little girl. She told me that she still sees her mother all the time. 'Giving her to the temple' might have only meant allowing her to join officially, not how I took it.

No wonder she doesn't mind. Her mother didn't abandon her at all.

That also explains how the kid helped get Talos out of there and didn't end up exiled or killed. Her mother is the head of the temple.

The two peer up at us—mostly at Talos who's

kinda large—as we approach. Zanjaya's tail quivers in excitement at seeing me.

"It's time for me to return to my world," I say. "It's quite possible that I will never be here again, so it seemed wrong to leave without telling you how grateful I am for your help."

"The Blind Chanters wrote of this ages ago," says Zaoma. "There is mention of a being from an upper realm, darkness, war… reunification."

Zanjaya raises her hands, tracing a rectangle in midair. A section of what looks like smooth brown stone appears as an illusion within. I think this is her version of showing me a picture on her cell phone. Drawn upon the rock—similar to cave paintings from long ago—is a crude representation of a human female form with long, dark hair, a white garment, and wings, surrounded by writing that sorta looks like Chinese characters, but isn't— it's Drajjan writing, obviously.

She says, "Sam, I was playing in the street when you arrived. From the instant I first saw you, I knew what the Blind Chanters foresaw was happening right in front of me."

"Except I'm not from the upper realms," I say.

"Which is what mother and the others said. However, the Blind Chanters only recorded what they *saw.* They did not *know.*" Zanjaya grins. "You *look* like a being from a higher realm, even if you're from a lower one. They painted what their inner eye revealed."

Smart kid.

Zaoma gazes upward. "The writings did not speak of the one you call Talos. I did not put much hope in that you were the being they saw. But, in case you were, it seemed that it would be best to aid the one who aids you. As such, my daughter was not punished. Indeed, she is now seen as a bit of a hero."

Zanjaya beams.

"I am grateful for your help," says Talos. "If ever you need help, summon me."

They both nod, bowing slightly. "And if ever you return to this place, it would be an honor to share body heat with you," says Zaoma. She turns to me. "You as well, Samantha Moon."

I blink.

That is the equivalent of a human inviting a friend over socially. Being in close quarters within their dwellings preserves the body heat of all, sends Talos over our mind link.

Ahh. I smile at her. "I would like that… however, I don't expect to be here again. The airfare is kind of expensive."

Both Zaoma and Zanjaya peer at me quizzically.

"I mean, it was a fluke for me to be here at all and it nearly killed Talos."

"Oh. Yes." Zaoma makes an odd hand gesture. "May Zaa safeguard you both."

"Thank you. And may she watch over you as well."

After exchanging this weird little handshaky-cheek-touchy gesture with both of them, I hop on

LOST MOON

Talos and we leap skyward.

***

Talos is quiet and reserved on the hours-long flight to the Vale of Torment.

Fortunately, he's radiating happiness. Mostly. Bunch of sad in there too. Even if I'm stuck in an 'aesthetically unpleasing' human wrapper, he deeply loves my soul and it pains him not to be physically in my presence. I'd argue that being inside my head is much closer than having me here in the flesh next to him, but my physical body being next to him is closer to what he remembers of my former incarnation as a dragon.

For him, this moment is bittersweet. He is happy the Seven Wisdoms won't bar him from linking with me. He's happy at the idea of me rejoining my family on Earth, too. However, my leaving this world saddens him a great deal. I suspect that without the ever present risk of me disintegrating for being here too long, he'd probably have tried to talk me into staying—or at least coming back here once my kids have grown old and passed into another cycle of reincarnation. Having to constantly watch me for total molecular separation is a bit too risky, even for him. He'd rather we be apart than take the chance a small oversight might destroy me.

Eventually, after flying over miles and miles of rippled grey silt and black rocks, the chaos of the dimensional bridge—Poendraz's home—comes into view ahead. Lightning arcs across the dome formed by the interaction of discordant planar energies, creating a field that resembles a massive soap bubble over the entire Vale of Torment. Sheets of brilliant green or blue plasma as big as city blocks appear out of thin air, stretching over the bubble as smears of vibrant glowing color. Each lasts only seconds before dissipating. It's astonishingly beautiful, but my need to get home keeps me from gawking at it for long.

"This is as far as I am able to go," says Talos.

"Why is that, really? Are you worried that the third-dimensionality might compromise the ideals of your evolved dragon self?"

He emits a somber laugh. "If one of our kind finds ourselves completely in the third dimension—as opposed to a mere projection—it affects us on a deep internal level. Before long, we devolve into creatures little more than animals. Our evolved souls require the energy and fourth-dimensional space to thrive."

"Wow... really?"

"Human legends of dragons as village-burning beasts are based on fact. A handful of us have slipped over in the past. And some of us really did raze whole towns, and feast on your kind. Fortunately, it is quite rare a thing as we now know what fate lies in store."

"But the Cibalor wanted to invade the third dimension. Wouldn't they have become savage beasts if they did that?"

"Yes. However, the reason they do not wield a great amount of magic is that they have spent several thousand years attempting to use magic to shield them from that effect. Whether or not it would have worked, I cannot say."

"Hope they're serious about not invading. I've got my hands full with demons and whatever Elizabeth is planning. I don't have space on my schedule to stop a dragon invasion, too."

He laughs. "You wouldn't need to. Human weaponry has come quite far since the last time a dragon crossed the boundary. The Cibalor still see your people as having only arrows and swords. Through your eyes, I have come to understand the world is not as they remember. An attempt to invade Earth would not end well for them. Our kind would be easy prey for fighter craft, missiles, tanks, even machine guns. Any warfare now would be rather short lived, especially as our magic would be much less powerful in that dimension."

I fake wipe sweat off my brow. "Whew. Maybe you can tell them that?"

"A reasonable request." He sighs. "Go, Sam. Return to your world. I will travel to the Canyon of Rifts and wait. When you are ready to re-establish our connection, find a quiet place to meditate and concentrate on calling me as you always have, via the single flame. It will take longer than usual for me to find you the first time… but I *will* find you."

"Of that, I have no doubt, big guy." I hop up onto my wings and fly around in front of him, resting my cheek against his. "I would tell you that you're the dearest of friends, but 'friend' isn't a strong enough word."

"You do not need your words, Sam, for I already know your heart."

Aww, dammit. Something's in my eye.

For a few minutes, we hover together in silence. Even though I have to go, leaving feels cruel.

"You must. Your children do not know what happened to you."

I wasn't so sure about that. In fact, knowing Tammy had re-established a mind link with me when the portal briefly opened had given me the peace of mind I needed to continue my mission here. Of course, if that dimensional rip really went to some mid-ground demi-plane, it might not have been her at all in my mind, but the demon messing with me.

Well, either way. With luck, I would be on my way home soon enough.

With that, I pat his face, then wipe a tear off my cheek. "See you on the other side, my friend."

"I'm going to miss you, Samantha Moon."

I kiss Talos on the forehead, then dive toward the churning maelstrom. True to her word, neither lightning nor plasma cause me harm while flying through the storm. The chaos keeps its distance. I cruise over the verdant grassland below up to the 500-story tower, heading straight for the topmost set of open archways and landing upon the massive windowsill. There are many things about this fourth-dimensional world that are unsettling and plain weird. But, the one I like the least is feeling like a two-inch-tall faerie.

This tower is too damn large.

Fortunately, Poendraz—the beyond massive red dragon—is still here, though she's curled up like a sleeping cat against the wall on the left. Darn. Guess there's a wait. I glide in, heading for the five-story-tall book. The instant my body passes the edge of the windowsill, Poendraz opens her eyes.

Those first two seconds are terrifying.

She glowers at me like a classical dragon catching a thief sneaking into its cave hoping to steal the horde of treasure. However, upon realizing who I am—and my likely reason for being here—the anger fades from her expression.

"You have returned. What news? Have my children spoken with my avatar?" asks Poendraz, sitting up and stretching in a rather catlike manner—if cats had wings.

"About that…" I fly over and hover next to her enormous eye. I explain everything that's happened since I last saw her. The instant I mention the Lumarae, Cibalor and Drajjan have agreed to reunite, tears of joy gather at the corners of her eyes.

"For such a tiny creature, you are most resourceful! I hardly expected you would be able to convince them to talk to me. Never did I imagine you capable of what you've done."

I offer a sheepish smile, pretty sure she knew

full well what happened already. "Had a lot of help. Can I ask you something?"

"Of course." She settles in a sejant pose.

"A little while ago, I wound up going into dimensions where my kind are not meant to be. I belong in the third dimension."

She nods once.

"To get there, a creator named Van Gogh inserted me into a painting. Is there a way for you to help me go back home to the third dimension, to write me into my specific world even if the bridge that's anchored here doesn't connect there?"

"That is the least I can do to repay you for reuniting my children." She ambles across the room to the podium and plops down by her book. After dipping one claw into her enormous ink well, she begins to write. "The shelf to your left. There is a box on the third tier, black with silver markings."

I spin, looking around. Sure enough, a massive box sits where indicated. To me, it's about the size of a cargo truck.

"Lift the lid and hop inside," says Poendraz.

Faerie in a music box? Seriously? Wait, maybe this is some kind of symbolic thing, right? Or even necessary. The Red Rider had a box that served as a gateway to another dimension, too.

I land on the shelf, grab the lid, and heave it up. It's damn heavy, but I manage. Much to my astonishment and utmost relief, the box contains Arizona. Specifically, Canelo. More specifically, I'm staring down a short, rectangular tunnel at the scrub brush near Mindy Hogan's house.

"Thank you!" I call out.

"The thanks are all mine. You have done this old creature's heart well. Farewell, tiny one."

Nothing left for me to do but jump.

I send a mental 'See you soon' to Talos, and dive into the box.

Chapter Thirty
Heck of a Fifteen Minutes

A short drop down a narrow tunnel ends with me in free fall about ten stories over the Arizona desert.

Thankfully, my wings are already out and it's a simple matter to stretch them, catch the wind, and glide to a reasonably soft landing.

Samantha Moon is back in the building. Rather, on Earth.

I wiggle my bare feet. Wow, I've been walking on powdery silt and smooth stone so long that being barefoot on actual dirt feels strange.

Mom! shouts Tammy in my head, her voice tinged with panic even worse than the time I hadn't texted her back in under twenty minutes. *Where are you?*

Slight dimensional wrong turn.

Gawd, Mom. What the heck are you wearing?

Did you go to a toga party?

My cheeks warm with blush. Uhh, no. Not exactly. It's magic.

Wait. You're naked under that thing?

Aren't we all naked under our clothes?

Okay, fine, but can't you summon something cute to put on?

I stare down at myself and sigh. Yes, I'm 'dressed' somewhere between an actress in a Greek stage play and one of Raphael's paintings of angels. Yeah, let me try to fix this. A moment of concentration causes a light flash and the 'toga' changes into a babydoll top and jeans. Still barefoot. I sigh at my toes. Not quite getting it right yet, but this is probably better anyway. Leaving bare footprints while appearing to wear shoes would confuse people.

And I'm being dumb. I'm back home in my dimension... where my bedroom at home is only a thought away. I'm no longer stuck with only magic to wear.

A screamed cheer in the distance draws my attention to people spilling out of Mindy's house about a football field away. Looks like my kids, Allison, Mindy Hogan, and her parents all running toward me. Ack. Illusory clothing is not going to cut it for the inevitable hug storm coming my way.

Sec, Tam Tam. Be right back.

I summon the single flame, teleport home to my bedroom, throw on a real outfit as fast as I can, then teleport back to the same spot in the desert to find

Tammy explaining to the others that I'll be right back. Anthony is wearing the second outfit he brought with him. The Fire Warrior is as equally hostile to clothing as Talos.

Within seconds of my return, my kids clamp onto me. Allison hovers for a second or three, but becomes impatient, so runs around behind me to add herself to the group embrace.

Mindy, her hair smelling of fake strawberry, bounces on her toes cry-laughing and saying 'ohmigod' over and over again. She can't seem to decide if she wants to cover her mouth with both hands, stuff them in her pockets, fold her arms, or fuss at her hair.

"Mom, what the heck happened?" asks Anthony. "You just fell out of the air and wouldn't get up."

"Or transform back to yourself," adds Tammy.

"We thought you died," says Anthony.

Tammy nods, sniffling. "My link dropped."

Art and Louise stand close behind Mindy, both of them staring at me like some long lost daughter they haven't seen in thirty years.

"Sorry guys. It's a long, long, loooong story."

Tammy squeezes me, frowning. "Long? But I got a little peek a couple minutes later, so I figured out what happened."

"A couple minutes?" I lean back from the hug enough to look her in the eye. "We tried to stop the demon from entering *days* later."

Art looks at his wristwatch—wow, people still

wear those? "Been about sixteen minutes give or take since the big lizard critter fell out of the sky. Which, I take it, is also you?"

"Technically"—Anthony holds up one finger—"it's Mom's mind inside Talos' body. Which, come to think of it, is super weird."

"Dork," mutters Tammy.

I raise my finger in a parody of my son. "Well, if we're getting technical, that was Talos creating a secondary projection of himself. He's a lot bigger in person."

Tammy grasps my head and makes me look at Mindy. "Someone's been waiting her turn to talk to you."

With that, Mindy squeals out a series of sounds that I think she intended as speech—just don't ask me to translate. After a few minutes of aggressive hugging, it occurs to me that I can read her mind. Aha! She said—or tried to say—'It worked' with about 1,500 exclamation points after it.

Whoa. The energy coming off her is frenzied and chaotic. As I step back, she goes full chipmunk on methamphetamines on me.

"Ohmigod, I can't believe it! You guys did it. The demon's gone. I'm not a damn zombie anymore! I'm back to normal. Seriously can't believe this all happened. I'm such an idiot! I swear I'm never gonna do any kind of medical testing again. You guys are so awesome! I'm gonna keep going to school. Might still move home at the end of the year. I can't believe I'm back. I'm alive. Am

I alive?"

"Yes," I say.

"Oh, thank god! Thank god!"

Allison creates a few small 'fireworks' in the air with magic to celebrate our victory over demonic possession.

"Reckon you did something right," says Louise. "My daughter's got espresso for blood again. She always was a fidgety little thing."

That explains the way the elder Hogans are looking at me as though we'd resurrected their daughter. Considering she'd suffered a demonic possession and not an actual dark master infusion, the girl never actually died—just damn sure looked like it.

"Sorry if I smell like fruit. I had to take a shower. Black demon slime went *everywhere*." Mindy finally lets go of me, backs up a step, and presses a hand to her chest. "I have a heartbeat!"

Art wipes a tear.

"If it makes you feel any better," I say, "the demon fooled me. You didn't become an undead. Allie's the one who figured out what really happened."

Mindy ambush hugs Allison again, machine-gunning her with thank yous.

Wow, watching this young lady now makes it quite obvious to me how her parents knew right away something had been wrong before. It would take an entire bottle of valium to turn this hyperactive Mindy into the deadened version of her

LOST MOON

I first saw.

"So, elephant in the desert?" asks Allison.

"What?" my kids and I ask at the same time.

"Elephant in the room, but we're in a desert now… oh, forget it." Allison nods toward the Hogans. "Should they remember all this weirdness? Or would they be better off believing none of this ever happened?"

"Umm." Mindy stares pleadingly at me. "Please, don't erase my mind. I don't wanna make the same dumb mistake again. Never gonna volunteer for any weird medical stuff ever again, I promise. I knew I shouldn't have done that. I knew it. So stupid. Dumb." She bonks herself upside the head.

Louise doesn't seem opposed to the idea of losing all memory of the paranormal, at least if her facial expression is any indication. A quick peek into her head confirms that. Art's on the fence, arguing with himself over which would be better. He definitely seems quite able to handle knowing the truth. The guy's unflappable. Space aliens could land in his field and he'd probably react with an 'aww, damn. Not again.' He'd prefer not to deal with the memory, but to protect his daughter, he wants to keep it.

I think we should let them remember, says Tammy via telepathy. *Besides, they just watched Ant get all huge and burny, Allie throwing magic all over the place, and you turning into a big dragon. Plus, dozens of demons dying all over the place. It would be a real pain in the butt to erase all of that without any gaps.*

"There's also the very slight chance that the 'forces of evil' might seek to go after you again," I say to Mindy.

She gasps. "No! Why would they? I'm nobody special."

"You've been possessed once by a rather powerful entity," says Allison. "That has left you spiritually vulnerable sort of the way a bent piece of metal is never as strong as it used to be."

"Oh." She looks down, fidgeting at her shirt.

"But, I think I can help with that part." Allison smiles. "A couple of shielding incantations, maybe a protective talisman. You weren't specifically targeted originally, just happened to be the person who picked up that cursed bracelet, so it's like Sam said, unlikely. But I'll still help you out with some defense."

"Cool." Mindy flashes a brittle smile.

"I think we're going to let your memories remain intact for your protection," I say to Art and Louise. Of course, I say "we" but really, I'm the only one who can alter memories of the group. Lucky me. I glance at the Hogan family. "Goes without saying, none of you should talk about any of this."

"Bah." Art chuckles. "Who'd believe it, anyway?"

Mindy hugs her mother, apologizing all over again for being dumb and volunteering for medical testing.

"Ms. Moon, Miss. Lopez, kids, you gave us our daughter back. That's a thing we can never really say thank you enough for. But…" Art waves for us to follow. "Y'all gotta be tired. Fighting demons is hungry work. You folks up for a barbecue?"

"It's almost nine at night, Art," says Louise.

"Nonsense! It's time for a celebration!"

"Just please don't cook anything with brains in it." Mindy gags.

Allison and Tammy shudder at the idea of eating brains.

Yeah. I do, too. Even after tunneling out of a dragon's stomach, I'd rather do that again than eat brains.

"Gah! I can't believe I ate that stuff." Mindy shivers.

"I don't know," says Anthony. "I hear they taste like chicken."

"Such. A. Dork," says Tammy.

Chapter Thirty-One
Old Family Recipe

Monday, paradoxically enough, is a welcome return to normal.

The barbecue at the Hogans' place last night was a fun, if low key, time. I think Anthony's got a crush on Mindy, but nothing more than a fifteen-year-old seeing a girl he thinks is pretty and getting a little star struck. He knows she's too old for him and she thinks of him as a kid. Well, more like a kid brother or cousin. The Hogans have kind of adopted us as extended family.

So, yeah… Mindy Hogan's back on track for a reasonably normal life. The universe has one less greater demon in it, and the 'forces of evil' are no doubt a little more annoyed at me than they were before this all started.

Yeah, so what else is new?

Another thing about Monday, it's a lazy Sam

LOST MOON

day. One thing about being my own boss with the private investigation stuff is days off happen whenever necessary. Today I have deemed it necessary.

So, I spend hours chilling out with Judge Judy while the kids are at school. It's kinda dark of me to think, but it's tempting to wish someone makes her into a vampire so she'll never go off the air. Then again, if that happened, she wouldn't appear on camera. Damn. Suppose there is no choice but to prepare myself for the inevitable tragedy of outliving that show. At least I'll have them all on DVD.

Within minutes of his arrival home from school, Anthony goes over to his friend Jim's house while Tammy puts in a few hours at a nearby Wendy's. Yeah, kid's first job. With her new thought-shielding necklace on Tammy actually enjoys being in public again. Each new stranger no longer represents an onslaught of memories, fears, phobias and God knows what else.

Well, God and my daughter.

And OMG, if she isn't the cutest little worker bee in her ballcap and apron. Yes, she has long since forbidden me to eat there, especially after I took an album-full of pictures. Tammy taking an order, Tammy getting fries, Tammy working the drive thru. Tammy glaring at me. Tammy turning her back on me. I loved them all!

Anyway, a little after six, both kids arrive home. Tammy gets started on homework in the dining room while Anthony goes to the kitchen... and get this, he's making us dinner. Okay, that has to be Danny's influence. I still haven't made up my mind how I feel about that, but my son doesn't mind him. His being a supernatural entity in his own right with a link to the Fire Warrior means that my *very* ex-husband can't possess him. Also, considering that Danny hadn't truly become a full dark master, his soul is basically the equivalent of an ectoplasmic turd that keeps popping back up every time the bowl is flushed.

Tammy gasps from the dining room, then snickers.

Poor kid. Danny was, after all her father, but she's fully aware of how much of a shit he was to me for most of her life. Once she got out of her wild stage, she resented him for treating me like that and using her and Anthony as weapons against me. The first time she told me it wasn't my fault, and Danny had been cruel to me… wow. I got chills. Talk about feeling vindicated, and more than a little choked up.

That's the thing with kids. They start off adoring their parents, followed by a phase where the parents are a giant pain in the ass. Later, when they get older, suddenly we're best friends again. At least, that's how the 'average' family is supposed to work. I never ended up in the 'best friend' zone with my mother. We don't have bad blood per se, but she's always been so spacey, she never really felt like a parent at all. More like we grew up with our crazy aunt who occasionally realized she had small people in the house with her.

Tammy's only seventeen, but after all the weird stuff we've been through together, she's already getting into the sort of relationship with me that most mother-daughters don't have until the kid's in their thirties. Not going to complain. I guess it's a side effect of her being able to literally see how much I love them both.

Anthony? He's somehow skipping over the surly, bratty stage entirely. Tammy thinks he's a 'suck up' or a 'goody goody.'

"He is," mutters Tammy from the dining room. "Boys aren't supposed to be that nice."

"Random conversation alert!" pipes my son from the kitchen, which he often does when either Tammy or I accidentally vocalize our inner conversations.

My son is his own guardian angel though, so maybe that contributes.

Speaking of Danny, the aroma of spaghetti sauce coming from the kitchen almost gives me a flashback to thirteen years ago. If Anthony keeps this up, he might end up as a professional chef someday. He actually does enjoy cooking, so it's a real possibility.

That aroma is a double-edged sword, but when dinner is ready, I decide to have some since food tastes normal to me again. Even with the opal ring the alchemist made to let me eat, things still didn't quite have the full flavor. Either way, my non-undead self can once again enjoy the process of eating, even if it doesn't provide any nutrition.

The sauce is so damn much like what Danny used to make it leaves me feeling maudlin the whole time we eat. Staring across the table at an empty chair isn't enough that I miss him though. After what he did to me and the kids, I'm well past the point of ever having any feelings for him again. But... I suppose there's an outside chance of no longer hating him.

It's not Danny I miss, it's the normal life we could never have. And that's not a complaint about all the supernatural stuff. If none of that happened to me, my son would've been dead as a small boy, so there's no lamentation on my part. And Danny more than likely would be part owner of a strip club in Colton.

Gah.

Though, in the interest of fairness, I suspect he only got involved with that sleazy element after his mind cracked under the stress of my death. As far as Danny believed, his wife had died and been replaced with an evil clone. But, really, how many people ever truly feel like they're having a *normal* life? Guarantee almost everyone you ask will feel like they're doing something wrong or can't get it right. Or feel disadvantaged in this way, or lacking in that way. No one ever really feels normal.

Tammy gives me a 'yeah, Mom, but we're *far* from normal' look, with a hint of a grin.

Somewhere to the east, Mindy Hogan's having a reasonably ordinary night with her roommates. As far as I know, they remained oblivious to the truth about her and bought my story about someone being sick in her family. With Mindy once again as fidgety as a hamster on crack, they think she's feeling better. The one girl did, however, call in a priest to bless the bathroom after what happened in there. She thinks a demon caused the stench that made her pass out. And yanno… she's not actually wrong.

Tammy sputters half-chewed spaghetti while laughing.

I wonder what our life might have been like if Danny had actually managed to 'cure' me. Yeah, I know my situation is way different. For me, this is a one way trip. Unlike Mindy, I *actually* died. And no, there's no jealousy of her getting her life back. In a way, I *did* get my life back. Granted, it took a trip across ninety-nine dimensions to do so, but in a technical sense, my body is 'alive' again.

Honestly, at this point in my life, I wouldn't change much. Things worked out okay for me… though, Elizabeth is still out there somewhere.

Tammy shivers at that thought in my head. She looks worried for a second or two, then sits up, confident. "We'll be ready for her, Mom."

Anthony, seemingly following our "random" conversation, mumbles something incoherent past a full mouth of pasta and gives me a thumbs-up.

Heh. The kids seem not to be too worried. But can anyone really be ready for Elizabeth… hmm.

Maybe we might be after all.

Chapter Thirty-Two
Rest

Wednesday, a little after noon, I hit Starbucks for a quick feeding as well as a caramel macchiato. My critical needs met, it's time to head out for some privacy. After stashing the Momvan in my driveway, I go inside to the bedroom, draw the curtains, and strip.

An illusion spell provides what appears to be an ordinary sundress. I check myself in the mirror to make sure it's opaque. Once confident no one can tell the difference between this and real clothes, I teleport once again to the remote part of woods where Allison and I had been experimenting with my witchy abilities.

The woods are serene, no people around. Only me, the rustle of a breeze in the branches, and the calls of a few birds. I take a seat on the dirt, close my eyes, and summon the single flame. It appears in my mind's eye... but no Talos within. Damn.

It's a startling, and quite discouraging event, but hardly unexpected. Still, experiencing it bothers me more than I thought it would. However, it will take more than the lack of instant success to make me give up. Like a meditating Shaolin monk, I focus on quieting my thoughts, blocking out all worry, anxiety, or other emotions. Over and over again, I picture the dancing fire, picture Talos's voice, imagine him sitting patiently in the Canyon of Rifts awaiting this moment.

Momentary worry makes me falter. I'd been stuck in that dimension for what felt like two weeks, yet only fifteen minutes passed here. It's now Wednesday, more or less four days since my return. Would that be months and months to him? For a being like Talos who has already lived over ten thousand years and is immortal by nature, it's probably not that big a deal.

Still, worry becomes guilt at making him sit there waiting, but it's nothing he didn't *want* to do.

Again, I clear my mind and summon the flame. Still no Talos.

Five minutes becomes twenty, then an hour. I refuse to give in to doubt, and in so doing, stop worrying about how long this is taking. All that matters is the darkness upon the backs of my eyelids and the little fire flicker hovering in my mind's eye.

I imagine seeing Talos within, popping up across dimensions. I imagine drawing him closer and closer like a camera zooming in. Without warning, the flame grows, twisting and fluttering, gliding nearer. And taking shape within it, is one familiar dragon. Rather than the smaller version of himself I usually see within the flame, this is his true, massive form.

That was much faster than expected, says Talos in my head.

I grin, overjoyed. "It's good to hear your voice again. And faster? It's been almost four days. Felt like forty years."

He chuckles. *I thought you might have gotten caught up in some complications from the demon situation. I am glad to see that is not the case.*

"Is our link repaired?"

Almost. I am completing the incantation now.

"What should I do?"

Merely wait. Keep talking.

I ramble about Mindy, the barbecue, the kids, Anthony being excited about a 'big raid' or something tonight in his online game. His virtual friends are going to take on a new 'boss' or some such thing they've never tried before. Coincidentally enough, it's a giant dragon that's so big, a whole group of characters get into a battle with other creatures while standing on that dragon's back.

Tingles spread down my body.

All is as it should be. I have re-established our connection across the dimensional boundary.

"Do you want to go for a fly?" I ask.

I would love nothing more… but, alas, my essence is weakened from the death of my projection. I lack the strength to project myself across. His deep sigh rattles my brain. *Forgive me, Samantha. As soon as my essence mends, I will be able to send a shadow of myself to you as before.*

"It's perfectly fine. Take a break, please. Go rest and recover. You deserve it."

Thank you. Now that we are connected again, it might be possible for me to rest.

"You couldn't rest before? Why?"

Worry.

I mentally lean against his presence, as much of a 'hug' as it's possible to send across dimensions. "It's beyond awesome to know you've got my back again. If anything like this ever happens again, promise me you will tell me to retreat and come up with a better plan rather than pulling some kamikaze crap?"

My caution will be greater in the future.

Hesitation and dread fill my mind. "What aren't you telling me?"

Again, he sighs.

"Talos?"

Since we do not have to keep our link hidden, I spoke at length with Baxxus about what happened. If he is correct, your surviving the death of my projection was a matter of luck. Sam, you should have died.

"But I didn't."

This time. I will not risk your life again.

"Stopping Elizabeth and the dark masters has to come first. The damage they could potentially do to the Earth—and universe—isn't worth my life. I *really* hope it doesn't come to that, but if finally getting rid of her requires my butt going back to the Source, so be it."

He grumbles.

"That said, I don't wanna stop existing yet. My kids need me."

You will be saying that even when they're ninety.

I chuckle. "Damn right. And when they reincarnate, I'll pretend to be a long lost aunt or something. I'm not above messing with memories to be around them again."

You would do that, Samantha?

I rub my chin. "Nah. Most likely, I'll watch them from afar. Then again, Anthony might be one of these semi-immortals types, so he might be around a while."

"You lead a strange life, Samantha Moon."

"As do you, Talos."

Sam, have you considered taking a vacation?

Are you nuts? I can't afford a—oh wait. I can.

Take care of yourself, Sam. I'm here if you need me.

"You too, Talos. And thank you."

I open my eyes and take a deep breath of clean air.

Hmm. Vacation. That's not a bad idea. But… the kids have school. Can't pick up and go somewhere spontaneously just yet. But, summer isn't *that* far away. Only like, umm… seven months. Argh.

Yes, we need a vacation… eventually. And, wow, did Ireland really just pop into my mind?

Hmm. Interesting.

Maybe the kids and I will go somewhere once school's out.

But at the moment, I have a couch, a television, a DVD player, and Judge Judy.

One big question remains…

What shall I overindulge on this afternoon while watching TV?

Ice cream or wine?

Or both?

The End

To be continued in:
Banshee Moon
Vampire for Hire #19
Coming soon!

About J.R. Rain:

J.R. Rain is an ex-private investigator who now writes full-time. He lives in a small house on a small island with his small dog, Sadie. Please visit him at www.jrrain.com.

About Matthew S. Cox:

Originally from South Amboy NJ, **Matthew S. Cox** has been creating science fiction and fantasy worlds for most of his reasoning life. Since 1996, he has developed the "Divergent Fates" world, in which Division Zero, Virtual Immortality, The Awakened Series, The Harmony Paradox, and the Daughter of Mars series take place.

Matthew is an avid gamer, a recovered WoW addict, Gamemaster for two custom systems, and a fan of anime, British humour, and intellectual science fiction that questions the nature of reality, life, and what happens after it.

He is also fond of cats.

Please find him at: www.matthewcoxbooks.com

Printed in Great Britain
by Amazon